KING,
QUEEN,
KNAVE

Books by Vladimir Nabokov

Bend Sinister, a novel

The Defense, a novel

Despair, a novel

Eugene Onegin, by Alexander Pushkin,
  translated from the Russian, with a Commentary

The Eye, a novel

The Gift, a novel

Invitation to a Beheading, a novel

Laughter in the Dark or *Camera Obscura*, a novel

Lolita, a novel

Nabokov's Dozen, a collection of short stories

Nabokov's Quartet, a collection of short stories

Nikolai Gogol, a critical biography

Pale Fire, a novel

Pnin, a novel

Poems

The Real Life of Sebastian Knight, a novel

The Song of Igor's Campaign, Anon.,
  translated from Old Russian

Speak, Memory or *Conclusive Evidence*, a memoir

Spring in Fialta and Other Stories

Three Russian Poets, verse translation from the Russian

The Waltz Invention, a drama

Translated by Dmitri Nabokov in collaboration with the author

VLADIMIR NABOKOV

A NOVEL

KING, QUEEN, KNAVE

McGraw–Hill Book Company

New York   St. Louis   San Francisco   Bogotá
Guatemala   Hamburg   Lisbon   Madrid   Mexico   Montreal
Panama   Paris   San Juan   Saõ Paulo   Tokyo   Toronto

Library of Congress Catalog Number 68-22764

1 2 3 4 5 6 7 8 9 0 FGFG 8 6 5 4 3 2 1 0

First Paperback edition, 1981

The Library of Congress cataloged the first
  issue of this title as follows:
Nabokov, Vladimir Vladimirovich, 1899-1977
      King, queen, knave; a novel [by] Vladimir Nabokov.
    Translated by Dmitri Nabokov in collaboration with the
    author. [1st ed.]   New York, McGraw-Hill [1968]
      xi, 272 p.   22 cm.
Translation of Korol´, dama, valet   68-22764
      I. Title.

ISBN 0-07-045722-0

FOREWORD

Of all my novels this bright brute is the gayest. Expatriation, destitution, nostalgia had no effect on its elaborate and rapturous composition. Conceived on the coastal sands of Pomerania Bay in the summer of 1927, constructed in the course of the following winter in Berlin, and completed in the summer of 1928, it was published there in early October by the Russian émigré house "Slovo," under the title *Korol', Dama, Valet*. It was my second Russian novel. I was twenty-eight. I had been living in Berlin, on and off, for half a dozen years. I was absolutely sure, with a number of other intelligent people, that sometime in the next decade we would all be back in a hospitable, remorseful, racemosa-blossoming Russia.

In the autumn of the same year Ullstein acquired the German rights. The translation was made—competently, as I was assured—by Siegfried von Vegesack, whom I recall meeting in the beginning of 1929 when passing with my wife posthaste through Paris to spend Ullstein's generous advance on a butterfly safari in the Oriental Pyrenees. Our interview took place in his hotel where he lay in bed with a bad cold, wretched but monocled, while famous American authors were having quite a time in bars and so forth, as was, it is often said, their wont.

One might readily conjecture that a Russian writer in choosing a set of exclusively German characters (the appearances of my wife and me in the last two chapters are merely visits of inspection) was creating for himself insurmountable difficulties. I spoke no German, had no German friends, had not read a single German novel either in the original, or in translation. But in art, as in nature, a glaring disadvantage may turn out to be a subtle protective device. The "human humidity," *chelovecheskaya vlazhnost'*, permeating my first novel, *Mashen'ka* (published in 1926 by "Slovo," and also brought out in German by Ullstein), was all very well but the book no longer pleased me (as it pleases me now for new reasons). The émigré characters I had collected in that display box were so transparent to the eye of the era that one could easily make out the labels behind them. What the labels said was fortunately not too clear but I felt no inclination to persevere in a technique assignable to the French "human document" type, with a hermetic community faithfully described by one of its members—something not unsimilar, in a small way, to the impassioned and boring ethnopsychics which depress one so often in modern novels. At a stage of gradual inner disentanglement, when I had not yet found, or did not yet dare apply, the very special methods of re-creating a historical situation that I used ten years later in *The Gift*, the lack of any emotional involvement and the fairytale freedom inherent in an unknown milieu answered my dream of pure invention. I might have staged KQKn in Rumania or Holland. Familiarity with the map and weather of Berlin settled my choice.

By the end of 1966, my son had prepared a literal translation of the book in English, and this I placed on my lectern beside a copy of the Russian edition. I foresaw having to make a number of revisions affecting the actual text of a forty-year-old novel which I had not reread ever since its proofs had been corrected by an author twice younger than the reviser. Very soon I asserted that the original sagged considerably more than I had expected. I do not wish to spoil the pleasure of future collators by discussing the little changes I made. Let me only remark that my main purpose in making them was not to beautify a corpse but rather to permit a still breathing body to enjoy certain innate capacities which inexperience and eagerness, the haste of thought and the sloth of word had denied it formerly. Within the texture of the creature, those possibilities were practically crying to be developed or teased out. I accomplished the operation not without relish. The "coarseness" and "lewdness" of the book that alarmed my kindest critics in émigré periodicals have of course been preserved, but I confess to have mercilessly struck out and rewritten many lame odds and ends, such as for instance a crucial transition in the last chapter where in order to get rid temporarily of Franz, who was not supposed to butt in while certain important scenes in the Gravitz resort engaged the attention of the author, the latter used the despicable expedient of having Dreyer send Franz away to Berlin with a scallop-shaped cigarette case that had to be returned to a businessman who had mislaid it with the author's connivance (a similar object also figures, I see, in my *Speak, Memory*, 1966, and quite properly, too, for its shape is that of the famous *In Search of Lost Time* cake). I cannot say I feel I have been losing time over a dated novel. Its revised text may soften and entertain even such readers as are opposed, for religious reasons no doubt, to an author's thriftily and imperturbably resurrecting all his old works one after the other while working on a new novel that has now obsessed him for five years. But I do think that even a godless author owes too much to his juvenilia not to take advantage of a situation hardly ever twinned in the history of Russian literature and save from administrative oblivion the books banned with a shudder in his sad and remote country.

I have not said anything yet about the plot of *King, Queen, Knave*. This plot is basically not unfamiliar. In fact, I suspect that those two worthies, Balzac and Dreiser, will accuse me of gross parody but I swear I had not read their preposterous stuff at the time, and even now do not quite know what they are talking about under their cypresses. After all, Charlotte Humbert's husband was not quite innocent either.

Speaking of literary air currents, I must admit I was a little surprised to find in my Russian text so many *"monologue intérieur"* passages—no relation to *Ulysses*, which I hardly knew at the time; but of course I had been exposed since tender boyhood to *Anna Karenin*, which contains a whole scene consisting of those intonations, Eden-new a hundred years ago, now well used. On the other hand, my amiable little imitations of *Madame Bovary*, which good readers will not fail to distinguish, represent a deliberate tribute to Flaubert. I remember remembering, in the course of one scene, Emma creeping at dawn to her lover's château along impossibly unobservant back lanes, for even Homais nods.

As usual, I wish to observe that, as usual (and as usual several sensitive people I like will look huffy), the Viennese delegation has not been invited. If, however, a resolute Freudian manages to slip in, he or she should be warned that a number of cruel traps have been set here and there in the novel.

Finally, the question of the title. Those three court cards, all hearts, I have retained, while discarding a small pair. The two new cards dealt me may justify the gamble, for I have always had an ivory thumb in this game. Tightly, narrowly, closely, through the smart of tobacco smoke, one edge is squeezed out. Frog's heart—as they say in Russian Gulch. And Jingle Bells! I can only hope that my good old partners, replete with full houses and straights, will think I am bluffing.

VLADIMIR NABOKOV
March 28, 1967
Montreux

KING,
QUEEN,
KNAVE

1

The huge black clock hand is still at rest but is on the point of making its once-a-minute gesture; that resilient jolt will set a whole world in motion. The clock face will slowly turn away, full of despair, contempt, and boredom, as one by one the iron pillars will start walking past, bearing away the vault of the station like bland atlantes; the platform will begin to move past, carrying off on an unknown journey cigarette butts, used tickets, flecks of sunlight and spittle; a luggage handcart will glide by, its wheels motionless; it will be followed by a news stall hung with seductive magazine covers—photographs of naked, pearl-gray beauties; and people, people, people on the moving platform, themselves moving their feet, yet standing still, striding forward, yet retreating as in an agonizing dream full of incredible effort, nausea, a cottony weakness in one's calves, will surge back, almost falling supine.

There were more women than men as is always the case at partings. Franz's sister, with the pallor of the early hour on her thin cheeks, and an unpleasant, empty-stomach smell, dressed in a checked cape that surely one would never see on a city girl; and his mother, small, round, all in brown like a compact little monk. See the handkerchiefs beginning to flutter.

And not only did they slip away, those two familiar smiles; not only did the station depart removing its news-stand, its luggage cart, and a sandwich-and-fruit vendor with such nice, plump, lumpy, glossy red strawberries posi-tively crying to be bitten into, all their achenes proclaiming their affinity with one's own tongue's papillae—but alas gone now; not only did all this fall behind; the entire old burg in its rosy autumn morning mist moved as well: the great stone *Herzog* in the square, the dark cathedral, the shop signs—top hat, a fish, the copper basin of a barber. There was no stopping the world now. In grand style houses pass by, the curtains flap in the open windows of his home, its floors crackle a little, the walls creak, his mother and sister are drinking their morning coffee in the swift draft, the furniture shudders from the quickening jolts, and ever more rapidly, more mysteriously, travel the houses, the cathedral, the square, the sidestreets. And even though by now tilled fields had long been unfolding their patchwork past the railway car window, Franz still felt in his very bones the receding mo-tion of the townlet where he had lived for twenty years. Besides Franz, the wooden-benched third-class compart-ment contained two old ladies in corduroy dresses; a plump inevitably red-cheeked woman with the inevitable basket of eggs in her lap; and a blond youth in tan shorts, sturdy and angular, very much like his own rucksack, which was tightly stuffed and looked as if it had been hewed of yellow stone: this he had energetically shaken off and heaved onto the shelf. The seat by the door, opposite Franz, was occupied by a magazine with the picture of a breathtaking girl; and at a window in the corridor, his back to the compartment, stood a broad-shouldered man in a black overcoat.

The train was now going fast. Franz suddenly clutched his side, transfixed by the thought that he had lost his wallet which contained so much: the solid little ticket, and a stranger's visiting card with a precious address, and an inviolate month of human life in reichsmarks. The wallet was there all right, firm and warm. The old ladies began to stir and rustle, unwrapping sandwiches. The man in the corridor turned and, with a slight lurch, retreating half a step, and then overcoming the sway of the floor, entered the compartment.

Most of the nose had gone or had never grown. To what remained of its bridge the pale parchment-like skin adhered with a sickening tightness; the nostrils had lost all sense of decency and faced the flinching spectator like two sudden holes, black and asymmetrical; the cheeks and forehead showed a geographical range of shades—yellowish, pinkish, and very glossy. Had he inherited that mask? And if not, what illness, what explosion, what acid had disfigured him? He had practically no lips; the absence of eyelashes lent his blue eyes a startled expression. And yet the man was smartly dressed, well groomed and well built. He wore a double-breasted suit under his heavy overcoat. His hair was as sleek as a wig. He pulled up the knees of his trousers as he sat down with a leisurely movement, his gray-gloved hands opened the magazine he had left on the seat.

The shudder that had passed between Franz's shoulder blades now tapered to a strange sensation in his mouth. His tongue felt repulsively alive; his palate nastily moist. His memory opened its gallery of waxworks, and he knew, he knew that there, at its far end somewhere a chamber of horrors awaited him. He remembered a dog that had vomited on the threshold of a butcher's shop. He remembered a child, a mere toddler, who, bending with the diffi-

[3]

culty of its age, had laboriously picked up and put to its lips a filthy thing resembling a baby's pacifier. He remembered an old man with a cough in a streetcar who had fired a clot of mucus into the ticket collector's hand. These were images that Franz usually held at bay but that always kept swarming in the background of his life greeting with a hysterical spasm any new impression that was kin to them. After a shock of that sort in those still recent days he would throw himself prone on his bed and try to fight off the fit of nausea. His recollections of school seemed always to be dodging away from possible, impossible, contacts with the grubby, pimply, slippery skin of some companion or other pressing him to join in a game or eager to impart some spitterish secret.

The man was leafing through the magazine, and the combination of his face with its enticing cover was intolerably grotesque. The ruddy egg woman sat next to the monster, her sleepy shoulder touching him. The youth's rucksack rubbed against his slick sticker-mottled black valise. And worst of all, the old ladies ignoring their foul neighbor munched their sandwiches and sucked on fuzzy sections of orange, wrapping the peels in scraps of paper and popping them daintily under the seat. But when the man put down his magazine and, without taking off his gloves, himself began eating a bun with cheese, glancing around provokingly, Franz could stand it no longer. He rose quickly, he lifted like a martyr his pale face, shook loose and pulled down his humble suitcase, collected his raincoat and hat and, banging his suitcase awkwardly against the doorjamb, fled into the corridor.

This particular coach had been hooked on to the express at a recent station, and the air in it was still fresh. He immediately felt a sense of relief. But the dizziness had not quite passed. A wall of beech trees was flickering by the window in a speckled sequence of sun and shade. He began tentatively to walk along the corridor clutching at knobs and things, and peering into the compartments. Only one had a free seat; he hesitated and went on, shaking off the image of two pasty-faced children with dust-black hands, their shoulders hunched up in expectation of a blow from their mother right on the nape as they quietly kept sliding off the seat to play among greasy scraps of papers on the unmentionable floor at the passengers' feet. Franz reached the end of the car and paused, struck by an extraordinary thought. This thought was so sweet, so audacious and exciting, that he had to take off his glasses and wipe them. "No, I can't, out of the question," said Franz under his breath, already realizing, however, that he could not conquer the temptation. Then checking the knot of his tie with thumb and forefinger, he crossed in a burst of clangor the unsteady connecting plates, and with an exquisite sinking feeling in the pit of his stomach passed into the next car.

It was a second-class schnellzug car, and to Franz second-class was something brightly attractive, even slightly sinful, smacking of spicy extravagance like a sip of thick white liqueur or that enormous grapefruit resembling a yellow skull that he had once bought on the way to school. About first-class one could not dream at all—that was for diplomats, generals, and almost unearthly actresses! Second, though . . . second. . . . If he could only get up the courage. They said his late father (a seedy notary) had on occasion— long ago, before the war—travelled second-class. Yet, Franz could not make up his mind. He stopped at the beginning of the corridor, by the placard listing the car inventory, and now it was no longer a fence-like forest glancing by but vast meadows majestically gliding past, and, in the distance, parallel to the tracks, flowed a highway, along which sped lickety-split a lilliputian automobile.

The conductor just then making his rounds brought him out of his difficulty. Franz bought a supplement promoting his ticket to the next rank. A short tunnel deafened him with its resounding darkness. Then it was light again but the conductor had vanished.

The compartment that Franz entered with a silent unacknowledged bow was occupied by only two people—a handsome bright-eyed lady and a middle-aged man with a clipped tawny mustache. Franz hung up his raincoat and sat down carefully. The seat was so soft; there was such a cosy semi-circular projection at temple level separating one seat from the next; the photographs on the wall were so romantic —a flock of sheep, a cross on a rock, a waterfall. He slowly stretched out his long feet, slowly took a folded newspaper from his pocket. But he was unable to read. Benumbed with luxury he merely held the newspaper open and from behind it examined his fellow travellers. Oh, they were charming. The lady wore a black suit and a diminutive black hat with a little diamond swallow. Her face was serious, her eyes cold, a little dark down, the sign of passion, glistened above her upper lip, and a gleam of sun brought out the creamy texture of her neck at the throat with its two delicate transverse lines as if traced with a fingernail across it, one above the other: also a token of all kinds of marvels, according to one of his schoolmates, a precocious expert. The man must be a foreigner, judging by his soft collar and tweeds. Franz, however, was mistaken.

"I'm thirsty," said the man with a Berlin accent. "Too bad there's no fruit. Those strawberries were positively dying to be sampled."

"It's your own fault," answered the lady in a displeased

voice, adding a little later: "I still cannot get over it—it was such a silly thing to do."

Dreyer briefly cast up his eyes to a makeshift heaven and made no reply.

"It's your own fault," she repeated and automatically pulled at her pleated skirt, automatically noticing that the awkward young man with the glasses who had appeared in the door corner seemed to be fascinated by the sheer silk of her legs.

"Anyway," she said, "it's not worth discussing."

Dreyer knew that his silence irritated Martha unspeakably. There was a boyish gleam in his eye, and the soft folds about his lips were undulating because he was rolling a mint in his mouth. The incident that had irritated his wife was actually pretty silly. They had spent August and half of September in Tyrol, and now, on the way home, had stopped for a few days on business in that quaint little town, and there he had called on his cousin Lina with whom he had danced in his youth, some twenty-five years ago. His wife had flatly refused to accompany him. Lina, now a roly-poly creature with false teeth but just as talkative and amiable as ever, found that the years had left their mark on him but that it might have been worse; she served him excellent coffee, told him about her children, said she was sorry they were not at home, asked about Martha (whom she did not know) and his business (about which she was well informed); then, after a pious pause, she wondered if he could give her a piece of advice. . . .

It was warm in the room where around the aged chandelier, with gray little glass pendants like dirty icicles, flies were describing parallelograms, lighting every time on the same pendants (which for some reason amused him), and the old chairs extended their plush-covered arms with comical cordiality. An old pug dozed on an embroidered cushion. In reply to the expectant interrogatory sigh of his cousin he had suddenly said, coming to life with a laugh: "Well, why don't you have him come to see me in Berlin? I'll give him a job." And that was what his wife could not forgive him. She called it "swamping the business with poor relations"; but when you come down to it, how can one poor relation swamp anything? Knowing that Lina would invite his wife, and that Martha would not go in any circumstance, he had lied, telling his cousin that they were leaving the same evening. Instead, Martha and he had visited a fair and the splendid vineyards of a business friend. A week later at the station, when they had already settled down in their compartment, he had glimpsed Lina from the window. It was a wonder they had not run into her somewhere in town. Martha wanted to avoid her seeing them at all cost, and even though the idea of buying a nest of fruit for the trip appealed to him greatly he did not put his head out of the window, did not beckon with a soft "psst" the young vendor in the white jacket.

Comfortably dressed, in perfect health, a colored mist of vague pleasant thoughts in his head and a peppermint in his mouth, Dreyer sat with crossed arms, and the soft folds of the fabric in the crook of his arms matched the soft folds of his cheeks, and the outline of his clipped mustache, and the wrinkles fanning templeward from his eyes. With a peculiar blandly amused gleam in his eyes he gazed from under his brows at the green landscape gliding in the window, at Martha's handsome profile rimmed with sunlight, and the cheap suitcase of the bespectacled young man who was reading a newspaper in the corner by the door. Idly he considered that passenger, palpating him from all sides. He noted the so-called "lizard" pattern of the young fellow's green-and-garnet tie which obviously had cost ninety-five pfennigs, the stiff collar, and also the cuffs and front of his shirt—a shirt incidentally which only existed in an abstract form since all its visible parts, judging by a treacherous gloss, were pieces of starched armor of rather low quality but greatly esteemed by a frugal provincial who attaches them to an invisible undergarment made at home of unbleached cloth. As to the young man's suit, it evoked a delicate melancholy in Dreyer as he reflected not for the first time on the pathetically short life of every new cut: that kind of three-button, narrow-lapelled blue jacket with a pin stripe had disappeared from most Berlin stores at least five years ago.

Two alarmed eyes were suddenly born in the lenses, and Dreyer turned away. Martha said:

"It is all so silly. I wish you had listened to me."

Her husband sighed and said nothing. She wanted to go on—there were still lots of pithy rebukes she could make but she felt the young man was listening and, instead of words, leaned her elbow abruptly on the window side of the table leaf—pulling up the skin of her cheek with her knuckles. She sat that way until the flicker of woods in the window became irksome; she slowly straightened her ripe body, annoyed and bored, then leaned back and closed her eyes. The sun penetrated her eyelids with solid scarlet, across which luminous stripes moved in succession (the ghostly negative of the passing forest), and a replica of her husband's cheerful face, as if slowly rotating toward her, got mixed up in this barred redness, and she opened her eyes with a start. Her husband, however, was sitting relatively far, reading a book bound in purple morocco. He was reading attentively and with pleasure. Nothing existed beyond the sunlit page. He turned the page, looked around, and the outside world avidly, like a playful dog waiting for that moment, darted up to him with a bright bound. But pushing Tom away affectionately, Dreyer again immersed himself in his anthology of verse.

For Martha that frolicsome radiance was simply the stuffy air in a swaying railway car. It is supposed to be stuffy in a car: that is customary and therefore good. Life should proceed according to plan, straight and strict, without freakish twists and wiggles. An elegant book is all right on a drawing-room table. In a railway car, to allay boredom, one can leaf through some trashy magazine. But to imbibe and relish . . . poems, if you please . . . in an expensive binding . . . a person who calls himself a businessman cannot, must not, dare not act like that. But for that matter, perhaps, he may be doing it on purpose, to spite me. Just another of his show-off whims. Very well, my friend, keep showing off. How nice it would be to pluck that book out of his hands and lock it up in a suitcase.

At that instant the sun seemed to lay bare her face, flowing over her smooth cheeks and lending an artificial warmth to her eyes with their large elastic-looking pupils amid the dove-gray iris and adorable dark lids slightly creased like violets, radiantly lashed and rarely blinking as if she were constantly afraid of losing sight of an essential goal. She wore almost no make-up—only in the minute transverse fissures of her full lips there seemed to be drying traces of orange-red paint.

Franz, who had been hiding behind his newspaper in a state of blissful nonexistence, living on the outside of himself, in the chance motions and chance words of his travelling companions, now started to assert himself and openly, almost arrogantly, looked at the lady.

Yet only a moment ago his thoughts always tending to morbid associations had blended, in one of those falsely harmonious images that are significant within the dream but meaningless when one recalls it, two recent events. The transition from the third-class compartment, where a noseless monster reigned in silence, into this sunny plush room appeared to him like the passage from a hideous hell through the purgatory of the corridors and intervestibular clatter into a little abode of bliss. The old conductor who had punched his ticket a short while ago and promptly vanished might have been as humble and omnipotent as St. Peter. Pious popular prints that had frightened him in childhood came to life again. He transformed the conductor's click into that of a key unlocking the gates of paradise. So a grease-painted gaudy-faced actor in a miracle play passes across a long stage divided into three parts, from the jaws of the devil into the shelter of angels. And Franz, in order to drive away the old obsessive fantasy, eagerly started to seek human, everyday tokens that would break the spell.

Martha helped him. While looking sideways out of the window she yawned: he glimpsed the swell of her tense tongue in the red penumbra of her mouth and the flash of her teeth before her hand shot up to her mouth to stop her soul from escaping; whereupon she blinked, dispersing a tickling tear with the beat of her eyelashes. Franz was not one to resist the example of a yawn, especially one that resembled somehow those luscious lascivious autumn strawberries for which his hometown was famous. At the moment when, unable to overcome the force prying his palate, he convulsively opened his mouth, Martha happened to glance at him, and he realized, snarling and weeping, that she realized he had been looking at her. The morbid bliss he had shortly before experienced as he looked at her dissolving face now turned into acute embarrassment. He knit his brows under her radiant and indifferent gaze and, when she turned away, mentally calculated, as though his fingers had rattled across the counters of a secret abacus, how many days of his life he would give to possess this woman.

The door slid open, and an excited waiter, the herald of some frightful disaster, thrust his head in, barked his message, and dashed on to the next compartment to cry his news.

Basically Martha was opposed to those fraudulent frivolous meals, with the railway company charging you exorbitant prices for mediocre food, and this almost physical sensation of needless expense, mixed with the feeling that someone, snug and robust, wanted to cheat her proved to be so strong that were it not for a ravenous hunger she would certainly not have gone that long vacillating way to the dining car. She vaguely envied the bespectacled young man who reached into the pocket of his raincoat hanging beside him and pulled out a sandwich. She got up and took her handbag under her arm. Dreyer found the violet ribbon in his book, marked his page with it, and after waiting a couple of seconds as if he could not immediately make the transition from one world to the other, gave his knees a light slap and stood up too. He instantly filled the whole compartment, being one of those men who despite medium height and moderate corpulence create an impression of extraordinary bulk. Franz retracted his feet. Martha and her husband lurched past him and went out.

He was left alone with his gray sandwich in the now spacious compartment. He munched and gazed out of the window. A green bank was rising there diagonally until it suffused the window to the top. Then, resolving an iron chord, a bridge banged overhead and instantly the green slope vanished and open country unfurled—fields, willows, a golden birch tree, a winding brook, beds of cabbage. Franz finished his sandwich, fidgeted cozily, and closed his eyes.

Berlin! In that very name of the still unfamiliar metropolis, in the lumber and rumble of the first syllable and in the light ring of the second there was something that excited him like the romantic names of good wines and bad women. The express seemed already to be speeding along the famous avenue lined for him with gigantic ancient lindens beneath which seethed for him a flamboyant crowd. The express sped past those lindens grown so luxuriantly out of the avenue's resonant name, and ("derlin, derlin" went the bell of the waiter summoning belated diners) shot under an enormous arch ornamented with mother-of-pearl spangles. Farther on there was an enchanting mist where another picture postcard turned on its stand showing a translucent tower against a black background. It vanished, and, in a brilliantly lit-up emporium, among gilded dummies, limpid mirrors, and glass counters, Franz strolled about in cut-away, striped trousers, and white spats, and with a smooth movement of his hand directed customers to the departments they needed. This was no longer a wholly conscious play of thought, nor was it yet a dream; and at the instant that sleep was about to trip him up, Franz regained control of himself and directed his thoughts according to his wishes. He promised himself a lone treat that very night. He bared the shoulders of the woman that had just been sitting by the window, made a quick mental test (did blind Eros react? clumsy Eros did, unsticking its folds in the dark); then, keeping the splendid shoulders, changed the head, substituting for it the face of that seventeen-year-old maid who had vanished with a silver soup ladle almost as big as she before he had had time to declare his love; but that head too he erased and, in its place, attached the face of one of those bold-eyed, humid-lipped Berlin beauties that one encounters mainly in liquor and cigarette advertisements. Only then did the image come to life: the bare-bosomed girl lifted a wine glass to her crimson lips, gently swinging her apricot-silk leg as a red backless slipper slowly slid off her foot. The slipper fell off, and Franz, bending down after it, plunged softly into dark slumber. He slept with mouth agape so that his pale face presented three apertures, two shiny ones (his glasses) and one black (his mouth). Dreyer noticed this symmetry when an hour later he returned with Martha from the dining car. In silence they stepped over a lifeless leg. Martha put her handbag on the collapsible window table, and the bag's nickel clasp with its cat's eye immediately came to life as a green reflection began dancing in it. Dreyer took out a cigar but did not light it.

The dinner, particularly that wiener schnitzel, had turned out to be pretty good, and Martha was not sorry now that she had agreed to go. Her complexion had grown warmer, her exquisite eyes were moist, her freshly painted lips glistened. She smiled, only just baring her incisors, and this contented, precious smile lingered on her face for several instants. Dreyer lazily admired her, his eyes slightly narrowed, savoring her smile as one might an unexpected gift, but nothing on earth could have made him show that pleasure. When the smile disappeared he turned away as a satisfied gawker drifts away after the bicyclist has picked himself up, and the street vendor has replaced on his cart the scattered fruit.

Franz crossed his legs like one very lame and slow but did not wake up. Harshly the train began braking. There glided past a brick wall, an enormous chimney, freight cars standing on a siding. Presently it grew dark in the compartment: they had entered a vast domed station.

"I'll go out, my love," said Dreyer, who liked to smoke in the open air.

Left alone, Martha leaned back in the corner, and having nothing better to do looked at the bespectacled corpse in the corner, thinking indifferently that this, perhaps, was the young man's stop and he would miss it. Dreyer strode along the platform, drummed with five fingers on the windowpane as he passed, but his wife did not smile again. With a puff of smoke he moved on. He strolled leisurely, with a bouncing gait, his hands clasped behind his back, and his cigar thrust forward. He reflected that it would be nice some day to be promenading like this beneath the glazed arches of a remote station somewhere on the way to Andalusia, Bagdad or Nizhni Novgorod. Actually one could set off any time; the globe was enormous and round, and he had enough spare cash to circle it completely half-a-dozen times. Martha, though, would refuse to come, preferring a trim suburban lawn to the most luxuriant jungle. She would only sniff sarcastically were he to suggest they take a year off. "I suppose," he thought, "I ought to buy a paper. I guess the stock market is also an interesting and tricky subject. And let us see if our two aviators—or is it some wonderful hoax?—have managed to duplicate in reverse direction that young American's feat of four months ago. America, Mexico, Palm Beach. Willy Wald was there, wanted us to accompany him. No, there is no breaking her down. Now then, where is the newsstand? That old sewing machine with its arthritic pedal wrapped up in brown paper is so clear right now, and yet in an hour or two I shall forget it forever; I shall forget that I looked at it; I shall forget everything. . . ." Just then a whistle blew, and the baggage car moved. Hey, that's my train!

Dreyer made for the newsstand at a smart trot, selected a coin from his palm, snatched the paper he wanted, dropped it, retrieved it, and dashed back. Not very gracefully, he hopped onto a passing step, and could not open the door immediately. In the struggle he lost his cigar but not his paper. Chuckling and panting, he walked through one car, another, a third. In the next to last corridor a big fellow in a black overcoat who was pulling a window shut moved to let him by. Glancing at him as he passed, Dreyer saw the grinning face of a grown man with the nose of a baby monkey. "Curious," thought Dreyer; "ought to get such a dummy to display something funny." In the next car he found his compartment, stepped across the lifeless leg, by now a familiar fixture, and quietly sat down. Martha was apparently asleep. He opened the paper, and then noticed that her eyes were fixed upon him.

"Crazy idiot," she said calmly and closed her eyes again. Dreyer nodded amiably and immersed himself in his paper.

The first chapter of a journey is always detailed and slow. Its middle hours are drowsy, and the last ones swift. Presently Franz awoke and made some chewing motions with his lips. His travelling companions were sleeping. The light in the window had dimmed, but in compensation the reflection of Martha's little bright swallow had appeared in it. Franz glanced at his wrist, at the watch face sturdily protected by its metal mesh. A lot of time, however, had escaped from that prison cell. There was a most repulsive taste in his mouth. He carefully wiped with a special square of cloth his glasses, and made his way out into the corridor in search of the toilet. As he stood there holding on to an iron handle, he found it strange and dreadful to be connected to a cold hole where his stream glistened and bounced, with the dark head-long-rushing naked earth so near, so fateful.

An hour later the Dreyers also woke up. A waiter brought them café-au-lait in bulky cups, and Martha criticized each sip she took. Dusk deepened in the faded fields which seemed to run faster and faster. Then rain began to patter softly against the window: a rillet would snake down the glass, stop hesitantly, and then again resume its quick downward zigzag course. Outside the corridor's windows a narrow orange sunset smouldered beneath a black thunderhead. Presently the light went on in the compartment. Martha looked at length in a little mirror, baring her teeth and raising her upper lip.

Dreyer, still replete with the pleasant warmth of slumber, looked at the dark-blue window, at the raindrops, and thought that tomorrow was Sunday, and that in the morning he would go to play tennis (which he had recently taken up with the desperate zeal of middle age), and that it would be a shame if the weather interfered with his plans. He asked himself if he had made any progress, unconsciously tensing his right shoulder, and remembered the beautifully groomed, sun-swept court in his favorite Tyrol resort, and the fabled player who had arrived for a local match in a white flannel overcoat with an English club muffler around his neck and three rackets under his arm, and then unhurriedly with professional gestures had taken off that coat, and the long striped scarf, and the white sweater under the coat, and then with a flash of his arm bared to the elbow had ringingly offered poor Paul von Lepel the indolent and terrible present of the first practice ball.

"Autumn, rain," said Martha slamming her handbag shut.

"Oh, just a drizzle," Dreyer corrected her softly.

The train, as if it were already within the magnetic field of the metropolis, was now travelling with incredible speed. The windowpanes had grown completely dark—one could not even distinguish the sky. The fiery stripe of an express flashed by in the opposite direction, and was cut off with a bang forever. It had been a hoax after all—that flight to America. Franz, who had returned to the compartment, suddenly clutched convulsively at his side. Another hour passed and in the murky gloom there appeared distant clusters of light, diamond-like conflagrations.

Soon Dreyer stood up. Franz, with a chill of excitement in all his frame, stood up too. The ritual of arrival had begun. Dreyer pulled down his bags (he enjoyed handing them to porters through the window). Franz, standing on tiptoe, pulled at his suitcase too. Their backs collided elastically, and Dreyer laughed. Franz started putting on his raincoat, failed to find the armhole at the first poke, donned his bottle-green hat, and went out into the corridor with his reluctant suitcase. More lights specked the darkness now and suddenly a street with an illuminated tram was revealed seemingly under his very feet; it disappeared again behind house walls that were being rapidly shuffled and dealt out again.

"Come on, hurry!" implored Franz.

A minor station flew past, just a platform, a half-opened jewel box, and all grew dark again as if no Berlin existed within miles. At last a topaz light spread out over a thousand tracks and rows of wet railway cars. Slowly, surely, smoothly, the huge iron cavity of the station drew in the train, which at once grew sluggish, and then, with a jolt, redundant.

Franz descended into the smoky damp. As he passed by the car he had lived in, he saw his tawny-mustached travelling companion lowering a window and hailing a porter. For a moment he regretted to have parted forever with that adorable, capricious, sloe-eyed lady. Together with the hurrying crowd he walked down the tremendously long platform, surrendered his ticket to its taker with an impatient hand, and continued past innumerable posters, counters, flower shops, people burdened with unnecessary bags, to an archway and freedom.

2

Golden haze, puffy bedquilt. Another awakening, but perhaps not yet the final one. This occurs not infrequently: You come to, and see yourself, say, sitting in an elegant second-class compartment with a couple of elegant strangers; actually, though, this is a false awakening, being merely the next layer of your dream, as if you were rising up from stratum to stratum but never reaching the surface, never emerging into reality. Your spellbound thought, however, mistakes every new layer of the dream for the door of reality. You believe in it, and holding your breath leave the railway station you have been brought to in immemorial fantasies and cross the station square. You discern next to nothing, for the night is blurred by rain, your spectacles are foggy, and you want as quickly as possible to reach the ghostly hotel across the square so as to wash your face, change your shirt cuffs and then go wandering along dazzling streets. Something happens, however—an absurd mishap—and what seemed reality abruptly loses the tingle and tang of reality. Your consciousness was deceived: you are still fast asleep. Incoherent slumber dulls your mind. Then comes a new moment of specious awareness: this golden haze and your room in the hotel, whose name is "The Montevideo." A shopkeeper you knew at home, a nostalgic Berliner, had jotted it down on a slip of paper for you. Yet who knows? Is this reality, *the* final reality, or just a new deceptive dream?

Lying on his back Franz peered with myopic agonizingly narrowed eyes at the blue mist of a ceiling, and then sideways at a radiant blur which no doubt was a window. And in order to free himself from this gold-tinted vagueness still so strongly reminiscent of a dream, he reached toward the night table and groped for his glasses.

And only when he had touched them, or more precisely the handkerchief in which they were wrapped as in a winding sheet, only then did Franz remember that absurd mishap in a lower layer of dream. When he had first come into this room, looked around, and opened the window (only to reveal a dark backyard and a dark noisy tree) he had, first of all, torn off his soiled collar that had been oppressing his neck and had hurriedly begun washing his face. Like an imbecile, he had placed his glasses on the edge of the washstand, beside the basin. As he lifted the heavy thing in order to empty it into the pail, he not only knocked the glasses off the edge of the stand, but sidestepping in awkward rhythm with the sloshing basin he held, had heard an ominous crunch under his heel.

In the process of reconstructing this event in his mind, Franz grimaced and groaned. All the festive lights of Friedrichstrasse had been stamped out by his boot. He would have to take the glasses to be repaired: only one lens was still in place and that was cracked. He palpated rather than re-examined the cripple. Mentally he had already gone out of doors in search of the proper shop. First that, and then the important, rather frightening visit. And, remembering how his mother had insisted that he make the call on the very first morning after his arrival ("it will be just the day when you can find a businessman at home"), Franz also remembered that it was Sunday.

He clucked his tongue and lay still.

Complicated but familiar poverty (that cannot afford spare sets of expensive articles) now resulted in primitive panic. Without his glasses he was as good as blind, yet he must set out on a perilous journey across a strange city. He imagined the predatory specters that last night had been crowding near the station, their motors running and their doors slamming, when still safely bespectacled but with his vision dimmed by the rainy night he had started to cross the dark square. Then he had gone to bed after the mishap without taking the walk he had been looking forward to, without getting his first taste of Berlin at the very hour of its voluptuous glitter and swarming. Instead, in miserable self-compensation, he had succumbed again, that first night, to the solitary practice he had sworn to give up before his departure.

But to pass the entire day in that hostile hotel room amid vague hostile objects, to wait with nothing to do until Monday, when a shop with a sign (for the seeing!) in the shape of a giant blue pince-nez would open—such a prospect was unthinkable. Franz threw back the quilt and, barefoot, padded warily to the window.

A light-blue, delicate, marvellously sunny morning welcomed him. Most of the yard was taken up by the sable velvet of what seemed to be a spreading tree shadow above which he was just able to distinguish the blurry orange-red hue of what looked like rich foliage. Booming city, indeed! Out there all was as quiet as in the remote serenity of a luminous rural autumn.

Aha, it was the room that was noisy! Its hubbub comprised the hollow hum of irksome human thoughts, the clatter of a moved chair, under which a much needed sock had long been hiding from the purblind, the plash of water, the tinkle of small coins that had foolishly fallen out of an elusive waistcoat, the scrape of his suitcase as it was dragged to a far corner where there would be no danger of one's tripping over it again; and there was an additional background noise —the room's own groan and din like the voice of a magnified seashell, in contrast with that sunny startling miraculous stillness preserved like a costly wine in the cool depths of the yard.

At last Franz overcame all the blotches and banks of fog, located his hat, recoiled from the embrace of the clowning mirror and made for the door. Only his face remained bare. Having negotiated the stairs, where an angel was singing as she polished the banisters, he showed the desk clerk the address on the priceless card and was told what bus to take and where to wait for it. He hesitated for a moment, tempted by the magic and majestic possibility of a taxi. He rejected it not only because of the cost but because his potential employer might take him for a spendthrift if he arrived in state.

Once in the street he was engulfed in streaming radiance. Outlines did not exist, colors had no substance. Like a woman's wispy dress that has slipped off its hanger, the city shimmered and fell in fantastic folds, not held up by anything, a discarnate iridescence limply suspended in the azure autumnal air. Beyond the nacrine desert of the square, across which a car sped now and then with a new metropolitan trumpeting, great pink edifices loomed, and suddenly a sunbeam, a gleam of glass, would stab him painfully in the pupil.

Franz reached a plausible street corner. After much fussing and squinting he discovered the red blur of the bus stop which rippled and wavered like the supports of a bathhouse when you dive under it. Almost directly the yellow mirage of a bus came into being. Stepping on somebody's foot, which at once dissolved under him as everything else was dissolving, Franz seized the handrail and a voice—evidently the conductor's—barked in his ear: "Up!" It was the first time he had ascended this kind of spiral staircase (only a few old trams served his hometown), and when the bus jerked into motion he caught a frightening glimpse of the asphalt rising like a silvery wall, grabbed someone's shoulder, and carried along by the force of an inexorable curve, during which the whole bus seemed to heel over, zoomed up the last steps and found himself on top. He sat down and looked around with helpless indignation. He was floating very high above the city. On the street below people slithered like jellyfish whenever the traffic froze. Then the bus started again, and the houses, shade-blue on one side of the street, sun-hazy on the other, rode by like clouds blending imperceptibly with the tender sky. This is how Franz first saw the city—fantasmally tinted, ethereal, impregnated with swimming colors, in no way resembling his crude provincial dream.

Was he on the right bus? Yes, said the ticket dispenser.

The clean air whistled in his ears, and the horns called to each other in celestial voices. He caught a whiff of dry leaves and a branch nearly brushed against him. He asked a neighbor where he should get off. It turned out to be a long way yet. He began counting the stops so as not to have to ask again, and tried in vain to distinguish cross streets. The speed, the airiness, the odor of autumn, the dizzy mirror-like quality of the world all merged into so extraordinary a feeling of disembodiment that Franz deliberately moved his neck in order to feel the hard head of his collar stud, which seemed to him the only proof of his existence.

At last his stop came. He clambered down the steep stairs and cautiously stepped onto the sidewalk. From receding heights a faceless traveller shouted to him: "On your right! First street on your—" Franz, vibrating responsively, reached the corner and turned right. Stillness, solitude, a sunny mist. He felt he was losing his way, melting in this mist, and most important, he could not distinguish the house numbers. He felt weak and sweaty. Finally, spying a cloudy passer-by, he accosted him and asked where number five was. The pedestrian stood very near him, and the shadow of foliage played so strangely over his face that for an instant Franz thought he recognized the man from whom he had fled the day before. One could maintain with almost complete certainty that this was a dappled whim of sun and shade; and yet it gave Franz such a shock that he averted his eyes. "Right across the street, where you see that white fence," the man said jauntily, and went on his way.

Franz did not see any fence but found a wicket, groped for the button and pressed it. The gate emitted an odd buzzing sound. He waited a little and pressed again. Again the wicket buzzed. No one came to open it. Beyond lay the greenish haze of a garden with a house floating there like an indistinct reflection. He tried to open the gate himself, but found it unyielding. Biting his lips he rang once more and held his finger on the button for a long time. The same monotonous buzzing. He suddenly realized what the trick was: leaned against the gate as he rang, and it opened so angrily that he nearly fell. Someone called to him: "Whom do you want?" He turned toward the voice and distinguished a woman in a light-colored dress standing on the gravel path that led to the house.

"My husband is not home yet," the voice said after a little pause when Franz had replied.

Slitting his eyes he made out the flash of earrings and dark smooth hair. She was neither a fearful nor fanciful woman but in his clumsy eagerness to see better he had come up so close that for a ridiculous moment she thought this impetuous intruder was about to take her head between his hands.

"It's very important," said Franz. "You see, I'm a relative of his." Stopping in front of her he produced his wallet and began to rummage in it for the famous card.

She wondered where she had seen him before. His ears were of a translucent red in the sun, and tiny drops of sweat gemmed his innocent forehead right at the roots of his short dark hair. A sudden recollection, like a conjuror, put eyeglasses on the inclined face and immediately removed them again. Martha smiled. At the same time Franz found the card and raised his head.

"Here," he said. "I was told to come. On a Sunday."

She looked at the card and smiled again.

"Your uncle has gone to play tennis. He will be back for lunch. But we've already met, you know."

"*Bitte?*" said Franz, straining his eyes.

Later, when he remembered this meeting, the mirage of the garden, that sun-melting dress, he marvelled at the length of time it had taken him to recognize her. At three paces he was able to make out a person's features at least as clearly as a normal human eye would through a gauze veil. Rather naively he told himself that he had never seen her hatless before, and had not expected her to wear her hair with a parting in the middle and a chignon behind (the only particular in which Martha did not follow the fashion); still it was not so simple to explain how it could have happened that, even in that dim perception of the phantom form, there had not worked again and at once the same tremor, the same magic that had fascinated him the day before. It seemed to him afterwards that on that morning he had been plunged in a vague irreproducible world existing for one brief Sunday, a world where everything was delicate and weightless, radiant and unstable. In this dream anything could happen: so it did turn out after all that Franz had not awakened in his hotel bed that morning but had merely passed into the next stratum of sleep. In the unsubstantial radiance of his myopia, Martha bore no resemblance at all to the lady in the train who had glowed like a picture and yawned like a tigress. Her madonna-like beauty that he had glimpsed and then lost now appeared in full as if this were her true essence now blooming before him without any admixture, without flaw or frame. He could not have said with certitude if he found this blurry lady attractive. Nearsightedness is chaste. And besides, she was the wife of the man on whom depended his whole future, out of whom he had been ordered to squeeze everything he possibly could, and this fact made her seem at the very moment of acquaintance more distant, more unattainable than the glamorous stranger of the preceding day. As he followed Martha up the path to the house he gesticulated, kept apologizing for his infirmity, broken glasses, closed shops, and extolling the marvels of coincidence, so intoxicating was his desire to dispose her favorably toward him as quickly as possible.

On the lawn near the porch stood a very tall beach umbrella and under it a small table and several wicker armchairs. Martha sat down, and Franz, grinning and blinking, sat down beside her. She decided that she had stunned him completely with the sight of her small but expensive garden which contained among other things five beds of dahlias, three larches, two weeping willows, and one magnolia, and did not bother to ascertain if those poor wild eyes could distinguish a beach umbrella from an ornamental tree. She enjoyed receiving him so elegantly *auf englische Weise*, dazzling him with undreamt-of wealth, and was looking forward to showing him the villa, the miniatures in the parlor, and the satinwood in the bedroom, and hearing this rather handsome boy's moans of respectful admiration. And, since generally her visitors were people from her own circle whom she had long since grown tired of dazzling, she felt tenderly grateful to this provincial with his starched collar and narrow trousers for giving her an opportunity to renew the pride she had known in her first months of marriage.

"It's so quiet here," said Franz. "I thought Berlin would be so noisy."

"Oh, but we live almost in the country," she answered, and feeling herself seven years younger, added: "the next villa over there belongs to a count. A very nice old man, we see a lot of him."

"Very pleasant—this quiet simple atmosphere," said Franz, steadily developing the theme and already foreseeing a blind alley.

She looked at his pale pink-knuckled hand with a nice long index lying flat on the table. The thin fingers were trembling slightly.

"I have often tried to decide," she said, "whom does one know better—somebody one has been in the same room with for five hours or somebody one has seen for ten minutes every day during a whole month."

"*Bitte?*" said Franz.

"I suppose," she went on, "the real factor here is not the amount of time but that of communication—the exchange of ideas on life and living conditions. Tell me, how are you related to my husband exactly? Second cousin, isn't it? You're going to work here, that's nice, boys like you should be made to work a lot. His business is enormous—I mean, my husband's firm. But then I'm sure you've already heard about his celebrated emporium. Perhaps emporium is too strong a word, it carries men's things only, but there is everything, everything—neckties, hats, sporting goods. Then there's his office in another part of the town and various banking operations."

"It will be hard to begin," said Franz, drumming with his fingers. "I'm a little scared. But I know your husband is a wonderful man, a very kind good man. My mother worships him."

At this moment there appeared from somewhere, as if in token of sympathy, the specter of a dog which turned out upon closer examination to be an Alsatian. Lowering its head, the dog placed something at Franz's feet. Then it retreated a little, dissolved momentarily, and waited expectantly.

"That's Tom," said Martha. "Tom won a prize at the show. Didn't you, Tom" (she spoke to Tom only in the presence of guests).

Out of respect for his hostess, Franz picked up the object the dog was offering him. It proved to be a wet wooden ball covered with tangible tooth marks. As soon as he took up the ball, raising it up to his face, the specter of the dog emerged with a bound from the sunny haze, becoming alive, warm, active, and nearly knocking him off his chair. He quickly got rid of the ball. Tom vanished.

The ball landed right among the dahlias but of course Franz did not see this.

"Fine animal," he observed with revulsion as he wiped his wet hand against the chintzed chair arm. Martha was looking away, worried by the storm in the flowerbed which Tom was trampling in frantic search of his plaything. She clapped her hands. Franz politely clapped too, mistaking admonishment for applause. Fortunately at that moment a boy rode by on a bicycle, and Tom, instantly forgetting the ball, lunged headlong toward the garden fence and dashed along its entire length barking furiously. Then he immediately calmed down, trotted back and lay down by the porch steps under Martha's cold eye, lolling his tongue and folding back one front paw like a lion.

As Franz listened to what Martha was telling him, in the vibrant petulant tones he was getting used to, about the Tyrol, he felt that the dog had not gone too far away, and might bring back any moment that slimy object. Nostalgically he remembered a nasty old lady's nasty old pug (a relative and great enemy of his mother's pet) that he had managed to kick smartly on several occasions.

"But somehow, you know," Martha was saying, "one felt hemmed in. One imagined those mountains might crash down on the hotel, in the middle of the night, right on our bed, burying me under them and my husband, killing everybody. We were thinking of going on to Italy but somehow I lost the lust. He's pretty stupid, our Tom. Dogs that play with balls are always stupid. A strange gentleman arrives but for him it's a brand-new member of the family. This is your first visit, isn't it, to our great city? How do you like it here?"

Franz indicated his eyes with a polite pinkie: "I'm quite blind," he said. "Until I get some new glasses, I cannot appreciate anything. All I see are just colors, which after all is not very interesting. But in general I like it. And it's so quiet here, under this yellow tree."

For some reason the thought crossed his mind—a streak of

[30]

fugitive fancy—that at that very moment his mother was returning from church with Frau Kamelspinner, the taxidermist's wife. And meanwhile—wonder of wonders—he was having a difficult but delicious conversation with this misty lady in this radiant mist. It was all very dangerous; every word she said might trip him.

Martha noticed his slight stammer and the nervous way he had of sniffing now and then. "Dazzled and embarrassed, and so very young," she reflected with a mixture of contempt and tenderness, "warm, healthy young wax that one can manipulate and mold till its shape suits your pleasure. He should have shaved, though, before coming." And she said by way of experiment, just to see how he would react:

"If you plan to work at a smart store, my good sir, you must cultivate a more confident manner and get rid of that black down on your manly jaws."

As she had expected, Franz lost what composure he had.

"I shall get new spectables, I mean respectacles," he expostulated, or so his flustered lisp sounded.

She allowed his confusion to spin itself out, telling herself that it was very good for him. Franz really did feel most uncomfortable for an instant but not quite in the way she imagined. What put him off was not the remonstrance but the sudden coarseness of her tone, a kind of throaty "hep!," as if, to set the example, she were jerking back her shoulders at the word "confident." This was not in keeping with his misty image of her.

The jarring interpolation passed quickly: Martha melted back into the glamorous haze of the world surrounding him and resumed her elegant conversation.

"Autumn is chillier around here than in your native orchards. I love luscious fruit but I also like a crisp cold day.

There is something about the texture and temperature of my skin that simply thrills in response to a breeze or a keen frost. Alas, I have to pay for it."

"Back home there is still bathing," observed Franz. He was all set to tell her about the celebrated limpid lyrical river running through his native town under arched bridges, and then between cornfields and vineyards; about how nice it was to go swimming there in the buff, diving right off the little "nicker raft" you could hire for a few coppers; but at that instant a car honked and drew up at the gate, and Martha said: "Here is my husband."

She fixed her eyes on Dreyer, wondering if his aspect would impress the young cousin, and forgetting that Franz had seen him before and could hardly see him now. Dreyer came at his fast bouncy walk. He wore an ample white overcoat with a white scarf. Three rackets, each in a differently colored cloth case—maroon, blue, and mulberry—protruded from under his arm; his face with its tawny mustache glowed like an autumn leaf. She was less vexed by his exotic attire than that the conversation had been interrupted, that she was no longer alone with Franz, that it was no longer exclusively she who engrossed and amazed him. Involuntarily her manner toward Franz changed, as if there had been "something between them," and now came the husband, causing them to behave with greater reserve. Besides, she certainly did not want to let Dreyer see that the poor relative whom she had criticized before knowing him had not turned out too bad after all. Therefore when Dreyer joined them she wanted to convey to him by means of an inconspicuous bit of pantomime that his arrival would now liberate her at last from a boring guest. Unfortunately Dreyer as he approached did not take his eyes off Franz who, peering at the gradually condensing light part of the mottled mist, got up and was preparing to make a bow. Dreyer, who was observant in his own way and fond of trivial mnemonic tricks (he often played a game with himself, trying to recollect the pictures in a waiting room, that pathetic limbo of pictures), had immediately, from a distance, recognized their recent travelling companion and wondered if perhaps he had brought the unopened letter from a milliner that Martha had mislaid during the journey. But suddenly another, much more amusing, thought dawned upon him. Martha, accustomed to the fireworks of his face, saw his cropped mustache twitch and the rays of wrinkles on the temple side of his eyes multiply and quiver. The next instant he burst out laughing so violently that Tom, who had been jumping around him, could not help barking. Not only the coincidence tickled Dreyer but also the conjecture that Martha had probably said something nasty about his relative while the relative had been sitting right there in the compartment. Just what Martha had said, and whether Franz could have heard it, he would never be able to recall now but something there had surely been, and this itchy uncertainty intensified the humorous aspect of the coincidence. In the no-time of human thought he also recalled— while the dog drowned his cousin's greeting—how an acquaintance once had rung him up while he was taking a tumultuous shower, and Martha had shouted through the bathroom door, "That stupid old Waooroohluoo io oalling" and five paces away the telephone receiver on the table was cupping its ear like an eavesdropper in a farce.

He laughed as he shook Franz's hand, and was still laughing when he dropped into one of the wicker chairs. Tom continued to bark. Suddenly Martha lunged forward and, rings blazing, gave the dog a really hard slap with the back of her hand. It hurt, and with a whimper Tom slunk away.

"Delightful," said Dreyer (the delight quite gone), wiping his eyes with an ample silk handkerchief. "So you are Franz —Lina's boy. After such a coincidence we must do away with formalities—please don't call me sir but Uncle, dear Uncle."

"Avoid vocatives," thought Franz quickly. Nevertheless, he began to feel at ease. Dreyer, blowing his nose in the haze, was indistinct, absurd, and harmless like those total strangers who impersonate people we know in our dreams and talk to us in phony voices like intimate friends.

"I was in fine form today," Dreyer said to his wife, "and you know something, I'm hungry. I imagine young Franz is hungry too."

"Lunch will be served in a minute," said Martha. She got up and disappeared.

Franz, feeling even more at ease, said: "I must apologize —I've broken my glasses and can hardly distinguish anything, so I get mixed up a little."

"Where are you staying?" asked Dreyer.

"At the Video," said Franz. "Near the station. It was recommended to me by an experienced person."

"Fine. Yes, you are a good dog, Tom. Now first of all you must find a nice room, not too far from us. For forty or fifty marks a month. Do you play tennis?"

"Certainly," replied Franz, remembering a backyard, a secondhand brown racket purchased for one mark at a bric-a-brac shop from under the bust of Wagner, a black rubber ball, and an uncooperative brick wall with a fatal square hole in which grew one wallflower.

"Fine. So we can play on Sundays. Then you will need a decent suit, shirts, soft collars, ties, all kinds of things. How did you get on with my wife?"

Franz grinned, not knowing the answer.

[34]

"Fine," said Dreyer. "I suspect lunch is ready. We'll talk about business later. We discuss business over coffee around here."

His wife had come out on the porch. She gave him a long cold glance, coldly nodded, and went back into the house. "That hateful, undignified, genial tone he always must take with inferiors," she reflected as she passed through the ivory-white front hall where the impeccable, hospitable white comb and white-backed brush lay on the doily under the pier glass. The entire villa, from whitewashed terrace to radio antenna, was that way—neat, clean-cut, and on the whole unloved and inane. The master of the house deemed it a joke. As for the lady, neither aesthetic nor emotional considerations ruled her taste; she simply thought that a reasonably wealthy German businessman in the nineteen-twenties, in Berlin-West, ought to have a house exactly of that sort, that is, belonging to the same suburban type as those of his fellows. It had all the conveniences, and the majority of those conveniences went unused. There was, for example, in the bathroom a round, face-sized swivel mirror—a grotesque magnifier, with an electric light attached. Martha had once given it to her husband for shaving but very soon he had grown to detest it: it was unbearable every morning to see one's brightly illuminated chin swollen to about three times its natural volume and studded with rusty bristles that had sprouted overnight. The chairs in the parlor resembled a display in a good store. A writing desk with an unnecessary upper stage, consisting of unnecessary little drawers, supported, in place of a lamp, a bronze knight holding a lantern. There were lots of well dusted but uncaressed porcelain animals with glossy rumps, as well as varicolored cushions, against which no human cheek had ever nestled; and albums —huge arty things with photographs of Copenhagen porcelain and Hagenkopp furniture—which were opened only by the dullest or shyest guest. Everything in the house, including the jars labelled sugar, cloves, chicory, on the shelves of the idyllic kitchen, had been chosen by Martha, to whom, seven years previously, her husband had presented on its green-turfed tray the freshly built little villa, still empty and ready to please. She had acquired paintings and distributed them throughout the rooms under the supervision of an artist who had been very much in fashion that season, and who believed that any picture was acceptable as long as it was ugly and meaningless, with thick blobs of paint, the messier and muddier the better. Following the count's advice, Martha had also bought a few old oils at auctions. Among them was the magnificent portrait of a noble-looking gentleman, with sidewhiskers, wearing a stylish morning coat, who stood leaning on a slender cane, illuminated as if by sheet lightning against a rich brown background. Martha bought this with good reason. Right beside it, on the dining-room wall, she placed a daguerreotype of her grandfather, a long-since-deceased coal merchant who had been suspected of drowning his first wife in a tarn around 1860, but nothing was proved. He also had sidewhiskers, wore a morning coat, and leaned on a cane; and his proximity to the sumptuous oil (signed by Heinrich von Hildenbrand) neatly transformed the latter into a family portrait. "Grandpa," Martha would say, indicating the genuine article with a wave of her hand that indolently included in the arc it described the anonymous nobleman to whose portrait the deceived guest's gaze shifted.

Unfortunately, though, Franz was able to make out neither the pictures nor the porcelain no matter how skillfully Martha directed his attention to the room's charms. He perceived a delicate blend of color, felt the freshness of abundant flowers, appreciated the yielding softness of the carpet underfoot, and thus perceived by a freak of fate the very quality that the furnishings of the house lacked but that, in Martha's opinion, ought to have existed, and for which she had paid good money: an aura of luxury, in which, after the second glass of pale golden wine, he began slowly to dissolve. Dreyer refilled his glass, and breakfastless Franz, who had not dared to partake of the enigmatic first course, realized that his lower extremities had by now dissolved completely. He twice mistook the bare forearm of the servant maid for that of Martha but then became aware that she sat far away like a wine-golden ghost. Dreyer, ghostly too, but warm and ruddy, was describing a flight he had made two or three years ago from Munich to Vienna in a bad storm; how the plane had tossed and shaken, and how he had felt like telling the pilot "Do stop for a moment"; and how his chance travelling companion, an old Englishman, kept calmly solving a crossword puzzle. Meanwhile Franz was experiencing fantastic difficulties with the vol-au-vent and then with the dessert. He had the feeling that in another minute his body would melt completely leaving only his head, which, with its mouth stuffed with a cream puff, would start floating about the room like a balloon. The coffee and the curaçao all but finished him. Dreyer, slowly rotating before him like a flaming wheel with human arms for spokes, began discussing the job awaiting Franz. Noting the state in which the poor fellow was, he did not go into details. He did say, however, that very soon Franz would become an excellent salesman, that the aviator's principal enemy is not wind but fog, and that, as the salary would not be much at first, he would undertake to pay for the room and would be glad if Franz dropped in every evening if he desired, though he would not be surprised if next year air service were established between Europe and America. The merry-go-round in Franz's head never stopped; his armchair travelled around the room in gliding circles. Dreyer considered him with a kindly smile, and, in anticipation of the tongue-lashing Martha would give him for all this jollity, kept mentally pouring out upon Franz's head the contents of an enormous cornucopia, for he had to reward Franz somehow for the exhilarating fun lavished upon him by the imp of coincidence through Franz. He must reward not only him, but cousin Lina too for that wart on her cheek, for her pug, for the rocking chair with its green sausage-shaped nape rest bearing the embroidered legend "Only one little half hour." Later, when Franz, exhaling wine and gratitude, bade his uncle good-by, carefully descended the steps to the garden, carefully squeezed through the gate, and, still holding his hat in his hand, disappeared round the corner, Dreyer imagined what a nice nap the poor boy would have back in his hotel room, and then himself felt the blissful weight of drowsiness and went up to the bedroom.

There, in an orange peignoir, her bare legs crossed, her velvety-white neck nicely set off by the black of her low thick chignon—Martha sat at her dressing table polishing her nails. Dreyer saw in the mirror the gloss of her smooth bandeaux, her knit brows, her girlish breasts. A robust but untimely throb dispelled sleepiness. He sighed. It was not the first time he regretted that Martha regarded afternoon lovemaking as a decadent perversion. And since she did not raise her head, he understood she was angry.

He said softly—trying to make matters worse so as to stop regretting: "Why did you disappear after lunch? You might have waited until he left."

Without raising her eyes Martha answered: "You know perfectly well we've been invited today to a very important and very smart tea. It wouldn't hurt if you got cleaned up too."

"We still have an hour or so," said Dreyer. "Actually I thought I'd take a nap."

Martha remained silent as she worked rapidly with the chamois polisher. He threw off his so-called Norfolk jacket, then sat down on the edge of the couch, and began taking off his red-sand-stained tennis shoes.

Martha bent even lower and abruptly said: "Amazing how some people have no sense of dignity."

Dreyer grunted and leisurely got rid of his flannel trousers, then of his white silk socks.

A minute or so later Martha chucked something with a clatter onto the glass surface of her dressing table and said: "I'd like to know what that young man thinks of you now. No formalities, call me Uncle. . . . It's unheard-of."

Dreyer smiled, wiggling his toes. "Enough playing on public courts," he said. "Next spring I'll join a club."

Martha abruptly turned toward him and, leaning her elbow on the arm of her chair, dropped her chin on her fist. One leg crossed over the other was swinging slightly. She surveyed her husband, incensed by the look of half-mischief, half-desire in his eyes.

"You've got what you wanted," she continued. "You've taken care of your dear nephew. I bet you've made him heaps of promises. And will you please cover your obscene nudity."

Draping himself in a dressing gown, Dreyer made himself comfortable on the cretonne couch. What would happen, he wondered, if he now said something like this: You too have your peculiarities, my love, and some of them are less pardonable than a husband's obscenity. You travel second-class instead of first because second is just as good and the saving is colossal, amounting to the stupendous sum of twenty-seven marks and sixty pfennigs which would otherwise have disappeared into the pockets of the swindlers who invented first-class. You hit a lovable and loving dog because a dog is not supposed to laugh aloud. All right: let's assume this is all right. But allow me to play a little too—leave me my nephew. . . .

"Evidently you do not wish to speak to me," said Martha. "Oh, well. . . ." She went back to work on her gem-like nails. Dreyer reflected: If only just once you let yourself go, come, come on, have some good fun and a good fit of crying. After that surely you'll feel better.

He cleared his throat, preparing the way for words, but as had happened more than once, decided at the last minute not to say anything. There is no knowing if it was from a wish to irritate her with silence or simply the result of contented laziness, or perhaps an unconscious fear of dealing a final blow to something he wanted to preserve. Leaning back against the three-cornered cushion, his hands thrust deep into his dressing-gown pockets, he remained contemplating silent Martha; presently his gaze roamed away to his wife's wide bed under its white blanket cover, batiste trimmed with lace, washable, ninety by ninety inches, and severely separated from his, also lace-covered, by a night table on which sprawled a leggy rag doll with a black face. This doll, and the bedspreads, and the pretentious furniture were both amusing and repelling.

He yawned and rubbed the bridge of his nose. Perhaps it would be wiser to change at once and then read for half an hour on the terrace. Martha threw off her orange peignoir, and as she drew back her elbows to adjust a necklace her angelically lovely bare shoulder blades came together like folding wings. He wondered wistfully how many hours must pass till she let him kiss those shoulders; hesitated, thought better of it, and went to his dressing room across the passage.

As soon as the door had noiselessly closed behind him, Martha sprang up and furiously, with a wrenching twist, locked it. This was utterly out of character: a singular impulse she would have been at a loss to explain, and all the more senseless since she would need the maid in a minute, and would have to unlock the door anyway. Much later, when many months had passed, and she was trying to reconstruct that day, it was this door and this key that she recalled most vividly, as if an ordinary door key happened to be the correct key to that not quite ordinary day. However, in wringing the neck of the lock she failed to dispell her anger. It was a confused and turbulent seething that found no release. She was angry that Franz's visit had given her a strange pleasure, and that for this pleasure she had to thank her husband. The upshot was that in their arguments about inviting or not inviting a poor relative she had been wrong, and her wayward and wacky husband right. Therefore she tried not to acknowledge the pleasure so that her husband might remain in the wrong. The pleasure, she knew, would soon be repeated, and she also knew that had she been absolutely sure her attitude would have caused her husband not to receive Franz again, she might not have said what she had said just now. For the first time in her married life she experienced something that she had never expected, something that did not fit like a legitimate square into the parquet pattern of their life after the dismal surprises of their honeymoon. Thus, out of a trifle, out of a chance stay in a ridiculous provincial town, something had started to grow, joyful and irreparable. And there was no vacuum cleaner in the world that could instantly restore all the rooms of her brain to their former immaculate condition. The vague quality of her sensations, the difficulty of figuring out logically just why she had liked that awkward, eager, provincial boy with tremulous long fingers and pimples between his eyebrows, all this vexed her so much that she was ready to curse the new green dress laid out on the armchair, the plump posterior of Frieda who was rummaging in the lower drawer of the commode, and her own morose reflection in the mirror. She looked at a jewel in which an anniversary was coldly reflected, and remembered that her thirty-fourth birthday had passed the other day, and with a strange impatience began consulting her mirror to detect the threat of a wrinkle, the hint of a sagging fold. Somewhere a door closed softly, and the stairs creaked (they were not supposed to creak!), and her husband's cheerful off-key whistle receded out of earshot. "He is a poor dancer," thought Martha. "He may be good at tennis but he will always be a poor dancer. He does not like dancing. He does not understand how fashionable it is nowadays. Fashionable and indispensable."

With muted resentment against inefficient Frieda, she thrust her head through the soft, gathered circumference of the dress. Its green shadow flew downward past her eyes. She emerged erect, smoothed her hips, and suddenly felt that her soul was temporarily circumscribed and contained by the emerald texture of that cool frock.

Below, on the square terrace, with its cement floor and the purple and pink asters on its wide balustrade, Dreyer sat in a canvas chair by a garden table, and with his open book resting in his lap gazed into the garden. Beyond the fence, the black car, the expensive Icarus, was already waiting inexorably. The new chauffeur, his elbows placed on the fence from the outside, was chatting with the gardener. A cold late-afternoon lucency penetrated the autumn air; the sharp blue shadows of the young trees stretched along the sunny lawn, all in the same direction as if anxious to see which would be first to reach the garden's white lateral wall. Far off, across the street, the pistachio facades of apartment houses were very distinct, and there, melancholically leaning on a red quilt laid on the window sill, sat a bald little man in shirt-sleeves. The gardener had already twice taken hold of his wheelbarrow but each time had turned again to the chauffeur. Then they both lit cigarettes. And the wispy smoke was clearly set off as it floated along the glossy black side of the car. The shadow seemed to have moved just a bit farther but the sun still bore down triumphantly on the right from behind the corner of the count's villa, which stood on higher ground with taller trees. Tom walked indolently along the flowerbed. From a sense of duty and without the least hope of success, he started after a low-flitting sparrow, and then lay down by the wheelbarrow with his nose on his paws. The very word terrace—how spacious, how cool! The pretty ray of a spiderweb stretched obliquely from the corner flower of the balustrade to the table standing beside it. The cloudlets in one part of the pale clean sky had funny curls, and were all alike as on a maritime horizon, all hanging together in a delicate flock. At last having heard all there was to hear and told all there was to tell, the gardener moved off with his wheelbarrow, turning with geometrical precision at the intersections of gravel paths, and Tom, rising lazily, proceeded to walk after him like a clockwork toy, turning when the gardener turned. *Die toten Seelen* by a Russian author, which had long been slipping down Dreyer's knee, slid onto the flags of the floor, and he felt too lazy to pick it up. So pleasant, so spacious. . . . The first to finish would be no doubt that apple tree over there. The chauffeur got into his seat. It would be interesting to know just what he was thinking about now.

This morning his eyes had oddly twinkled. Could it be that he drinks? Wouldn't that be a scream, a tippling chauffeur. Two men in top hats, diplomats or undertakers, went by; the top hats and black coats floated by along the fence. Out of nowhere came a Red Admirable butterfly, settled on the edge of the table, opened its wings and began to fan them slowly as if breathing. The dark-brown ground was bruised here and there, the scarlet band had faded, the fringes were frayed—but the creature was still so lovely, so festive. . . .

3

On Monday Franz splurged: he purchased what the optician assured him was an American article. The rims were of tortoise shell—allowing no doubt for the well-known fact that chelonians are frequently and variously mocked. When the proper lenses had been inserted and he donned his new spectacles, Franz experienced at once a feeling of comfort and peace in his heart as well as behind his ears. The haze dissolved. The unruly colors of the universe were confined once more to their official compartments and cells.

There still remained one thing he had to do in order to establish and affirm himself in this freshly marked-out world: he had to find himself a dwelling place. Franz smiled indulgently and smugly as he recalled Dreyer's promise of the previous day to pay for many luxuries. Uncle Dreyer was a somewhat fantastic but highly useful institution. And Uncle was perfectly right: how indeed could Franz do without some decent clothes? First, however, let us find that room.

No sun today. A sober chill emanated from the low drab sky. Berlin taxis turned out to be a very dark green with a neat black-and-white checkered border across the doors.

Here and there a blue mailbox had been freshly painted in celebration of autumn and looked singularly shiny and sticky. He found the streets of this quarter disappointingly quiet, as actually streets in a great city were not supposed to be. It was fun to memorize their names and the whereabouts of useful shops and offices—pharmacy, grocery, post office, police station. Why did the Dreyers insist on living so far from the center? He was displeased that there were so many vacant lots, so many little parks and lawny squares, so many pines and birches, houses under construction, vegetable gardens. It all reminded him too much of his backwoods home. He thought he recognized Tom in a dog being walked by a plump but not uncomely housemaid. Children were playing ball or whipping their tops right on the asphalt. He too had once played like that. Only one thing really told him he was in the metropolis: some strollers wore marvellous clothes! For instance, plus-fours, very baggy below the knee, so as to make the wool-stockinged shin look handsomely slender. That particular style he had never seen before, though boys in his hometown also wore knickerbockers. Then there was the high-class fop in a double-breasted jacket, very wide in the shoulders, and ultra-tight around the hips, and with incredibly elephantine trouser legs the tremendous cuffs of which practically concealed his shoes. The hats, too, were splendid, and the flamboyant ties; and the girls, the girls. Kind Dreyer!

He walked slowly shaking his head, clucking his tongue, looking around every moment. The kissable cuties, he thought almost aloud, and inhaled with a hiss through clenched teeth. What calves! What bottoms! Enough to drive one crazy!

At home when walking along the cloyingly familiar streets, he had experienced, of course, the same aching reaction to fugitive charm many times a day. But in his morbid shyness he did not dare look too insistently in those days. Here it was a different matter. He was disguised as a stranger, and these girls were accessible, (again that hiss), they were accustomed to avid glances, they welcomed them, and it was possible to accost any one of them, and start a brilliant and brutal conversation. He would do just that but first he had to find a room in which to rip off her dress and possess her. Forty to fifty marks, Dreyer had said. That meant fifty, at least.

Franz decided to act systematically. At the door of every third or fourth house a small notice board announced rooms for rent. He consulted a newly bought map of the city, checked once again the distance from Uncle's villa and found he was close enough. A nice, new-looking house with a nice green door to which a white card was affixed attracted him, and he blithely rang the bell. Only after he had pressed it he noticed that the sign said "fresh paint"! But it was too late. A window opened on his right. A bob-haired, bare-shouldered young girl in a black slip, clutching a white kitten to her breast, peered out at Franz. His lips went dry in the arid blast. The girl was enchanting: a simple little seamstress, no doubt, but enchanting, and let us hope not too expensive. "Whom do you want?" she asked. Franz gulped, smiled foolishly, and said with quite unexpected impudence, by which he himself was at once embarrassed: "Maybe you, eh?"

She looked at him with curiosity.

"Come on," said Franz awkwardly, "let me in."

The girl turned away and was heard to say to someone in the room: "I don't know what he wants. Better ask him yourself." Over her shoulder appeared the head of a middle-aged man with a pipe between his teeth. Franz tipped his hat, turned on his heel, and walked on. He noticed that he was still grinning horribly and emitting a thin moan. "Nonsense," he thought with rage, "it's nothing. Forget it."

It took him two hours to inspect eleven rooms in four different blocks. Strictly speaking, any one of them was delightful. But each had a tiny defect. One, for example, had not been tidied up yet, and as he looked into the dull eyes of the woman in mourning who was answering his questions with a kind of listless despair, Franz decided her husband had just died in that very room which she was rather fraudulently offering him. Another room had a simpler shortcoming: it cost five marks more than the price mentioned by Dreyer; otherwise it was perfect. The third room revealed brown stains on the walls, and a mousetrap in the corner. The fourth was connected with a smelly toilet that could also be reached from the corridor and was used by a neighbor's family. The fifth. . . . But in a singularly short time these rooms with their virtues and flaws became confused in Franz's mind, and only one remained immaculate and distinct: the one that cost fifty-five marks. He had a sudden feeling there was no reason to prolong his quest, and that anyway he would not venture to decide by himself, fearing to make a bad choice and deprive himself of a million other rooms; on the other hand, it was hard to imagine anything better than the room that had caught his fancy. It gave on a pleasant by-street with a delicatessen shop. A palace-like affair that the landlord said would be a movie house was being built on the corner, and this gave life to the surroundings. A picture above the bed showed a naked girl leaning forward to wash her breasts in a misty pond.

"Good," he reflected. "It is now a quarter to one. Time for a meal. A brilliant idea: eat at the Dreyers'. I'll ask them what I should pay particular attention to when making my choice, and if he does not think that five extra marks. . . ."

Cleverly using his map (and promising himself incidentally that as soon as he had taken care of business he would go by subway to what was surely the gayest part of this sprawling city), Franz arrived without difficulty at the villa. It was painted a grainy gray, and had a solid, compact, one might even say appetizing, look. In the garden heavy red apples hung in clusters on the young trees. As he walked up the crunching path, he saw Martha standing on the porch step. She wore a hat and a moleskin coat, and was checking the dubious whiteness of the sky, trying to decide whether or not to open her umbrella. She did not smile when she noticed Franz.

"My husband is not at home," she said, fixing him with her beautiful cold eyes. "He is lunching in town today."

Franz glanced at the handbag jutting from under her arm, at the artificial purple pansy pinned to the huge collar of her coat, at the stubby umbrella with its sparkling knob, and realized that she too was leaving.

"Pardon me for having disturbed you," he said, inwardly cursing his fate.

"Oh, it's perfectly all right," said Martha, and they both moved in the direction of the gate. Franz wondered what to do next—bid her good-by? Go on walking beside her? Martha with a displeased expression kept looking straight ahead, her full warm lips half open. Then she quickly wet them and said: "This is so unpleasant. I have to walk. We wrecked the car last night."

There had indeed been an unpleasant accident on the way home after a tea and a dance. In an ill-timed attempt to pass a truck, the chauffeur had first hit a wooden railing where the tram tracks were being repaired, and swerving sharply had collided with the side of the truck; the Icarus had spun around and crashed into a pole. While this motorized frenzy was in progress, Martha and her husband had assumed all imaginable positions, and had finally found themselves on the floor. Dreyer had asked sympathetically if she were not hurt. The shock, the search for the beads of her necklace, the crowd of gawkers, the vulgar aspect of the smashed car, the foul-mouthed truck driver, the arrogant policeman who was not amused by Dreyer's jokes—all this brought Martha to a state of such irritation that she had had to take two sleeping pills, and had slept only two hours.

"A wonder I did not get killed," she said sullenly. "But even our chauffeur was not hurt, which is a pity." And slowly stretching out her hand, she helped Franz open the wicket which he was vainly pushing and rattling.

"No question about it, cars are dangerous playthings," he said noncommitally. Now it was definitely time to take leave.

Martha noticed and approved his hesitation.

"Which way are you going?" she asked, transferring her umbrella from right hand to left. The glasses he had got were very becoming. He looked like the actor Hess in *The Hindu Student*, a movie.

"Don't know myself," said Franz, smirking rather freely. "You see I was just coming to ask Uncle's advice about the room." This first "Uncle" came out unconvincingly, and he resolved not to repeat it for a while so as to let the word ripen on its twig.

"I can help too," said Martha. "Tell me what's the trouble."

Imperceptibly they had begun to move and were now

walking slowly along the wide sidewalk on which broken chestnuts and claw-like crisp leaves lay here and there. Franz blew his nose and began telling her about the room.

"Why, that's unheard of," Martha interrupted. "Fifty-five? I'm sure you can haggle a little."

A forethrill of triumph went through Franz but he decided not to rush things.

"The landlord is a closefisted old codger, the devil himself would not make him budge."

"You know what?" Martha said suddenly. "I would not mind going there and talking to him myself."

Franz exulted. What luck! To say nothing of how splendid it was to stroll along with this red-lipped beauty in her moleskin coat! The sharp autumn air, the susurration of tires —this was the life! Add a new suit and a flaming tie—and his happiness would be complete.

"Where is Mr. Tom today?" he inquired. "I thought I saw him going for a walk."

"No, he's locked up in the gardener's shed. He's a good dog but a little neurotic. As I always say, dogs are acceptable pets if they are clean."

"Cats are cleaner," said Franz.

"Oh, I abominate cats. Dogs understand when you scold them, but cats are hopeless—no contact with human beings, no gratitude, nothing."

"We shot lots of stray ones back home, a school friend and I. Especially along the river in spring."

"There's something wrong with my left heel," said Martha. "I need your support for a moment." She placed two light fingers upon his shoulder as she glanced backward and downward. It was nothing. With the tip of her umbrella she scraped off the dead leaf her heel had transfixed.

They reached the square. At least two future stories of the new corner house could be discerned through the scaffolding of the present.

Martha pointed with her umbrella. "We know," she said, "the man who works for the partner of the director of the cinema company who is building that house there."

It would not be ready till sometime next year. The workmen were moving as in a dream.

Franz frantically racked his brain for some more fruitful theme. The coincidence!

"I still can't forget how strangely we met on the train. It's incredible!"

"Yes, a coincidence," said Martha, thinking her own thoughts.

"Listen," she said as they started to climb the steep staircase of the fifth floor, "I'd rather my husband did not know I helped you. No, there is no mystery here. Simply, I would rather he did not."

Franz made a bow. It was no concern of his. Yet he wondered if what she had said were flattering or insulting. Hard to decide. They had now been standing for some time before the door. No one answered the bell. Franz rang again. The door flew open. A little old man with hanging braces and no collar thrust out a rumpled face, and let them in silently.

"I'm back again," said Franz. "Could I see the room once more?"

The old fellow made a kind of rapid salute and shuffled ahead through a long darkish passage.

"Good heavens, what a squalid hole," thought Martha squeamishly. Was she right in coming here? She imagined her husband's mischievous smile: You reproached me, and now you're helping him yourself.

The room, however, turned out to be reasonably bright and clean. By the left-hand wall stood a wooden, probably creaky bed, a washstand, and a stove. On the right, two chairs and a pretentious armchair of moth-eaten plush. There was a small table in the center and a chest-of-drawers in a corner. Over the bed hung a picture. Puzzled, Franz stared at it. A bare-bosomed slave girl on sale was being leered at by three hesitant lechers. It was even more artistic than the bathing September nymph. *She* must have been in some other room—yes, of course, in the one with the stench.

Martha felt the mattress. It was firm and hard. She took off one glove, stroked the bed table, and consulted the face of her finger. A fashionable song she liked, *Black-eyed Natasha*, came from two different radios on two different levels, mingling buoyantly with the musical clanking of construction work somewhere outside.

Franz looked hopefully at Martha. She pointed her umbrella at the barish right-hand wall and inquired in a neutral voice without looking at the old man: "Why did you remove the couch? Obviously, you had something here before."

"The couch was beginning to sag and is being repaired," answered the old man and cocked his head.

"You will put it back later," observed Martha, and raising her eyes, she switched on the light for an instant. The old man looked up too.

"All right," said Martha and again extended her umbrella. "You furnish sheets, don't you?"

"Sheets?" repeated the old man after her with surprise. Then, cocking his head to the other side, he pursed his lips, thought for a moment, and replied: "Yes, we can dig up some sheets."

"And how about service and cleaning?"

The old man poked himself in the chest.

"I do everything," he said. "I *make* everything. I alone."

Martha went over to the window, looked at a truck with planks in the street, then walked back.

"And how much was it you wanted?" she asked with indifference.

"Fifty-five," alertly said the man.

"Including electricity and morning coffee?"

"Has the gentleman got a job?" the old man inquired, nodding in the direction of Franz.

"Yes," promptly said Franz.

"Fifty-five for everything," said the old man.

"That is expensive," said Martha.

"That is not expensive," said the old man.

"That is extremely expensive," said Martha.

The old man smiled.

"Oh well," shrug-sighed Martha and turned toward the door.

Franz realized that the room was about to float away forever. He squeezed and tortured his hat as he tried to catch Martha's eye.

"Fifty-five," the old man repeated pensively.

"Fifty," said Martha.

The old man opened his mouth, and closed it again firmly.

"Very well," he said at last. "But the lights have to be out by eleven."

"Naturally," flowed in Franz. "Naturally—I quite understand."

"When do you wish to move in?" asked his landlord.

"Today, right now," said Franz. "I just have to get my suitcase from the hotel."

"How about a small deposit?" the old man proposed with a subtle smile.

The room itself seemed to be smiling. How strange to recall the cluttered attic of his youth! His mother at the Singer machine while he tried to sleep. How could he have endured it so long? When they emerged again onto the street, there remained in his consciousness a warm hollow formed as it were by his new room's sinking into a soft mass of minor impressions. As she bade him good-by at the corner, Martha saw the glitter of gratitude behind his glasses. And as she headed for the photo shop with some undeveloped Tyrol snapshots, she recalled the conversation with legitimate pride.

A drizzle had set in. The doors of flower shops opened wide to catch the moisture. Now it was really raining. She could not find a taxi; raindrops were managing to get under her umbrella and wash the powder off her nose. A dull restlessness replaced elation. Both yesterday and today were novel and absurd days, and certain not quite intelligible, but significant, outlines were showing through confusedly. And, like that darkish solution in which mountain views would presently float and grow clear, this rain, this delicate pluvial damp, developed shiny images in her soul. Once again a rain-soaked, ardent, strong, blue-eyed man, a vacational acquaintance of her husband's, took advantage of a cloudburst in Zermatt to bluster her into the recess of a porch and push against her and pant out his passion, his sleepless nights, and she shook her head, and he vanished behind the corner of memory. Once again in her drawing room that fool of a painter, a languid rascal with dirty fingernails, glued his lips to her bare neck and she waited a moment to make out what she felt, and feeling nothing, struck him in the face with her elbow. Once again—and this image was a recent one—a wealthy businessman, an American with bluish-gray hair and a long upper lip, murmured as he played with her hand that certainly she would come to his hotel room, and she smiled and regretted vaguely that he was a foreigner. In the company of these chance phantoms rapidly touching her with cold hands, she reached home, shrugged her shoulders and cast them aside as casually as she did her open umbrella which she left on the porch to dry.

"I'm an idiot," she said. "What's the matter? What's wrong with me? Why worry? It must happen sooner or later. It is inevitable."

Her mood changed again. With pleasure she gave Frieda a dressing down because the dog had somehow got back into the house and tracked dirt on the carpet. She devoured a pile of small sandwiches at tea. She called the garage to find out if Dreyer had rented a car as he had promised. She called the cinema to reserve two tickets for the première on Friday; then called her husband; and then old Mrs. Hertwig when it turned out that Dreyer would be busy. And Dreyer was indeed very busy. He had grown so absorbed in an unexpected offer from another firm, in a series of cautious negotiations and courteous conferences that for several days he did not remember Franz; or rather he would remember him at the wrong moments—while relaxing neck-deep in warm water; while driving from office to factory; while smoking a cigarette in bed. Franz would appear gesticulating wildly at the wrong telescope end of his mind; Dreyer would mentally promise to attend to him soon, and immediately would start thinking about something else.

To Franz that was no comfort. When the first agreeable excitement of housewarming had passed, he asked himself what he should do next. Martha had taken down his landlord's telephone number but nothing happened after that. He did not dare to phone himself nor did he dare call on the Dreyers without warning, not trusting chance, which last time had so magnificently transfigured his inopportune visit. He must wait. Evidently, sooner or later, he would be summoned. But he did not relish the delay. At half past seven on the very first morning the landlord in person brought him a sticky cup of weak coffee and on a saucer two lumps of sugar, one with a brown corner, and remarked in an admonishing tone: "Now don't be late for work. Drink this and jump into your clothes. Do not flush the toilet too hard. Take care not to be late."

Franz decided that he had no alternative but leave the house for the whole day in order to perform the job that the old fellow had invented for him, and stay out until five or six, and then have a bite in town before returning. Thus perforce he explored the city, or rather what seemed to him its most metropolitan section. The obligatory nature of those excursions envenomed the novelty. By evening he would be much too exhausted to carry out his plan, his old glorious plan, of sauntering along seductive streets and taking a good preliminary look at genuine harlots. But how to get there? His map seemed to be curiously misleading. One cloudless day, having strayed far enough, he found himself on a broad dreary boulevard with many steamship line offices and art shops: he glanced at the street sign and realized it was the world-famous avenue that had seemed so sublime in his dreams. Its rather skimpy lindens were shedding their leaves. The winged arch at one end was sheathed in scaffolding. He traversed wildernesses of asphalt. He walked along a canal: in one place there was a rainbow-like splotch of oil on the water, and an intoxicating aroma of honey, reminding him of childhood, wafted from a barge where pink-shirted men were unloading mountains of pears and apples; from a bridge he saw two women in glistening bathing caps, intently snorting and rhythmically striking out with their arms as they swam side by side. He spent two hours in a museum of antiquities, examining with awe statues and sarcophagi, and the revolting profiles of brown men driving chariots. He took long rests in shabby pubs and on the fairly comfortable benches of an immense park. He plunged into the depths of the subway and, perched on a red leather seat, looking at the shiny stangs, up which raced golden reflections, waited impatiently for the coaly clattering blackness to be replaced at last by paradises of luxury and sin that kept eluding him. He also wanted very much to find Dreyer's emporium about which they used to speak with such reverence in his hometown. The fat telephone directory, however, listed only his home and office. Evidently it must have some other name. And continuing to remain unaware that the heart of the city had moved to the west, Franz dismally wandered through the central and northern streets where he thought the smartest stores and the liveliest trade must be.

He did not dare buy anything, and this tormented him. In this short time he had already managed to spend quite a bit of money and now Dreyer had disappeared. Everything was somehow uncertain, everything filled him with uneasiness. He tried to make friends with his landlord who so insistently turned him out of the house for the whole day. But the old man was untalkative and kept lurking in the unknown depths of his little apartment. The first night, however, he met Franz in the corridor, warned him again that the water closet chain should be pulled very gently or it would be jerked off and explained to him at length the mysteries of the district police station for which he supplied him with some forms where Franz had to fill in name, marital status, and place of birth. "And another thing," said the old fellow, "about that lady friend of yours. She must not visit you here. I know you are young. I was young once myself. I would be quite ready to give you my permission but there is my wife, you see—she happens to be away temporarily—but I know she would never allow such visits."

Franz flushed and hastily nodded in assent. His landlord's assumption flattered and excited him. He imagined her fragrant, warm-looking lips, her creamy skin, but cut short the habitual swell of desire. "She is not for me," he thought glumly, "she is remote and cold. She lives in a different world, with a very rich and still vigorous husband. She'd send me packing if I were to grow enterprising; my career would be ruined." On the other hand, he thought he might find himself a sweetheart anyway. She too would be shapely, sleek, ripe-lipped and dark-haired. And with this in mind he decided to take certain measures. In the morning, when the landlord brought him his coffee, Franz cleared his throat and said: "Listen, if I paid you a small supplement, would you. . . . Would I. . . . What I mean is, could I entertain anyone if I wished?"

"That depends," said the old man.

"A few extra marks," said Franz.

"I understand," said the old man.

"Five marks more per month," said Franz.

"That's generous," said the old man, and as he turned to go added in a sly admonitory tone: "But take care not to be late for work."

Thus Martha's haggling had all been for nought. Having resolved to pay the extra sum secretly, Franz knew perfectly well he had acted rashly. His money was melting away, and still Dreyer did not telephone. For four days running he left the house in disgust punctually at eight, returning at nightfall in a fog of fatigue. He was completely fed up by now with the celebrated avenue. He sent a postcard to his mother with a view of the Brandenburg Gate, and wrote that he was well, and that Dreyer was a very kind uncle. There was no use frightening her, though perhaps she deserved it. And only on Friday night, when Franz was already lying in bed and saying to himself with a tremor of panic that they had all forgotten him, that he was completely alone in a strange city, and thinking with a certain evil joy that he would stop being faithful to the radiant Martha presiding over his nightly surrenders and ask lewd old Enricht, his landlord, to let him have a bath in the grimy tub of the flat and direct him to the nearest brothel. At that instant Enricht in a sleepy voice called him to the telephone.

With terrible haste and excitement, Franz pulled on his pants and rushed barefoot into the passage. A trunk managed to bang him on the knee as he made for the gleam of the telephone at the end of the corridor. Owing perhaps to his being unaccustomed to telephones, he could not identify at first the voice barking in his ear. "Come to my house this minute," the voice said clearly at last. "Do you hear me? Please hurry, I am waiting for you."

"Oh, how are you, how are you?" Franz babbled, but the telephone was dead. Dreyer put down the receiver with a flourish and continued rapidly jotting down the things he had to do tomorrow. Then he glanced at his watch, reflecting that his wife would be back from the cinema any moment now. He rubbed his forehead, and then with a sly smile took from a drawer a bunch of keys, and a sausage-shaped flashlight with a convex eye. He still had his coat on, for he had just come home and without shedding it had strode right to his study as he always did when he was in a hurry to write something down or telephone someone. Now he noisily pushed back his chair, and began taking off his voluminous camel-hair coat as he walked to the front hall to hang it up there. Into its capacious pocket he dropped the keys and the flashlight. Tom, who was lying by the door, got up and rubbed his soft head against Dreyer's leg. Dreyer resonantly locked himself up in the bathroom where three or four senile mosquitoes slept on the whitewashed wall. A minute later, turning down and buttoning up his sleeves at the wrists, he proceeded with another leisurely homy gait toward the dining room.

The table was laid for two, and a dark red Westphalian ham reposed on a dish, amid a mosaic of sausage slices. Large grapes, brimming with greenish light, hung over the edge of their vase. Dreyer plucked off one and tossed it in his mouth. He cast a sidelong glance at the salami but decided to wait for Martha. The mirror reflected his broad back clothed in gray flannel and the tawny strands of his smoothly brushed hair. He turned around quickly as though feeling that someone was watching him, and moved away; all that remained in the mirror was a white corner of the table against the black background broken by a crystal glimmer on the sideboard. He heard a faint sound from the far side of that stillness: a little key was seeking a sensitive point in the stillness; it found and pierced that point, and gave one crisp turn, and then everything came to life. Dreyer's gray shoulder passed and repassed in the mirror as he paced hungrily round the table. The front door slammed and in came Martha. Her eyes glistened, she was wiping her nose firmly with a Chanel scented handkerchief. Behind her came the fully awakened dog.

"Sit down, sit down, my love," said Dreyer briskly, and turned on the sophisticated electric current to warm the tea water.

"Lovely film," she said. "Hess was wonderful, though I think I liked him better in *The Prince*."

"In what?"

"Oh you remember, the student at Heidelberg disguised as a Hindu prince."

Martha was smiling. In fact, she smiled fairly often of late, which gladdened Dreyer ineffably. She was in the pleasant position of a person who has been promised a mysterious treat in the near future. She was willing to wait awhile, knowing that the treat would come without fail. That day she had summoned the painters to have them brighten up the south side of the terrace wall. A banquet scene in the film had made her hungry, and now she intended to betray her diet, then roll into bed, and perhaps allow Dreyer his long-deferred due.

The front-door bell tinkled. Tom barked briskly. Martha raised her thin eyebrows in surprise. Dreyer got up with a chuckle, and, chewing as he went, marched into the front hall.

She sat half-turned toward the door, holding her raised cup. When Franz, jokingly nudged on by Dreyer, stepped into the dining room, clicked his heels, and quickly walked up to her, she beamed so beautifully, her lips glistened so warmly that within Dreyer's soul a huge merry throng seemed to break out in deafening applause, and he thought that after a smile like that everything was bound to go well: Martha, as she once used to, would tell him in breathless detail the entire foolish film as the preface and price of a submissive caress; and on Sunday, instead of tennis, he would go riding with her in the rustling, sun-flecked, orange-and-red park.

"First of all, my dear Franz," he said, drawing up a chair for his nephew, "have a bite of something. And here is a drop of kirsch for you."

Like an automaton, Franz stuck out his hand across the table, aiming for the proffered snifter, and knocked over a slender vase enclosing a heavy brown rose ("Which should have been removed long ago," reflected Martha). The liberated water spread across the tablecloth.

He lost his composure, and no wonder. In the first place, he had not expected to see Martha. Secondly, he had thought Dreyer would receive him in his study and inform him about a very, very important job that had to be tackled immediately. Martha's smile had stunned him. He ascertained to himself the reason for his alarm. Like the fake seed a fakir buries in the ground only to draw out of it at once, with manic magic, a live rose tree, Martha's request that he conceal from Dreyer their innocent adventure—a request to which he had barely paid attention at the time—now, in the husband's presence had fabulously swelled, turning into a secret erotic bond. He also remembered old Enricht's words about a lady friend, and those words confirmed as it were the bliss and the shame. He tried to cast off the spell— but, meeting her unbearably intense gaze, dropped his eyes and helplessly continued to dab the wet tablecloth with his handkerchief despite Dreyer's trying to push his hand away. Moments ago he had been lying in bed and now here he sat, in this resplendent dining room, suffering as if in a dream because he could not halt the dark streamlet that had rounded the saltcellar, and under cover of the plate's rim was endeavoring to reach the edge of the table. Still smiling (the tablecloth would have to be changed tomorrow anyway), Martha shifted her gaze to his hands, to the gentle play of the knuckles under the taut skin, to the hairy wrist, to the long groping fingers, and felt oddly aware she had nothing woollen on her body that night.

Abruptly Dreyer got up and said: "Franz, this is not very hospitable, but it can't be helped. It's getting late, and you and I must be on our way."

"On our way?" Franz uttered in confusion, thrusting the wet ball of his handkerchief into his pocket. Martha glanced at her husband with cold surprise.

"You'll understand presently," said Dreyer, his eyes twinkling with an adventurous light that was all too familiar to Martha. "What a bore," she thought angrily, "what is he up to?"

She stopped him for a moment in the front hall and asked him in rapid whisper: "Where are you going, where are you going? I demand to be told where you are going."

"On a wild spree," replied Dreyer, hoping to provoke another marvellous smile.

She winced in disgust. He patted her on the cheek and went out.

Martha wandered back to the dining room and stood lost in thought behind the chair Franz had vacated. Then with irritation she lifted the tablecloth where the water had been spilled, and slipped a plate bottom up under it. The looking glass, which was working hard that night, reflected her green dress, her white neck under the dark weight of her chignon, and the gleam of her emerald earrings. She remained unconscious of the mirror's attention, and as she slowly went about putting the fruit knives away her reflection would reappear every now and then. Frieda joined her for a minute or two. Then the light in the dining room clicked off, and, nibbling at her necklace, Martha went upstairs to her bedroom.

"I bet he wants me to think he is kidding because he isn't. I bet it's exactly the way it will be," she thought. "He'll fix him up with some dirty slut. And that will be the end of it."

As she undressed, she felt she was about to cry. Just you wait, just you wait till you get home. Especially if you were pulling my leg. And what manners, what manners! You invite the poor boy and then whisk him away. In the middle of the night! Disgraceful!

Once again, as so many times previously, she went over all her husband's transgressions in her memory. It seemed to her that she remembered them all. They were numerous. That did not prevent her, however, from assuring her married sister Hilda, when the latter would come from Hamburg, that she was happy, that her marriage was a happy one.

And Martha really did believe that her marriage was no different from any other marriage, that discord always reigned, that the wife always struggled against her husband, against his peculiarities, against his departures from the accepted rules, and all this amounted to happy marriage. An unhappy marriage was when the husband was poor, or had landed in prison for some shady business, or kept squandering his earnings on kept women. Therefore Martha never complained about her situation, since it was a natural and customary one.

Her mother had died when Martha was three—a not unusual arrangement. A first stepmother soon died too, and that also ran in some families. The second and final stepmother, who died only recently, was a lovely woman of quite gentle birth whom everybody adored. Papa, who had started his career as a saddler and ended it as the bankrupt owner of an artificial leather factory, was desperately eager she marry the "Hussar," as for some reason he dubbed Dreyer, whom she barely knew when he proposed in 1920, at the same time that Hilda became engaged to the fat little purser of a second-rate Atlantic liner. Dreyer was getting rich with miraculous ease; he was fairly attractive, but bizarre and unpredictable; sang off-key silly arias and made her silly presents.

As a well-bred girl with long lashes and glowing cheeks, she said she would make up her mind the next time he came to Hamburg. Before leaving for Berlin he gave her a monkey which she loathed; fortunately, a handsome young cousin with whom she had gone rather far before he became one of Hilda's first lovers taught it to light matches, its little jersey caught fire, and the clumsy animal had to be destroyed. When Dreyer returned a week later, she allowed him to kiss her on the cheek. Poor old Papa got so high at the party that he beat up the fiddler, which was pardonable—seeing all the hard luck he had encountered in his long life. It was only after the wedding, when her husband cancelled an important business trip in favor of a ridiculous honeymoon in Norway—why Norway of all places?—that certain doubts began to assail her; but the villa in Grunewald soon dissipated them, and so on, not very interesting recollections.

4

In the darkness of the taxi (the unfortunate Icarus was still being repaired, and the rented substitute, a quirky Oriole, had not been a success), Dreyer remained mysteriously silent. He might have been asleep, had not his cigar glowed rhythmically. Franz was silent too, wondering uneasily where he was being taken. After the third or fourth turn he lost all sense of direction.

Up to now he had explored, besides the quiet quarter where he lived, only the avenue of lindens and its surroundings at the other end of the city. Everything that lay between those two live oases was a *terra incognita* blank. He gazed out of the window and saw the dark streets gradually acquiring a certain limpidity, then dimming again, then again welling with light, waning once more, brightening again, until having matured in the darkness they suddenly burst forth scintillating with fabulous colors, gemmed cascades, blazing advertisements. A tall steepled church glided past under the umber sky. Presently, skidding slightly on the damp asphalt, the car drew up at the curb.

Only then did Franz understand. In sapphire letters with a diamond flourish prolonging the final vowel, a glittering forty-foot sign spelled the word D*A*N*D*Y—which now he remembered hearing before, the fool that he was! Dreyer took him under the arm and led him up to one of the ten radiantly lit display windows. Like tropical blossoms in a hothouse, ties and socks vied in delicate shades with the rectangles of folded shirts or drooped lazily from gilded bows, while in the depths an opal-tinted pajama with the face of an Oriental idol stood fully erect, god of that garden. But Dreyer did not allow Franz to dally in contemplation. He led him smartly past the other windows, and there flashed by in turn an orgy of glossy footwear, a Fata Morgana of coats, a graceful flight of hats, gloves, and canes, and a sunny paradise of sports articles; then Franz found himself in a dark passageway where stood an old man in a black cape with a badge on his visored cap next to a slender-legged woman in furs. They both looked at Dreyer. The watchman recognized him and put his hand to his cap. The bright-eyed prostitute glanced at Franz and modestly moved away. As soon as he disappeared behind Dreyer in the gloom of a courtyard, she resumed her talk with the watchman about rheumatism and its cures.

The yard formed a triangular dead end between window-less walls. There was an odor of damp mingled with that of urine and beer. In one corner, either something was dumped, or else it was a cart with its shafts in the air. Dreyer produced the flashlight from his pocket, and a skimming circle of gray light outlined a grating, the moving shadows of descending steps, an iron door. Taking a childish delight in choosing the most mysterious entrance, Dreyer unlocked the door. Franz ducked and followed him into a dark stone passage where the round of flitting light now picked out a door. If any illegal attempt had been made to tamper with it, it would have emitted a wild ringing. But for this door too Dreyer had a small noiseless key, and again Franz ducked. In the murky basement through which they walked one could distinguish sacks and crates piled here and there and something like straw rustled underfoot. The mobile beam turned a corner, and yet another door appeared. Beyond it rose a bare staircase that melted into the blackness. They shuffled up the stone steps, explorers of a buried temple. With dream-like unexpectedness they emerged presently into a vast hall. The light glanced across metallic gallows, then along folds of drapery, gigantic wardrobes, swinging mirrors and broad-shouldered black figures. Dreyer stopped, put away his light and said softly in the dark "Attention!" His hand could be heard fumbling, and a single pear-shaped bulb brightly illuminated a counter. The remainder of the hall—an endless labyrinth—remained submerged in darkness, and Franz found it a little eerie to have this one nook singled out by the strong light. "Lesson One," Dreyer said solemnly, and with a flourish went behind the counter.

It is doubtful if Franz benefited from this fantastic night lesson—everything was too strange, and Dreyer impersonated a salesman with too much whimsy. And yet, despite the baroque nonsense there was something about the angular reflections and the surrounding spectral abyss, where vague fabrics that had been handled and re-handled during the day reposed in weary attitudes, which long remained in Franz's memory and imparted a certain dark luxurious coloring, at least at first, to the basic background against which his everyday salesman's toil began to sketch later its plain, comprehensible, often tiresome pattern. And it was not on personal experience, not on the recollection of distant days when he actually had worked behind the counter, that Dreyer drew that night as he showed Franz how to sell neckties. Instead, he soared into the ravishing realm of inutile imagination, demonstrating not the way ties should be sold in real life, but the way they might be sold if the salesman were both artist and clairvoyant.

"I want a simple blue one," Franz, prompted by him, would say in a wooden schoolboy voice.

"Certainly, sir," Dreyer answered briskly and, whisking off several cardboard boxes from a shelf, nimbly opened them on the counter.

"How do you like this one?" he inquired not without a shadow of pensiveness, knotting a mottled magenta-and-black tie on his hand and holding it away a little as if admiring it himself in the capacity of an independent artist.

Franz was silent.

"An important technique," explained Dreyer, changing his voice. "Let's see if you got the point. Now you go behind the counter. In this box here there are some solid-colored ties. They cost four-five marks. And here we have stylish ones on the "orchid" side, as we say, at eight, ten, or even fourteen, the Lord forgive us. Now then, you are the salesman and I am a young man, a ninny if you'll excuse me—inexperienced, irresolute, easily tempted."

Franz self-consciously went behind the counter. Hunching his shoulders and narrowing his eyes as if he were near-sighted, Dreyer said in a high-pitched quaver: "I want a plain blue one. . . . And please, not too expensive." "Smile," he added in a prompter's whisper.

Franz bent low over one of the boxes, fumbled awkwardly and produced a plain blue tie.

"Aha, I caught you!" Dreyer exclaimed cheerfully. "I knew you had not understood, or else you are color-blind, and then good-by dear uncle and aunt. Why on earth must you give me the cheapest one? You should have done as I did—stun the ninny first with an expensive one, no matter what color. But be sure it's gaudy and costly, or costly and elegant, and maybe squeeze out of him 'an extra throb and an extra bob,' as they say in London. Here, take this one. Now knot it on your hand. Wait, wait—don't worry it like that. Swing it around your finger. Thus! Remember the slightest delay in the rhythm costs you a moment of the customer's attention. Hypnotize him with the flip of the tie you display. You must make it *bloom* before the idiot's eyes. No, that's not a knot, that's some kind of tumor. Watch. Hold your hand straight. Let's try this expensive vampire red. Now we suppose it is I who am looking at it, and I still don't yield to temptation."

"But I wanted a plain blue one," said Dreyer in a high voice—and then, again in a whisper: "Ah, no—keep pushing the vampire one in his stupid face, perhaps you'll wear him down. And watch him, watch his eyes—if he looks at the thing that's already something. Only if he does not look at all and begins to frown, and clear his damned throat—only then, you understand, only then give him what he requested—always choosing the dearest of the three plain blues, of course. But even as you yield to his coarse request, give, you know, a slight shrug, look at me now—and smile sort of disdainfully as if to say 'this isn't fashionable at all, frankly, this is for peasants, for droshky coachmen . . . but if you really want it'—"

"I'll take this blue one," said Dreyer in his comedy voice.

Franz grimly handed him the tie across the counter. Dreyer's guffaw awakened a rude echo. "No," he said, "no, my friend. Not at all. First, you lay it aside to your right, then you inquire if he does not need something else, for instance, handkerchiefs, or some fancy studs, and only after he has thought a bit and shaken his calf's head, only then produce this fountain pen (which is a present) and write out and give him the price slip for the cashier. But the rest is routine. No, keep it, I said. You will be shown that part tomorrow by Mr. Piffke, a very pedantic man. Now let's continue."

Dreyer hoisted himself a little heavily to a sitting position on the counter, casting as he did so a sharp black shadow that dived head first into the darkness which seemed to have moved closer the better to hear. He started to finger the silks in the boxes, and to instruct Franz how to remember ties by touch and tint, how to develop, in other words (lost on Franz), a chromatic and tactile memory, how to eradicate from one's artistic and commercial consciousness styles and specimens that had been sold out—so as to make room for new ones in one's mind, and how to determine the price in marks immediately and then add the pfennigs from the tag. Several times he jumped off the counter, gesticulating grotesquely, impersonating a customer irritated by everything he was shown; the brute who objected to his being told the price before he had asked for it; and the saint to whom price was no object; also an old lady buying a tie for her grandson, a fireman at Potsdam; or a foreigner unable to express anything comprehensible—a Frenchman who wants a *cravate*, an Italian who demands a *cravatta*, a Russian who pleads gently for a *galstook*. Whereupon he would reply at once to himself, pressing his fingers lightly against the counter, and for each occasion inventing a particular variety of intonation and smile. Then seating himself again and slightly swinging his foot in its glossy shoe (as his shadow flapped a black wing on the floor), he discussed the tender and cheerful attitude a salesman should have toward man-made things, and he confessed that sometimes one felt absurdly sorry for outmoded ties and obsolete socks that were still so neat and fresh but completely unwanted; an odd, dreamy smile hovered under his mustache, and alternately creased and smoothed out the wrinkles at the corners of his eyes and mouth—whilst extenuated Franz, leaning against a wardrobe, listened in a torpor to him.

Dreyer paused—and as Franz realized that the lesson was over, he could not help casting a covetous glance at the iridescent wonders now scattered, in real life, on the counter. Again producing his flashlight and turning off the switch on the wall, Dreyer led Franz over a waste of dark carpeting into the shadowy depths of the hall. He flung off in passing the canvas of a small table and trained his light on cuff links sparkling like eyes on their blue velvet cushion. A little further with playful nonchalance he tipped off its stand a huge beach ball which rolled soundlessly away into the dark, far, far, all the way to the Bay of Pomerania and its soft white sands.

They walked back along the stone passages, and as he was locking the last door Dreyer recalled not without pleasure the enigmatic disorder he had left behind while neglecting to think that perhaps someone else would be held responsible for it.

As soon as they emerged from the dark courtyard into the wetly gleaming street, Dreyer hailed a passing taxi and offered Franz a lift home.

Franz hesitated, staring at the festive vista (at last!) of the animated boulevard.

"Or do you have a date with a" (Dreyer consulted his wrist watch) "sleepy sweetheart?"

Franz licked his lips and shook his head.

"As you wish," said Dreyer with a laugh and, thrusting his head out of the cab, he shouted in parting: "Be at the store tomorrow, nine o'clock sharp."

The lustre of the black asphalt was filmed by a blend of dim hues, through which here and there vivid rends and oval holes made by rain puddles revealed the authentic colors of deep reflections—a vermilion diagonal band, a cobalt wedge, a green spiral—scattered glimpses into a humid upside-down world, into a dizzy geometry of gems. The kaleidoscopic effect suggested someone's jiggling every now and then the pavement so as to change the combination of numberless colored fragments. Meanwhile, shafts and ripples of life passed by, marking the course of every car. Shop windows, bursting with tense radiance, oozed, squirted, and splashed out into the rich blackness.

And at every corner, emblem of ineffable happiness, stood a sleek-hosed harlot whose features there was no time to study: another already beckoned in the distance, and beyond her, a third. And Franz knew without any doubt where those mysterious live beacons led. Every street lamp, its halo spreading like a spiky star, every rosy glow, every spasm of golden light, and the silhouettes of lovers pulsating against each other in every recess of porch and passage; and those half-opened painted lips that fleeted past him; and the black, moist, tender asphalt—all of it was assuming a specific significance and finding a name.

Saturated with sweat, limp with delicious languor, moving with the slow motion of a sleepwalker called back to his rumpled warm pillow, Franz went back to bed, without having noticed how he had re-entered the house and reached his room. He stretched, he passed his palms over his hairy legs, unglued and cupped himself, and almost instantly Sleep, with a bow, handed him the key of its city: he understood the meaning of all the lights, sounds, and perfumes as everything blended into a single blissful image. Now he seemed to be in a mirrored hall, which wondrously opened on a watery abyss, water glistened in the most unexpected places: he went toward a door past the perfectly credible motorcycle which his landlord was starting with his red heel, and, anticipating indescribable bliss, Franz opened the door and saw Martha standing near the bed. Eagerly he approached but Tom kept getting in the way; Martha was laughing and shooing away the dog. Now he saw quite closely her glossy lips, her neck swelling with glee, and he too began to hurry, undoing buttons, pulling a blood-stained bone out of the dog's jaws, and feeling an unbearable sweetness welling up within him; he was about to clasp her hips but suddenly could no longer contain his boiling ecstasy.

Martha sighed and opened her eyes. She thought she had been awakened by a noise in the street: one of their neighbors had a remarkably loud motorcycle. Actually, it was only her husband snoring away with particular abandon. She recalled she had gone to bed without awaiting his return, raised herself, and called to him sharply; then, reaching across the night table, she began roughly tousling his hair, the only trick that worked. His snoring ceased, his lips smacked once or twice. The light on the table flashed on showing the pink of her hand.

"The awakening of the lion," said Dreyer, rubbing his eyes with his fist like a child.

"Where did you go?" Martha asked, glaring at him.

He stared sleepily at her ivory shoulder, at the rose of a bared breast, at the long strand of ebony hair falling on her cheek, and gave a soft chuckle as he slowly leaned back on his pillows.

"I've been showing him Dandy," he muttered cozily. "A night lesson. He can now knot a tie on his paw or his tail. Very entertaining and instructive."

Ah, that was it. Martha felt so relieved, so magnanimous,

that she almost offered . . . but she was also too sleepy. Sleepy and very happy. Without speaking she switched off the light.

"Let's go riding Sunday—what do you say?" a voice murmured tenderly in the dark. But she was already lost in dream. Three lecherous Arabs were haggling over her with a bronze-torsoed handsome slaver. The voice repeated its question in an even more tender, even more questioning tone. A melancholy pause. Then he turned his pillow in quest of a cooler hollow, sighed, and presently was snoring again.

In the morning, as Dreyer was hurriedly enjoying a soft-boiled egg with buttered toast (the most delicious meal known to man) before dashing off to the emporium, Frieda informed him that the repaired car was waiting at the door. Here Dreyer remembered that in the past few days, and particularly after the recent smash, he had repeatedly had a rather amusing thought which he had somehow never brought to its conclusion. But he must act cautiously, in a roundabout manner. A blunt question would lead nowhere. The rascal would leer and deny everything. Would the gardener know? If he did, he would shield him. Dreyer gulped down his coffee and, blinking, poured himself a second cup. Of course, I could be mistaken. . . .

He sipped up the last sweet drop, threw his napkin on the table and hurried out; the napkin slowly crept off the edge of the table and fell limply onto the floor.

Yes, the car had been well repaired. It gleamed with its new coat of black paint, the chrome of its headlight rims, the blazon-like emblem that crested the radiator grill: a silver boy with azure wings. A slightly embarrassed smile bared the chauffeur's ugly gums and teeth as he doffed his blue cap and opened the door. Dreyer glanced at him askance.

"Hello, hello," he said, "so here we are together again." He buttoned all the buttons of his overcoat and continued: "This must have cost a tidy sum—I haven't looked at the bill yet. But that's not the point. I'd be willing to pay even more for the sheer fun of it. A most exhilarating experience, to be sure. Unfortunately, neither my wife nor the police saw the joke."

He tried to think of something else to add, failed, unbuttoned his coat again, and got into the car.

"I gave his physiognomy a thorough examination," he reflected to the accompaniment of the motor's gentle purr. "Still it is impossible to draw any conclusion yet. Of course, his eyes are sort of twinkly, of course, they have those little bags under them. But that may be normal with him. Next time I'll have to take a good sniff."

That morning, as agreed, he visited the emporium and introduced Franz to Mr. Piffke. Piffke was burly, dignified, and smartly dressed. He had blond eyelashes, baby-colored skin, a profile that had prudently stopped halfway between man and teapot, and a second-rate diamond on his plump auricular. He felt for Franz the respect due to the boss's nephew, while Franz gazed with envy and awe at the architectonic perfection of Piffke's trouser creases and the transparent handkerchief peeping out of his breast pocket.

Dreyer did not even mention the lesson of the night before. With his complete approval Piffke assigned Franz not to the tie counter, but to the sporting-goods department. Piffke went to work on Franz with zeal, and his training methods turned out to be very different from Dreyer's, containing as they did a great deal more arithmetic than Franz had expected.

Neither had he expected his feet to ache so much, from constant standing, or his face, from the mechanical expression of affability. As usual in autumn, that part of the emporium was much quieter than the others. Various body-building appliances, ping-pong paddles, striped woollen scarves, soccer boots with black cleats and white laces moved fairly well. The existence of public pools accounted for a continued small demand for bathing suits; but their real season had passed, while the time for skates and skis had not yet come. Thus no rush of customers hampered Franz's training and he had complete leisure to learn his job. His main colleagues were two girls, one red-haired and sharp-nosed, the other a stout energetic blonde inexorably accompanied by a sour smell; and an athletically built young man wearing the same kind of tortoise shell glasses as Franz. He casually informed Franz about the prizes he had won in swimming competitions, and Franz envied him, being himself an excellent swimmer. It was with Schwimmer's help that Franz selected the cloth for two suits and a supply of ties, shirts, and socks. It was he, too, who helped Franz to unravel some minor mysteries of salesmanship far more astutely than Piffke, whose true function was to promenade about the place and grandly arrange meetings between customer and salesman.

During the first few days Franz, dazed and self-conscious, and trying not to shiver (his department was over-ventilated and full of its own athletic drafts), simply stood in a corner trying not to attract attention, avidly following the actions of his colleagues, memorizing their professional movements and intonations, and then abruptly, with unbearable clarity, imagining Martha—the way she had of putting her hand to the back of her chignon, or glancing at her nails and emerald ring. Very soon, however, under the approving solicitous gaze of Mr. Schwimmer, Franz started selling on his own.

He remembered forever his first customer, a stout old man

who asked for a ball. A ball. At once this ball went off bouncing in his imagination, multiplying and scattering, and Franz's head became the playground for all the balls in the store, small, medium, and large—yellow leather ones with stitched sections, fluffy white ones bearing the violet signature of their maker, little black ones hard as stone, extra-light orange-and-blue ones of vacational size, balls of rubber, celluloid, wood, ivory, and they all rolled off in different directions leaving behind a single sphere shining in the middle of his mind when the customer added placidly: "I need a ball for my dog."

"Third shelf on your right, Tooth-Proof," came Schwimmer's prompt whisper, and Franz with a grin of relief and sweat on his brow started to open one wrong box after another but at last found what was needed.

In a month or so he had grown completely accustomed to his work; he no longer got flustered; would boldly bid the inarticulate to repeat their request; and would condescendingly counsel the puny and shy. Fairly well built, fairly broad-shouldered, slim but not skinny, he observed with pleasure his passage in a harem of mirrors and the glances of obviously infatuated shopgirls, and the flash of three silver clips over his heart: Uncle's fountain pen and two pencils, lilac and lead. He might have passed, indeed, for a perfectly respectable, perfectly ordinary salesman, were it not for a blend of details that only a detective of genius might have discerned—a predatory angularity of nostril and cheekbone, a strange weakness about the mouth as if he were always out of breath or had just sneezed, and those eyes, those eyes, poorly disguised by glasses, restless eyes, tragic eyes, ruthless and helpless, of an impure greenish shade with inflamed blood vessels around the iris. But the only detective around was an elderly woman always with the same parcel, who did not bother patrolling Sports but had quite a lot to do in the Neckties department.

Acting upon impeccable Piffke's delicately formulated suggestions, Franz acquired sybarite habits of personal hygiene. He now washed his feet at least twice a week and changed his starched collar and cuffs practically every day. Every evening he brushed his suit and shined his shoes. He used all sorts of nice lotions, smelling of spring flowers and Piffke. He hardly ever skipped his Saturday bath. He put on a clean shirt every Wednesday and Sunday. He made a point of changing his warm underwear at least once in ten days. How shocked his mother would be, he reflected, if she saw his laundry bills!

He accepted with alacrity the tedium of his job, but disliked intensely the necessity of having meals with the rest of the staff. He had hoped that in Berlin he would gradually get over his morbid juvenile squeamishness, but it kept finding mean opportunities to torture him. At table he sat between the plump blonde and the champion swimmer. Whenever she stretched toward the bread basket or the salt, her armpit flooded him with nausea reminding him of a detested spinster teacher at school. The champion on his other side had another infirmity—that of spitting whenever he spoke, and Franz found himself reverting to his schooldays' system of protecting his plate from the spray with forearm and elbow. Only once did he accompany Mr. Schwimmer to the public pool. The water proved to be much too cool and far from clean, and his colleague's roommate, a sunlamp-tanned young Swede, had embarrassing manners.

Basically, though, the emporium, the glossy goods, the brisk or suave dialogue with the customer (who always seemed to be the same actor changing his voice and mask), all this routine was a superficial trickle of repetitive events and sensations which touched him as little as if he was one of those figures of fashion with waxen or wooden faces in suits pressed by the iron of perfection, arrested in a state of colorful putrefaction on their temporary pedestals and platforms, their arms half-bent and half-extended in a parody of pastoral appeal. Young female customers and fleet-footed bob-haired salesgirls from other departments hardly excited him at all. Like the colored commercial stills advertising furniture or furs that succeed each other on the cinema screen for a long time, unaccompanied by music, before a fascinating film starts, all the details of his work were as inevitable as they were trivial. Around six it all stopped abruptly. And then the music would start playing.

Almost nightly—and what monstrous melancholy lurked in that "almost"—he would visit the Dreyers. He dined there only on Sundays, and not every Sunday at that. On weekdays, after a bite at the same cheap restaurant where he had lunched, he took the bus or walked to their villa. A score of evenings had gone by, and everything remained the same: The welcome buzz of the wicket, the pretty lantern illuminating the path through a pattern of ivy, the damp exhalation of the lawn, the gravel's crunch, the tinkle of the doorbell winging off into the house in quest of the maid, the burst of light, Frieda's placid face, and suddenly—life, the tender reverberations of radio music.

She was generally alone; Dreyer, a fantastic but punctual person, would arrive exactly in time for what Franz called supper, and the evening tea, and would always telephone when he thought he might be late. In his presence Franz felt uncomfortable to the point of numbness, and therefore managed to evolve in those days a certain air of grim familiarity in response to Dreyer's natural joviality. But while he was alone with Martha, he had a constant sensation of languorous pressure somewhere at the top of his spine; his chest felt tight, his legs weak; his fingers retained for a long time the cool strength of her handshake. He would compute within half an inch the exact degree to which she showed her legs while walking about the room and while sitting with her legs crossed, and he perceived almost without looking the tense sheen of her stocking, the swell of her left calf over the right knee; and the fold of her skirt, sloping, soft, supple, in which one would have liked to bury one's face. Sometimes, when she got up and walked past him to the radiola, the light would fall at such an angle as to let the outline of her thighs show through the light fabric of her skirt, and once she got a ladder-like run in her stocking and, licking her finger, quickly dabbed at the silk. Occasionally, the sensation of languid weight became too much for him, and taking advantage of her looking away, he would search her beauty for some little fault on which he could prop his mind and sober his fancy, and thus allay the relentless stir of his senses. Now and then he had the impression that he had indeed found the saving flaw—a hard line near the mouth, a pockmark above the eyebrow, a too prominent pout of those full lips in profile, a dark shadow of down above them, especially noticeable when the powder came off. But one turn of her head or the slightest change of expression would restore to her face such adorable charm that he slipped back into his private abyss even deeper. By means of those rapid glances he made a complete study of her, followed and forefelt her gestures, anticipated the banal but to him unique movement of her alertly raised hand when one end of a tiny comb would slacken its grip on her heavy bun. Most of all he was tormented by the grace and power of her bare white neck, by that rich delicately grained texture of skin and the fashionable glimpses of nudity allowed by short flimsy skirts.

At every new visit he added something to the collection of enchantments which he would gloat over later in his solitary bed, choosing the one his frenzied fancy would work on and spend itself. There was the evening when he saw a minute brown birthmark on her arm. There was the moment when she bent low from her seat to turn back the corner of a rug and he noticed the parting of her breasts and was relieved when the black silk of her bodice became taut again. There was also the night when she was getting ready for a dance, and he was stunned to observe that her armpits were as smooth and white as a statue's.

She questioned him about his childhood, his mother, a dull theme, his native town, an even duller one. Once Tom put his muzzle in Franz's lap and yawned, enveloping him in an unendurable odor—foul herring, carrion. "That is how my childhood smells," muttered Franz as he pushed the dog's head away. She did not hear or did not understand, and asked what he had said. But he did not repeat his confession. He talked about his school, about the dust and the boredom, about his mother's indigestible pies, and about the butcher next door, a dignified gentleman in a white waistcoat who at one time used to come to dinner every day, and eat mutton in a disgustingly professional manner. "Why disgustingly?" Martha interrupted in surprise. "God, what nonsense I'm spouting," he thought, and with mechanical enthusiasm described for the hundredth time the river, the boating, the diving, the beer-drinking under the bridge.

She would switch the radio from song to speech, and he would reverently listen to a Spanish lesson, a lecture on the benefits of athletics, to Mr. Streseman's conciliatory tones, and then—back to some bizarre nasal music. She would tell him in detail the plot of a film, the story of Dreyer's lucky speculations in the days of the inflation, and the gist of an article on the removal of fruit stains. And all the time she would be thinking: "How much longer would he need to get started?" and simultaneously she was amused and even a little touched that he was so unsure of himself and that without her help he would probably never get started at all. Gradually, however, vexation began to predominate. November was being squandered on trifles as money is squandered on trifles when you get stranded in some dull town. With a vague resentment, she recalled that her sister had already had at least four or five lovers in succession, and that Willy Wald's young wife had had two simultaneously. And yet Martha was already past thirty-four. It was high time. In turn, she had been given a husband, a beautiful villa, antique silver, an automobile; the next gift on her list was Franz. Yet it was all not quite so simple; there intruded an alien little breeze, a special ardor, a suspicious softness. . . .

It was no use trying to sleep. Franz opened his window. At the transit from autumn to winter, quirky nights occur when suddenly, out of nowhere, there passes a breath of warm humid air, a belated sigh of summer. He stood in his new zebra pajamas holding on to the window frame, then leaned out, morosely released a long spurt of saliva, and listened, waiting for it to splatter against the sidewalk. However, since he lived on the fifth floor, and not on the second as he had at home, Franz heard nothing. With a slow clatter he shut the window and went back to bed. That night he realized, as one becomes abruptly aware of suffering from a fatal illness, that he had already known Martha for more than two months, and was draining his passion in useless fantasies. And Franz told the pillow, in the half-obscene, half-grandiloquent idiom he affected when talking to himself: "Never mind—better betray my career than wait till my brain cracks. Tomorrow, yes, tomorrow, I'll grab her and tumble her, on the sofa, on the floor, on the table, on broken crockery . . ." Crazy Franz!

Tomorrow came. He went home after work, changed his socks, brushed his teeth, put on his new silk scarf and marched to the bus stop with martial determination. On the way he kept persuading himself that of course she loved him, that only out of pride she concealed her feeling, and that was a pity. If only she leaned toward him as if by chance, and brushed her cheek against his temple over a blurred album, or if she did again, as she had the other night—if she pressed for a moment her back to his before the front-hall mirror and said, turning her perfumed head: "I'm an inch taller than you," or if—but here he pulled himself together and soundlessly told the bus conductor: "That's weakness, and there should be no weakness." Let her be tonight even colder than usual—no matter—now, now, now. . . . As he rang the bell there flashed through his mind a poltroon's hope that perhaps by some chance Dreyer had already come home. Dreyer had not.

As Franz passed through the first two rooms, he pictured how in an instant he would push open that door over there, enter her boudoir, see her in a low-cut black dress with emeralds around her neck, immediately embrace her, hard, make her crunch, make her faint, make her spill her jewels; he pictured it so vividly that for a split second he saw before him his own receding back, saw his hand, saw himself opening the door, and because that sensation was a foray into the future, and it is forbidden to ransack the future, he was swiftly punished. In the first place, as he caught up with himself, he tripped and sent the door flying open. In the second, the room Martha called the boudoir was empty. In the third, when she came in she was wearing a beige dress with a high neck and a long line of buttons. In the fourth place, such a familiar helpless timidity came over him that all he could hope for was to speak more or less articulately.

Martha had decided that tonight he would kiss her for the first time. Characteristically, she chose one of her monthly days lest she succumb too soon, and in the wrong spot, to a yearning that otherwise she could no longer resist. In anticipation of that prudently circumscribed embrace she did not immediately settle down on the sofa near him. As tradition demanded, she turned on the radio, brought a little silver case with Libidettes (Viennese cigarettes), re-arranged the fold of a window curtain, turned on the opal glow of a table lamp, switched off the ceiling light, and (choosing the worst subject imaginable) began telling Franz how the day before Dreyer had started on some mysterious new project—a profitable one, let us hope; she picked up and placed on the back of a chair a pink woollen shawl, and only then gently sat down next to Franz, not quite comfortably folding one leg under her and adjusting the pleats of her skirt.

For no reason at all, he began extolling Uncle, saying how frightfully grateful he was, and how fond he had grown of him. Martha nodded absently. He would alternately puff on his cigarette, or hold it next to his knee, drawing the cardboard tip across the fabric of his trouser leg. The smoke like a flow of spectral milk crept along the clingy nap. Martha extended her hand and with a smile touched his knee as if playing with this phantom larva of smoke. He felt the tender pressure of her fingers. He was hungry, sweaty, and completely impotent.

" . . . And my mother in every letter, you know, sends him her respectful love, her regards, her thanks."

The smoke dissolved. Franz kept sniffing as he did when he was especially nervous. Martha got up and turned off the radio. He lit another cigarette. She had now thrown the pink shawl over her shoulders and, like a woman in some old-fashioned romance, gazed at him fixedly from the far corner of the settee. With a wooden laugh, he recounted an anecdote from yesterday's paper. Then, nudging the door with his paw, a very sad, very sleek, very hopeless Tom appeared, and Franz for the first time actually talked to the astonished animal. And at last, thank God, beloved Dreyer arrived.

Franz came home around eleven, and as he was proceeding along the passage on tiptoe to the foul little water closet he heard a chuckle coming from the landlord's door. The door was ajar. He peeped into the room as he passed. Old Enricht, clad only in his nightshirt, was standing on all fours with his wrinkled and hoary rear toward a brilliant cheval glass. Bending low his congested face, fringed with white hair, like the head of the professor in the "Hindu Prince" farce, he was peering back through the archway of his bare thighs at the reflection of his bleak buttocks.

5

There was indeed an air of mystery about Dreyer's new project. It all began one Wednesday in mid-November when he received a visit from a nondescript stranger with a cosmopolitan name and no determinable origin. He might have been Czech, Jewish, Bavarian, Irish—it was entirely a matter of personal evaluation.

Dreyer was sitting in his office (a huge quiet place with huge unquiet windows, with a huge desk, and huge leather armchairs) when, having traversed an olive-green corridor past glass expanses full of the hurricane-like clatter of typewriters, this nondescript gentleman was ushered in. He was hatless but wore a topcoat and warm gloves.

The card that had preceded him by a couple of minutes bore the title of "Inventor" under his name. Now Dreyer was fond, perhaps over-fond, of inventors. With a mesmeric gesture, he deposited his guest in the leathern luxury of an over-stuffed chair (with an ashtray affixed to its giant paw) and, toying with a red-and-blue pencil, sat down half-facing him. The man's thick eyebrows wiggled like furry black caterpillars, and the freshly shaven parts of his melancholy face had a dark turquoise cast.

The inventor began from afar, and this Dreyer approved. All business ought to be handled with that artful caution. Lowering his voice, the inventor passed with laudable smoothness from the preface to the substance. Dreyer laid down his pencil. Suavely and in detail the Magyar—or Frenchman, or Pole—stated his business.

"You say, then, that it has nothing to do with wax?" asked Dreyer. The inventor raised his finger. "Absolutely nothing, though I call it 'voskin,' a trade name that will be in all dictionaries tomorrow. Its main component is a resilient, colorless product resembling flesh. I particularly stress its elasticity, its pliability, its rippliability, so to speak."

"Speak by all means," said Dreyer. "And what about that 'electric impellent'—I don't quite understand; what do you mean, for example, by 'contractive transmission'?"

The inventor smiled a wise smile. "Ah, that's the whole point. Obviously, it would be much simpler if I showed you the blueprints; but it is also obvious that I'm not yet inclined to do so. I have explained how you can apply my invention. Now it's up to you to give me the funds for the construction of the first sample."

"How much would you need?" asked Dreyer with curiosity.

The inventor replied in detail.

"Don't you think," said Dreyer with a mischievous glint in his eye, "that perhaps your imagination is worth much more? I highly respect and value the imagination in others. If for example a man came to me and said: 'My dear *Herr Direktor*, I would like to dream a little. How much will you pay me for dreaming?' then, maybe, I would begin negotiations with him. Whereas you, my dear inventor, you offer at once something practical, factory production and so forth. Who cares about realization? I am duty-bound to believe in

[89]

a dream but to believe in the embodiment of that dream—Puh!" (one of Dreyer's lipbursts).

At first the inventor did not understand; then he understood and was offended.

"In other words, you simply refuse?" he asked gloomily.

Dreyer sighed. The inventor clucked his tongue, and leaned back in his chair clasping and unclasping his hands.

"This is my life's work," he said at last, staring into space. "Like Hercules, I have been struggling with the tentacles of a dream for ten years, mastering this softness, this flexibility, this plexibility, this stylized animation, if I may use the expression."

"*Of course* you may," said Dreyer. "I'd even say that's better than the—what was it—'ripplexibility'? Tell me," he began, picking up the pencil again—a good sign (though his interlocutor could not know it), "have you approached anyone else with that offer?"

"Well," said the inventor with perfectly mimicked sincerity, "I confess this is the first time. In fact, I have just arrived in Germany. This *is* Germany, isn't it?" he added, looking around.

"So I'm told," said Dreyer.

There was a fruit-bearing pause.

"Your dream is enchanting," said Dreyer pensively, "enchanting."

The other grimaced and flared up: "Stop harping on dreams, sir. They have come true, they have become flesh, in more senses than one, even though I may be a pauper, and cannot build my Eden and eidolons. Have you ever read Epicritus?"

Dreyer shook his head.

"Nor have I. But do give me a chance to prove that I am no quack. They told me you were interested in such innovations. Just think what a delight this would be, what an adornment, what an astounding, and permit me to say even artistic, achievement."

"What guarantee do you offer me?" asked Dreyer, relishing the entertainment.

"The guarantee of the human spirit," the inventor said trenchantly.

Dreyer laughed. "That's more like it. You revert to my original viewpoint."

He thought for a moment, then added: "I think I want to roll your offer around in my head. Who knows, maybe I'll see your invention in my next dream. My imagination must become steeped in it. At the moment I can say neither yes nor no. Now run along home. Where are you staying?"

"Hotel Montevideo," said the inventor. "An idiotically misleading name."

"But also a familiar one, though I can't remember why. Video, video. . . ."

"I see you have my friend's Pugowitz Tapwater Filter," said the inventor, pointing at the faucet in the corridor with the air of Rembrandt indicating a Claude Lorraine.

"Video, video," repeated Dreyer. "No, I don't know. Well, ponder our talk. Decide if you really want to kill a delightful fancy by selling it to the factory, and in a week or ten days I'll ring you up. And—pardon me for alluding to this—I hope you'll be a bit more communicative, a bit more trusting."

When his visitor had left, Dreyer sat motionless, his hands thrust deep into his trouser pockets. "No, he is not a charlatan," he reflected. "Or at least he is not aware of being one. Why not have a little fun? If it is all he says, the results really may be curious." The telephone emitted a discreet buzz, and for a time he forgot about the inventor.

That evening, however, he hinted to Martha that he was about to embark on a completely new project, and when she asked if it were profitable, he narrowed his eyes and nodded: "Oh, very, very profitable, my love." Next morning, as he was snorting under the shower, he decided not to receive the inventor again. At lunchtime, in a restaurant, he remembered him with pleasure and decided that the invention was something unique and irresistible. Upon coming home to supper he remarked to Martha casually that the project had fallen through. She was wearing her beige dress and was wrapped in a pink shawl, though it was quite warm in the house. Franz, whom he considered an amusing simpleton, was as usual jumpy and gloomy. He soon went home, saying he had smoked too much and had a headache. As soon as he had gone, Martha went up to the bedroom. In the boudoir on the tripod table by the sofa a silver box remained open. Dreyer took a Libidette from it and burst out laughing. "Contractive transmission! Animated flexibility! No, he can't be cheating. I think his idea is awfully attractive."

When he in turn went up to bed, Martha seemed to be asleep. After several centuries had elapsed, the bed table lamp went out. Presently she opened her eyes and listened. He was snoring. She lay on her back, gazing into the dark. Everything irritated her—that snoring, that gleam in the dark, probably in the looking glass, and incidentally, her own self.

"That was the wrong approach," she thought. "Tomorrow night I'll take drastic measures. Tomorrow night."

Franz, however, did not appear either the next evening or on Saturday. On Friday he had gone to a movie, and on Saturday, to a café with his colleague Schwimmer. At the cinema, an actress with a little black heart for lips and with eyelashes like the spokes of an umbrella was impersonating a rich heiress impersonating a poor office girl. The café turned out to be dark and dull. Schwimmer kept talking about the goings-on among boys in summer camps, and a rouged whore with a repulsive gold tooth was looking at them and swinging her leg, and half-smiling at Franz every time she shook off the ash of her cigarette.

It would have been so simple, thought Franz, to grasp her when she touched my knee. Agony. . . . Should I perhaps wait a while and not see her for a few days? But then life is not worth living. The next time I swear, yes, I swear. I swear by my mother and sister.

On Sunday his landlord brought him his coffee as usual at nine-thirty. Franz did not at once dress and shave as he did on weekdays, but merely pulled on his old dressing gown over his pajamas, and sat down at the table to write his weekly letter: "Dear Mama," he wrote in his crawling hand, "how are you? How is Emmy? Probably . . . —"

He paused, crossed out the last word and lapsed into thought, picking his nose, looking at the rainy day in the window. Probably they were on their way to church now. In the afternoon there would be coffee with whipped cream. He imagined his mother's fat florid face and dyed hair. What did she care about him? She had always loved Emmy more. She had still boxed his ears when he was seventeen, eighteen, even nineteen—last year, in fact. Once at Easter, when he was quite small but already bespectacled, she had ordered him to eat a little chocolate bunny that had been well licked by his sister. For having licked the candy meant for him Emmy received a light slap on the behind, but to him, for having refused to touch the slimy brown horror, she delivered such a backhand whack in the face that he flew off his chair, hit his head against the sideboard and lost consciousness. His love for his mother was never very deep but even so it was his first unhappy love, or rather he regarded her as a rough draft of a first love, for although he had craved for her affection because his schoolbooks of stories (*My Soldier Boy*, *Hanna Comes Home*) told him, as they had from immemorial time, that mothers always doted upon their sons and daughters, he actually could not stand her physical appearance, mannerisms, and emanations, the depressing, depressingly familiar odor of her skin and clothes, the bedbug-brown fat birthmark on her neck, the trick she had of scratching with a knitting needle the unappetizing parting of her chestnut hair, her enormous dropsical ankles, and all the kitchen faces she made by which he could unerringly determine what she was preparing—beer soup or bull hodes, or that dreadful local dainty *Budenzucker*.

Perhaps—in retrospection, at least—he had suffered less from her indifference, meanness, fits of temper, than from the embarrassment and detestation when she pinched his cheek in feigned fondness before a guest, usually the next-door butcher, or in the latter's presence forced him in folly and fun to kiss his sister's schoolmate Christina whom he adored from a distance, and to whom he would have apologized for those dreadful moments had she paid the least attention to him. Perhaps, in spite of everything, his mother missed him now? She never wrote anything about her feelings in her infrequent letters.

Still it was nice to feel sorry for oneself, it brought hot tears to one's eyes. And Emmy—she was a good girl. She would marry the butcher's assistant. Best butcher in town. Damn this rain. Dear Mama. What else? Maybe a description of the room?

He replaced his right slipper, which had aged more quickly than the left one and kept falling off his foot when he dangled it, and looked around.

"As I already wrote you, I have an excellent room, but I never described it to you properly. It has a mirror and a washstand. Above the bed there is the beautiful picture of a lady in an Oriental setting. The wallpaper has brownish flowers. In front of me, against the wall, there is a chest-of-drawers."

At that moment there came a light knock, Franz turned his head, and the door opened a crack. Old Enricht thrust his head in, winked, disappeared, and said to somebody on the other side of the door: "Yes, he is at home. Go right in."

She was wearing her beautiful moleskin coat thrown open over a veily, vapory dress; the rain that had caught her between taxi and entrance had had time to dot with dark stains her pearl-gray helmet-like hat; she stood pressing closely together her legs in apricot silk, as if on a parade. Still standing thus, she reached behind her and closed the door. She took off her gloves. Intently, unsmilingly, she stared at Franz as if she had not expected to see him. He covered his bare Adam's apple with his hand and uttered a long sentence but noticed with surprise that seemingly no words had been produced, as if he had tapped them out on a typewriter in which he had forgotten to insert a ribbon.

"Excuse me for bursting in like this," said Martha, "but I was afraid you might be ill."

Palpitating and blinking, his lower lip drooping, Franz began helping her to get rid of her coat. The silk lining was crimson, as crimson as lips and flayed animals, and smelled of heaven. He placed her coat and hat on the bed, and one last staunch little observer in the storm of his consciousness, after the rest of his thoughts had scattered, noted that this was like a train passenger marking the seat he is about to occupy.

The room was damp, and Martha, who had not much under her dress besides her gartered stockings, shivered.

"What's the matter?" she said. "I thought you would be glad to see me, and you don't say a word."

"Oh, I'm talking," answered Franz, doing his best to out-shout the hum around him.

Now they were standing face to face in the middle of the room, between the unfinished letter and the unmade bed.

"I don't care much for your dressing gown," she said, "but I love your pajamas. What nice stuff," she continued, rubbing it between finger and thumb near his open throat. "Look, he sleeps with his pen in his breast pocket, the perfect little businessman."

He began with her hands, burying his mouth in their warm palms, fondling her cold knuckles, kissing her bracelet. She gently plucked off his glasses and, as if blind herself, groped for his dressing-gown pockets, maddening him in the process. Her face was now sufficiently close to his and sufficiently removed from the invisible world for his next step. Holding her by the hips, he fed on her half-opened active mouth; she freed herself, fearing that his young impatience might resolve itself too soon; he nuzzled her in her deep soft neck.

"Please," he murmured, "please, I implore you."

"Silly," she said. "Why, of course. But you have to lock the door first."

He made for the door, automatically resuming his glasses and leaving in front of her, on the floor, his right slipper in token of his speedy return. Then, his desire exposed and his eyes wicked behind their strong lenses, he attempted to push her toward the bed.

"Wait, wait a moment, my sweet," she said, holding him with one cold hand and frantically fumbling in her bag with the other, "Look, you must put this on; I'll do it for you, you awkward brutal darling."

"Now," she cried when he was magnificently sheathed; and, baring her thighs, and not bothering to lie down, and revelling in his ineptitude, she directed his upward thrusts until they drove home, whereupon, her face working, she threw her head back and dug her ten nails in his nates.

As soon as it was over, Martha staggered and sat down hard on the edge of the bed against which she had been standing. Everything had been so wonderful that she did not immediately become aware of her second-best bag of imitation crocodile under her.

Franz wanted to continue at once but she said that first of all she must take off her dress and stockings, and make herself comfy in bed. The coat and hat were transferred to a chair. What Martha called "your macky" was rinsed and slipped on again. Franz and Martha admired each other. Her breasts were disappointingly small but charmingly shaped. "I never thought you'd be so lean and hairy," she said, stroking him. His vocabulary was even more primitive.

Presently the bed stirred into motion. It glided off on its journey creaking discreetly as does a sleeping car when the express pulls out of a dreamy station. "You, you, you," uttered Martha, softly squeezing him between her knees at every gasp, and following with moist eyes the shadows of angels waving their handkerchiefs on the ceiling, which was moving away faster and faster.

Now the room was empty. Objects lay, stood, sat, hung in the carefree postures man-made things adopt in man's absence. The mock crocodile lay on the floor. A blue-tinted cork, which had been recently removed from a small ink bottle when a fountain pen had to be refilled, hesitated for an instant, then rolled in a semi-circle to the edge of the oilcloth-covered table, hesitated again, and jumped off. With the help of the lashing rain the wind tried to open the window but failed. In the rickety wardrobe a blue black-spotted tie slithered off its twig like a snake. A paperback novelette on the chest-of-drawers left open at Chapter Five skipped several pages.

Suddenly the looking glass made a signal—a warning gleam. It reflected a bluish armpit and a lovely bare arm. The arm stretched—and fell back lifeless. Slowly, the bed returned to Berlin from Eden. It was greeted by a blast of music from the radio upstairs which changed immediately to excited speech which in its turn was replaced by the same music but now more remote. Martha lay with closed eyes, and her smile formed two sickle-shaped dimples at the sides of her tightly closed mouth. The once impenetrable black strands were now thrown back from her temples, and Franz as he lay beside her leaning on his elbow gazed at her tender naked ear, at her limpid forehead, and at last found again in this face that madonna-like something which, prone as he was to content himself with such comparisons, he had already noted three months ago.

"Franz," said Martha without opening her eyes, "Franz, it was paradise! I've never, never. . . ."

She left an hour later, promising her poor pet that next time she would take less cruel precautions. Before going she thoroughly studied every corner of the room, picked up Franz's pajamas, took out the fountain pen from its pocket and put it on the bed table, changed the position of the chair, observed that socks were torn and buttons missing, and said that a general fixing up was in order for the room— embroidered doilies, perhaps, and definitely a couch with two or three gay cushions. About that couch she reminded the landlord, whom she found very quietly walking up and down the corridor evidently waiting for a chance to sweep the room and collect the coffee things. Smiling now at her, now at Franz, rubbing his rustling palms, he said that as soon as his wife returned the couch would also return. Since in all truthfulness he had not taken any couch to be repaired (the vacant place had been occupied by a previous tenant's upright piano), he took great pleasure in answering Martha's precise questions. He was quite content with his life in general, gray old Enricht in his felt houseshoes with buckles, especially since the day he discovered that he had the remarkable gift of transforming himself into all kinds of creatures—a horse, a hog, or a six-year-old girl in a sailor cap. For actually (but this of course was a secret) he was the famed illusionist and conjuror Menetek-El-Pharsin.

Martha liked his courteous ways but Franz warned her that he was a little odd. "Oh, my darling," she said on the way downstairs, "this could not be better. This quiet old man is so much safer than would have been a nosy old crone. Au revoir, my treasure. You may give me a kiss—a quick one."

His street was decidedly dingy. Perhaps, when that "Ciné-palace" was finished, it would look better. A special poster in a wooden frame facing the sidewalk at a strategic point depicted an illusory future—a soaring edifice of glittering glass which stood aloof in a spacious area of blue air, although actually ugly tenement houses snuggled up to its very slowly rising walls. The scaffolded half-finished stories above the promised cinema were to contain an exhibition hall for rent, a beauty salon, a photographic atelier, many other attractions.

In one direction the street terminated in a dead end, in the other it ran into a small square where a modest open-air market was set up on Tuesdays and Fridays. From there two streets branched out: to the left, a crooked alley which used to flaunt red flags on the days of political celebration, and on the right, a long populous street; one noticed there a large store where every article cost a quarter be it a bust of Schiller or a kitchen pan. She was cold but happy. The street abutted on a stone portico with a white U on blue glass, a subway station. Then one turned left onto a rather nice boulevard. Then the houses stopped; here and there a villa was being built, or a wasteland was partitioned into small vegetable gardens. Then came houses again, big new ones, pink and pistachio. Martha turned past the last of these and was on her street. Beyond her villa there was a large avenue serviced by two trams, number 113 and 108, and one bus.

She passed quickly along the gravel path leading to the porch. At that instant the sun swept across the soft underbelly of the white sky, found a slit, and radiantly burst through. The small trees along the path responded immediately with all their moist droplets of light. The lawn scintillated in its turn. A sparrow's crystal wing flashed as it flew by.

When Martha entered the house, pink optical mottles drifted before her eyes in the comparative darkness of the front hall. In the dining room the table was not yet laid. In the bedroom the sudden sun was already carefully folded on the carpet and on the blue couch. She proceeded to change, smiling, sighing happily, acknowledging with thanks her reflection in the mirror.

A little later, as she stood in the center of the bedroom in a garnet-red dress, with smooth temples and just a touch of make-up, she heard Tom's idiotically lyrical bark downstairs followed by a stranger's loud voice. On her way at the turn of the staircase she met the ascending stranger who passed swiftly, whistling and tapping the banisters with his riding crop. "Hello, my love," he said without stopping, "I'll be down in ten minutes." And taking the last two or three steps in one ponderous stride, he grunted cheerfully and cast a downward glance at her retreating bandeaux. "Hurry up," she said, not looking back, "and please get rid of that horsy smell."

At lunch, in the midst of small talk and tinkle—that particular tinkle half-glass, half-metal, peculiar to the process of human feeding—Martha still did not recognize the master of the house with his mobile cropped mustache and his way of rapidly tossing into his mouth now a radish, now a bit of the roll he kept kneading on the tablecloth as he talked. Not that she experienced any special constraint. She was no Emma, and no Anna. In the course of her conjugal life she had grown accustomed to grant her favors to her wealthy protector with such skill, with such calculation, with such efficient habits of physical practice, that she who thought herself ripe for adultery had long grown ready for harlotry.

On her right sat a somewhat coarse-looking old man with a glamorous title; on her left there was plump Willy Wald with big red cheeks, and three even folds of fat over the back of his collar. Next to him sat his noisy mother, also corpulent, with the same prominent dark moist eyes. Her rasping voice kept abruptly passing into rich gurgling laughter, so different from her speech that a blind man might mistake her for two different people. Next to the old count sparkled young Mrs. Wald, who was powdered to a death-like pallor and had unnaturally arching eyebrows, and could keep her three gigolos as far as we were concerned. And between them, opposite Martha, concealed now by a fleshy dahlia, now by crystal facets, there sat talking and laughing a completely superfluous Mr. Dreyer. Everything except him was fine. The food, especially the goose, and the heavy profile of bald kindly Willy, and the conversation about cars, and the wit of the count, and his anecdote about the skin-lifting operation of an aging star, after which her chin was adorned with a new dimple that had been formerly her navel, which he communicated to her *sotto voce*. She did not talk much herself. But her silence was so vibrant, so responsive, with such an animated smile on her half-open glistening lips, that she seemed unusually talkative. Dreyer could not help admiring her from behind the fat pink corners of the dahlias. And the sensation that she was after all happy with him made him almost condone the unfrequency of her caresses.

"How can one love a man whose mere touch makes one feel sick," she confessed to Franz at one of their next meetings, when he began insisting she tell him if she loved her husband.

"Then I'm the first?" he asked eagerly. "The first?"

In answer she bared her shining teeth and slowly pinched his cheek. Franz clasped her legs and looked up at her, rolling his head as he tried to catch her fingers in his mouth. She was sitting in the armchair already dressed and ready to leave but unable to make herself go, and he huddled on his knees before her, tousled, with blinking glasses, in his new white braces. He had just put on her street shoes for her, for, while visiting him, she would wear bed slippers with crimson pompoms. This pair of slippers (his modest but considerate gift) our lovers kept in the lower drawer of the corner chest, for life not unfrequently imitates the French novelists. That drawer contained, moreover, a little arsenal of contraceptive implementa, gradually accumulated by Martha, who after a miscarriage in the first year of her marriage had developed a morbid fear of pregnancy. As he put the pretty slippers away till next time, he thought what a glamorous feminine touch all this added to the room, which had grown more attractive in other ways too. On the table three pink dahlias were on their last legs in a dark-blue vase with a single oblong reflection. Lacy doilies had appeared here and there, and soon the tenaciously anticipated couch was to move in weightily; Martha had already acquired two peacock cushions for it. In a container of celluloid a round cake of violet-scented beige soap adorned the washstand for Martha's use. The young man's own toiletry had been supplemented by a bottle of Anticaprine and a skin lotion with a spotted face on the label. All his things had been checked and counted; his underwear bore lovingly sewn-on monograms; one unforgettable morning she glided into the emporium, demanded to be shown the most elegant ties available, chose three of them and vanished with them, passing through his department and drowning alternately in the many mirrors, and the fact that she had not even glanced at him added a strange sparkle to that crystal tryst. They now hung in his wardrobe like trophies; and there was a slowly ripening intoxicating project: a tuxedo!

Love helped Franz to mature. This first affair resembled a diploma of which one could be proud. All day he was tormented by the desire to show this diploma to fellow salesmen but prudence restrained him from even hinting at it. Around half past five (Piffke, thinking this would please the boss, would let him go a little earlier than the others) he would come tearing breathlessly into his room. Soon Martha arrived with a couple of sandwiches from the neighboring delicatessen. The rather droll but endearing contrast between his thin body and one cocked part of it, shortish but exceptionally thick, would cause his mistress to croon in praise of his manhood: "Fatty is greedy! Oh, greedy! . . ." Or she might say: "I bet (she adored bets), I bet you a new sweater that you can't do it again." But time is no friend of lovers. At a little past seven she had to leave. She was as punctual as she was passionate. And around nine Franz would generally go and have supper at Uncle's.

Warm, warmly flowing happiness filled physical Franz to the brim, pulsated in wrist and temple, pounded in his breast, and issued from his finger in a ruby drop when he pricked himself accidentally at the store: he frequently had to deal with pins in his department (though not as much as the adjusting tailor, Kottmann, who resembled the "cat's-whiskers" fish found in the remote river of an abolished boy-hood, when with bristling mouth he circled around a chalk-marked customer). But on the whole his hands had now grown more nimble, and he no longer had trouble with the light lids and tissue paper of flat cardboard boxes as he had during the first weeks. Those rapid behind-the-counter exer-cises had as it were prepared his hands for other motions and contact, also rapid and nimble, causing Martha to purr with pleasure, for she particularly loved his forelimbs, and loved them most of all when with a succession of rhapsodic touches they would run all over her milk-white body. Thus a shop counter was the mute keyboard on which Franz had rehearsed his happiness.

But as soon as she had gone, as soon as supper hour ap-proached, and he had to face Dreyer, everything changed. As happens in dreams, when a perfectly harmless object in-spires us with fear and thereafter is frightening every time we dream of it (and even in real life retains disquietening overtones), so Dreyer's presence became for Franz a refined torture, an implacable menace. When for the first time after her visit, he had walked the short distance between the gate and the porch (yawning nervously and plucking at his glasses as he went); when for the first time in the capacity of clandestine lover of the lady of the house he had glanced askance at innocent Frieda and crossed the threshold rubbing his rain-wet hands, Franz was overwhelmed with such an eerie feeling that in his fright and confusion he had aimed a kick at Tom, who was welcoming him in the drawing room with an unexpected burst of affection; as Franz waited for his hosts, he superstitiously searched the bright eyes of the cushions for omens of disaster. A high-strung and abject coward in matters of feeling (and such cowards are doubly wretched since they lucidly perceive their cowardice and fear it), he could not help cringing when, with a banging of doors in a dramatic draft, Martha and Dreyer entered simultaneously from two different rooms as if on a too harshly lit stage. Then he snapped to attention and in this attitude felt himself ascending through the ceiling, through the roof, into the black-brown sky, while, in reality, drained empty, he was shaking hands with Martha, with Dreyer. He dropped back on his feet out of that dark nonexistence, from those unknown and rather silly heights, to land firmly in the middle of the room (safe, safe!) when hearty Dreyer described a circle with his index finger and jabbed him in the navel; Franz mimicked a gasp and giggled; and as usual Martha was coldly radiant. His fear did not pass but only subsided temporarily: one incautious glance, one eloquent smile, and all would be revealed, and a disaster beyond imagination would shatter his career. Thereafter whenever he entered this house, he imagined that the disaster had happened—that Martha had been found out, or had confessed everything in a fit of insanity or religious self-immolation to her husband; and the drawing room chandelier invariably met him with a sinister refulgence.

He would weigh every joke of Dreyer's, scrape at it, sniff

at it, with trepidation, checking it for some crafty allusion, but there was nothing. Luckily for Franz, his observant uncle's interest in any object, animated or not, whose distinctive features he had immediately grasped, or thought he had grasped, gloated over and filed away, would wane with its every subsequent reappearance. The bright perception became the habitual abstraction. Natures like his spend enough energy in tackling with all the weapons and vessels of the mind the enforced impressions of existence to be grateful for the neutral film of familiarity that soon forms between the newness and its consumer. It was too boring to think that the object might change of its own accord and assume unforeseen characteristics. That would mean having to enjoy it again, and he was no longer young. He had appreciated the poor bloke's simplicity and vulgarity almost at their first anonymous rendezvous in the train. Thenceforth, from the first moment of actual acquaintance, he had thought of Franz as of an amusing coincidence in human form: the form was that of a timid provincial nephew with a banal mind and limited ambitions. Similarly Martha, for more than seven years now, had remained the same distant, thrifty, frigid wife whose beauty would occasionally come alive and welcome him with the paradisal smile he had first fallen in love with. Neither of these images changed basically; they simply became more compactly filled up with fitting characteristics. Thus an experienced artist sees only that which is in keeping with his initial concept.

On the other hand, Dreyer would feel a kind of humiliating itching when an object did not immediately yield to his voracious eye, did not assume obediently such a posture as to give him a chance to wrestle with it. A couple of months had passed since the car accident. He had had time to make his will as he had intended to do all along on his fiftieth birthday (which, bless her cold heart, his only inheritor had let pass without a shadow of celebration), and still he could not determine a silly little thing about his chauffeur which if true would certainly lead to another accident sooner or later. With a twitch of his nostril he would probe the man's tobacco reek for a gayer smell; observed him when he went bow-legged around the car; and, at the most perilous hour—Saturday night—would unexpectedly summon him and laboriously conduct a trivial conversation while he watched whether the other did not behave in too free a fashion. He hoped that some day he would be told that the man, alas, was not fit to come, but alas that day never came. At times it seemed to him that the Icarus was taking the turns a little faster, a little more cheerfully than usual. It was just on such a day of carefree swerves, made especially interesting by the fact that the first real snow of the year had fallen on the eve and had now melted into a slippery mush, that he noticed a hatless man through the window who looked exactly as if he had hinges for joints, crossing the street with mincing steps. That reminded him of his talk with the amiable inventor. When he reached his office, he promptly had him called at the Montevideo, and was very pleased when old Sarah Reich, his secretary, announced that the inventor would be right over. However, neither Dreyer, nor Miss Reich (who had her own dreadful troubles), nor anyone at all in the world ever found out that the lonely and homesick inventor happened to live in the very same room where Franz had spent the night of his arrival; where a great ash tree, now leafless, was visible from the window; and where one could notice, if one looked very carefully, that some minute glass dust had become imbedded in the cracks of the linoleum by the washstand. It is significant that Fate should have lodged him there of all places. It was a road that Franz had travelled—and all at once Fate remembered and sent in pursuit this practically nameless man who of course knew nothing of his important assignment, and never found out anything about it, as for that matter no one else ever did, not even old Enricht.

"Welcome," said Dreyer, "sit down."

The inventor did.

"Well," asked Dreyer, toying with his favorite pencil.

The inventor blew his nose, carefully wrapped up the results, and spent a long time tucking the handkerchief—an article that some new invention should have long replaced—into his pocket.

"I come to you with the same offer," he said at last.

"Any additional details," suggested Dreyer, pencilling concentric blue circles on his blotter.

The inventor nodded and started to speak. The telephone on the desk buzzed. Dreyer gave his visitor a gentle smile and energetically put the receiver to his ear. "It's me. I forgot—did you say you would not be back for supper tonight?"

"That's right, my love."

"And you'll be home late?"

"After midnight. Meeting of the board and festivities. Go to a restaurant with Franz or something."

"I don't know. Maybe I shall."

"Wonderful," said Dreyer. "Goody-by. Oh, wait—if you want the car— Hullo!" But she had already hung up.

The inventor was pretending not to listen. Dreyer noticed this and said with a coy snicker: "That was my little girl friend."

The inventor smirked indulgently in response and resumed his explanations. Dreyer began a new set of concentric circles, Miss Reich brought a batch of letters and silently disappeared. The inventor continued to talk. Dreyer

[108]

threw down the pencil, reclined limply in his armchair and surrendered to the fascination.

"What was that?" he interrupted. "The noble slowness of a sleepwalker's progress?"

"Yes, if desired," said the inventor. "Or at the other extreme, the restrained agility of a convalescent."

"Go on, go on," Dreyer said, closing his eyes. "This is pure witchcraft."

6

An unprepossessing sullen little café, not far from where
Franz lives. Three men engrossed in a silent game of skat.
The wife of one of them, pregnant and veal-pale, sleepily
following their game. A plain girl with a nervous tic, leafing
through an old picture magazine and stopping at the messy
death of a riddle: an indelible pencil had rapaciously filled
in most of the crossword's blank squares. A lady in a moleskin coat (that impressed the proprietress of the place) and
a young man in tortoise shell glasses, sipping cherry brandy
and gazing into each other's eyes. A drunk in an unemployed-
looking cap tapping on the thick glass behind which coins
had bunched together forming a metal sausage—the losses
of all those who had put a coin in the slot and had moved
the handle to activate the little tin juggler while his tiny
bright balls followed the winding grooves. The counter,
chilled by beer foam, gives off a fish-like sheen. The proprietress has two green wool soccer balls for breasts. She
yawns as she looks toward a dark nook where the waiter,
half-concealed by a screen, is devouring a mountain of
mashed potatoes. On the wall behind her tocks a cuckoo
clock of carved wood surmounted by a pair of antlers and

beside it there is an oleograph depicting the meeting of Bismarck and Napoleon III. The rustle of the card players grows softer and softer. It has now stopped altogether.

"You chose well—we can be sure nobody will see us here."

He caressed her hand on the table: "Yes, but it's getting late, darling, maybe it's time to go."

"Your uncle won't be back till midnight or later. We have time."

"Forgive me for dragging you to such a squalid place."

"No-no, not at all. I told you, it's quite a good choice. Let's imagine you are a Heidelberg student. How nice you would look in a cerevis."

"And you are a princess incognito? I'd like us to drink champagne, with couples dancing around us, and beautiful Hungarian music."

She propped her elbow on the table, drawing back the skin of her cheek with her fist. Silence.

"Tell me, would you like to eat something? I'm afraid you have grown still thinner."

"Oh, what does it matter. All my life I've been unhappy. And now you are with me."

Motionless, the players gazed at their cards. The puffy woman leaned exhausted against her husband's shoulder. The girl had lapsed into thought and her face had ceased twitching. The picture magazine's pages drooped on their stick like a flag in the calm. Silence. Torpor.

Martha was the first to stir: Franz, too, tried to shake off that strange drowsiness; blinked, tugged at the lapels of his jacket.

"I love him but he is poor," she said jokingly. And suddenly her expression changed. She imagined that she, too, was penniless, and that here, in this shabby little tavern, among befuddled workmen and cheap floozies, in this deafening silence with only that clock clucking, a sticky wine glass before each, the two of them were whiling away their Saturday night.

She fancied with horror that this tender pauper really was her husband, her young husband, whom she would never, never give up. Darned stockings, two modest dresses, a broken comb, one room with a bloated mirror, her hands coarse from washing and cooking, this tavern where for one reichsmark you could get royally drunk. . . .

She felt so terrified that she dug her nails into his hand.

"What's happened? Dearest, I don't understand."

"Get up," she said, "pay and let's go. It's so stuffy in here, I can't breathe."

As she inhaled the matter-of-fact cold of the night, she instantly regained her wealth and, pressing against him, rapidly switched feet so as to be in step with him; he groped for and found her warm wrist among the folds of her furs.

Next morning, as she lay in bed in her pretty bright room, Martha recalled her fanciful fears with a smile. "Let us be realistic," she reassured herself. "It's all quite simple. I simply have a lover. That ought to embellish, not complicate, my existence. And that's just what it is—a pleasant embellishment. And if, by any chance—" But strange, she could find no specific direction for her thoughts; Franz's street terminated in a dead end which her mind reached invariably. She could not imagine, say, that Franz did not exist, or that some other admirer was floating out of a mist with a rose in his hand, for, as he came nearer, it was always Franz. This day like all days to come was suffused and colored by her passion for Franz. She tried to think of the past, of those impossible years when she did not yet know him, but it was not her own past she conjured up, it was his: his little town where she had happened to stop on her way grew up in her thoughts and there, in the haze, was Franz's white green-roofed house, never seen by her in real life but described by him many times, and the brick schoolhouse around the corner, and the frail little boy with glasses. What Franz had told her about his childhood was more important than anything she had actually experienced; and she did not understand why that was so, and argued with herself in an attempt to refute what impinged on her sense of conformity and clarity.

Particularly painful was that inner discord when she had to attend to some household project or ponder an important purchase that in no way concerned Franz. For example, at odd moments the idea of acquiring a new car kept cropping up; then she would tell herself that this had nothing to do with Franz, that he was being left out, and somehow cheated; and despite her long-standing dream of substituting a certain fashionable make of limousine for the somewhat seedy Icarus, all the fun of such an acquisition was spoiled. A dress that she would wear for Franz, or a Sunday dinner that she could compose of his favorite dishes—these matters were different. And at first all these misgivings and pleasures were strange to her as if she had grown ten years younger and was learning to live in a new way, and needed time to get accustomed to it.

Another perplexity stemmed from the fact that her house, of which she had grown even fonder since Franz had become practically a member of the family, contained someone else besides him and her. There he stuck out, tawny-mustached and ruddy, eating at one table with her and sleeping in the adjacent bed, and demanding her attention in one way or another. His financial affairs interested her even more than in that already very distant year when a lot of ballast jettisoned from the balloon of inflation had come pouring into his pockets where it turned into that alchemistical dream—*valuta*. As before, he told her little. This interest of hers in Dreyer's ventures did not combine organically with the new, piercing, moaning, and throbbing meaning of her life. She felt she could not be fully happy without such a blending of bank and bed, and yet she did not know how to achieve harmony, how to eliminate the discord. He had once shown her a slip of paper on which he had totalled up for her benefit his fortune in round numbers: "Is it enough?" he asked with a smile, "what do you think?" There were those 700,000 untouchable dollars in a safe in Hamburg. There was another fortune in stocks. There were considerable resources of a more fluid and changeable nature that constituted the blood system of his business. There was the will he had recently made which had cost her two nights of strenuous love-making but which had completely excluded, thank goodness, a wayward young brother in South Africa who, she suspected, was very much looking forward to his share.

"So we are practically millionaires," she said with one of those rare resplendent responses for which her husband was ready to pay considerably more than he owned: "On the saddleback, on the saddleback, darling," he answered.

No matter what happened, she meditated, at the exchange or in his frivolous transactions, there remained sufficient funds for many years of idle life—until, say, she was sixty, or, say, fifty-eight and Franz a still ardent forty-five. However, as long as Mr. Dreyer existed, he must continue to earn. Therefore veering from enthusiasm to a show of anxious gloom, she urged him to accumulate more in Hamburg and gamble less in Berlin, and coldly gave him back the slip of paper. They were standing by the desk where Parsifal held his lighted lantern, and one could tell by the peculiar stillness muffling the villa that snow was falling, smothering the garden in dark, dark white. December turned out to be colder than usual with spectacularly low temperatures to be eagerly noted by the forgetful old-timers of the press who had gone through the same rigmarole a couple of years earlier. Dreyer gave his watch a worried glance. The three of them were going to a variety show. Like a child he was afraid to be late. Martha reached for the newspaper lying on the table and looked through the advertisements and the local news, learning that a luxurious villa was for sale for 500,000 reichsmark, and that a car had overturned killing its occupant, the famous actor Hess, on his way to his sick wife's bedside. "Good God," she exclaimed, "this is unheard-of." In the adjacent boudoir Franz was listening without much interest to the radio's rich voice giving details of the crash.

The vast theater was crowded; its enormous stage was still curtained. They squeezed into one of those exceptionally narrow boxes in which one becomes so acutely aware what an uncomfortable, tangly and tingly thing a pair of human legs is. It was especially hard on lanky Franz. As if it were not enough that his lower extremities had grotesquely lengthened, Martha, strictly adhering to every rule of adultery, pressed the side of her silky knee against his awkwardly bent right leg while Dreyer, sitting to his left and a little behind, leaned lightly against his shoulder and kept tickling his ear with the corner of the program he was consulting. Poor Franz was torn between the fear that the husband might notice something and the delight of feeling the silky sparks coursing through his body.

"Such a huge theater," he muttered, slightly shifting his shoulder so as to escape from Dreyer's repulsive golden-haired hand. "I can imagine how much they make every night. Let me see—about two thousand seats—"

Dreyer, as he went through the program for the second or third time, exclaimed: "Ah, that will be good: trick cyclists."

The lights dimmed slowly. The pressure of Martha's knee increased recklessly, but then relaxed as the orchestra began to play a potpourri from *Lucia di Lammermoor* (which in the circumstances was pretty apt, though lost on our audience).

They were shown many entertaining things. Martha found the program very acceptable, Dreyer thought it a jolly good show, Franz loved every bit of it. A man in a top hat juggled dummy bottles to which he suddenly added his hat; four Japanese flew hither and thither on rhythmically creaking trapezes and while pausing in between stunts tossed to each other a bright handkerchief with which they fastidiously wiped their hands; a clown, constantly on the point of losing his baggy trousers, flopped all over the stage emitting a sharp whistle as he skidded before falling with a whack on his face; a horse, so white it might have been powdered, delicately played pace in time to music; a crazy family of cyclists extracted all that was humanly possible and more from the properties of the wheel; a black lustrous seal gave throaty cries like a drowning bather, and then slithered smooth and slick as if greased down a board into the green water of a pool where a half-naked girl greeted the happy beast with a kiss on the nose. Now and then Dreyer grunted with pleasure and nudged Franz. After the seal had received its ultimate reward, a live mackerel which it succulently snapped up in mid-air, and galloped off on its flappers, the curtain was drawn for the public to re-pick themselves, as the French say; when it opened again, a woman in silver shoes and a spangled evening dress stood bathed in light in the center of the darkened stage with a luminous violin to which she applied a star-flashing bow. The spotlight diligently drenched her now in pink now in green; a diadem shimmered on her brow. Her playing was languorous and really delicious and suffused Martha with such excitement, such exquisite sadness that she half-closed her eyes and found Franz's hand in the darkness; and he experienced the same sensation—a poignant rapture in harmony with their love. The musical phantasmagoria (as that item was listed) sparkled and swooned, the violin sang and moaned, the pink and the green were joined by blue and violet—and then Dreyer could stand it no longer.

"I have my eyes and ears closed," he said in a weepy whisper, "let me know when this obscene abomination is over."

Martha gave a start; Franz thought that all was lost, that he had seen them holding hands. At the same moment the stage grew black and the house thundered in an avalanche of applause.

"You understand absolutely nothing about art," said Martha dryly. "You only disturb other people who want to listen."

Dreyer exhaled in noisy relief. Then, with fussy gestures, with swift jerks of his eyebrows, like a man who is in a hurry to forget, he looked up the next number on the program.

"Ah, that's more like it," he said. "The Gutter-Perchers, whoever they are, and then a world-famous conjuror."

"Close call," Franz was thinking at that moment. "That time it was really a close call. Phew! . . . We've got to be extremely careful. . . . Of course, it's wonderful sitting here and knowing she's mine, and he sitting next to us and not knowing. But it is all so dangerous. . . ."

The performance concluded with a motion picture, as was still customary in circuses and music halls ever since the first "bioscope" was shown there as a fascinating curiosity. On the flickering screen, strangely flat after the live stage, a chimpanzee in degrading human clothes performed human actions degrading to an animal. Martha laughed heartily, remarking: "Just look how smart he is!" Franz clucked his tongue in amazement, and insisted in all seriousness that it was a dwarf in disguise.

When they came out into the frosty street lighted like yet another scene by the theater's electric signs, and the faithful Icarus rolled up with a kind of clownish zeal, Dreyer reproached himself for having neglected lately to observe his chauffeur's behavior. Now was the perfect moment to make a little check. As the chauffeur was hurriedly pulling on his fur gauntlets, Dreyer tried to catch with his nose the steam issuing from the man's mouth. The chauffeur met his glance and, baring his bad teeth, innocently raised his eyebrows.

"Chilly, chilly, isn't it," said Dreyer quickly.

"Not too bad," replied the chauffeur, "not too bad."

"Can't smell anything," thought Dreyer. "And yet I'm sure that while he was waiting. . . . Flushed face, merry eyes. Well, let's see how he is going to drive."

The chauffeur drove remarkably well. Franz, respectfully perched on the edge of one of the two folding seats of the luxurious vehicle, listened to the smooth hum of its speed, examined the artificial daisies in their little silver vase, the speaking tube hanging on its steel hook, the travelling clock which had its own concept of time, and the ashtray with one gold-tipped cigarette butt in it. A snowy night with aureoled street lights ran past the wide windows.

"I'll get out here," he said, recognizing a square and a statue. "It's just a short walk to my house from here."

"Oh, I'll take you there," replied Dreyer with a little yawn. "What's your exact address?"

Martha caught Franz's eye and shook her head. He understood. Dreyer, accustomed as he was to seeing his nephew nearly every evening at his house, had never bothered to ask where he actually lived, and this should be left in silent and propitious obscurity. Franz nervously cleared his throat and said:

"No, really, I'd like to stretch my legs."

"As you wish," said Dreyer in the middle of a yawn and, leaning across Franz, knocked on the glass partition with his fist.

"Why knock?" Martha observed crossly; "there's a tube for this purpose, isn't there?"

Franz found himself in a deserted white square. He put up the collar of his raincoat, thrust his hands into his pockets and, hunching over, walked quickly in the direction of his house. On Sundays, on the elegant street in the western section of the city, he would wear his new overcoat and walk quite differently. Now, however, was not the moment for that—the cold was intense. That big-city Sunday walk had not been easy to copy. It consisted of stretching one's arms well down and crossing one's hands (good gloves were essential) below the last button of one's overcoat as if to keep it in place as one advanced at a very slow strut, with toes pointing out at each step. Thus promenaded the Kurfürstendamm dandies, sometimes in pairs, now and then looking around at a girl without changing the position of their hands but merely giving a slight backward jerk of the shoulder.

Despite the cold, Franz felt multiplied and exaggerated as one does after a show, and he even began to whistle. "To hell with her husband. One must be braver. Such bliss is not bestowed on everyone. What was she doing now? She must be home and undressing. That yellow-bristled pig. Pestering her, no doubt. To hell with him! Now she is sitting on the

[119]

bed, peeling off her stocking. Three or four houses more, and she will be naked. I should buy her a lacy nightdress. Keep it among my pajamas. When I reach that street lamp, she will lower her head on the pillow. I cross the street, and she turns off the light. They share the same bedroom. No, he is getting old, he will leave her alone. One more block: she has fallen asleep. That's my street. Wonderful violinist—and so beautifully staged, there was really something heavenly about it. The conjuror was good too. Simple tricks, no doubt: make good money by deceiving people. Now she is sound asleep. She sees my house in dream and hears the divine violin. Damn this key. Always starts by behaving as if it had never been in this lock before. Stair light not working again. You could really come crashing down if you happened to trip. And this key is acting up, too."

In the dim corridor, by the slightly brighter door of his room, stood old Enricht shaking his head disapprovingly. He wore a mouse-gray dressing gown and checkered booties.

"Oh-oh-oh," he said. "Going to bed after midnight. Shame on you."

Franz was about to walk on but the old man clutched at his sleeve.

"I can't be angry tonight," he said with feeling. "It's a joyful occasion for me: the wife is back!"

"Congratulations," said Franz.

"But no joy is perfect," Enricht went on without releasing Franz's sleeve. "My little old lady arrived sick."

Franz gave a commiserating grunt.

"There she is," cried the landlord. "Sitting there in the armchair. Have a look."

He opened the door wider and over the back of the chair Franz glimpsed a gray head with something white pinned to its crown.

"See what I mean?" said the old man, staring at Franz with shining eyes. "And now good night," he added and, slipping into his room, closed the door.

Franz proceeded on his way. But then stopped short and went back. "Listen," he said through the door. "How about that couch?"

A hoarse, strained, old-womanish voice replied: "The couch is already in your room. I gave you my own couch."

"Two old crackpots," thought Franz with a squeamish grimace. True enough, the furniture family in his room had grown. It was a hard decrepit couch of a drab gray, patterned with forget-me-nots. Still, it was a couch. When Martha came the next day she wrinkled her nose and, keeping it wrinkled, felt the stuffing, located a sick spring, and raised the shabby fringe.

"Oh well, there is nothing to be done," she said at last. "I have no intention of quarrelling with his old lady. A pity she has returned. One more pair of ears. Put those two cushions there. Now it looks better." And soon they grew used to it, to its modest coloration and to the disapproving creaks it emitted in rhythm to their ebullient love-making.

It was not only a couch, however, that enriched Franz's room. Once, in a particularly benevolent moment, Dreyer gave him some extra cash from his waistcoat pocket (real green dollars!), and a fortnight later, just in time for Christmas, a new lodger appeared in Franz's wardrobe: the long awaited tuxedo.

"That's all very well," said Martha, "but it's not all. You have to learn to dance. Tomorrow night after supper we'll put a nice record on the phonograph, and I'll give you your first lesson. It will be rather fun to have Uncle watch us."

Franz arrived in his new dinner jacket. She reprimanded him for wearing it needlessly but found it very becoming. It was nine o'clock. Dreyer was expected any minute. He was very precise in this respect, always telephoning to say he would be so many minutes earlier or later, for he was extremely fond of hearing his wife's soft, smooth, formal voice over the phone—her voice in a kind of early Florentine perspective, so different from matter-of-fact reality. Martha was always surprised at his telephoning about those trifling minutes and seconds, and despite her own careful attitude toward measured time, her husband's punctuality in this respect puzzled and irritated her. Tonight he had not telephoned, and yet he was already half an hour late. Out of natural reverence toward the sacred crease of each trouser-leg, Franz avoided sitting down and walked around the room, skirting Martha's armchair but not daring to kiss her because of the maid's proximity.

"I'm hungry," said Martha. "I can't understand why he does not come."

"Let's start the phonograph. You'll teach me while we're waiting."

"I'm not in the mood. I said after supper."

Another ten minutes passed. She got up abruptly and summoned Frieda.

A succulent omelette and a bit of liver revived her. "Close it," she said to Franz, indicating the door left open by Frieda, whom a bad toothache had been afflicting all day. When Franz returned to his seat, Martha enveloped him in a smile of contented adoration. It so happened that this was the first time she was having supper at home alone with Franz. Yes, the dinner jacket could not be better. She must give him some nice cuff links instead of those stud-like horrors.

"Oh, my own big sweet darling," she said softly, stretching her arm toward him across the dinner cloth.

"Careful," whispered Franz, looking around. He did not

trust the pictures on the wall—the old baron in the frock coat and his redoutable double staring down, ready to pounce. The glittering sideboard was all eyes. Cloaked eavesdroppers lurked in the folds of the drapery. A famous practical joker, Curtius Dreyerson, might be crouching under the table. Good thing at least that Tom had stayed in the front hall. And the maid might come back any moment. In this castle one must take no liberties. Nevertheless, powerless to oppose her smiling desire, he stroked her bare arm. She slowly caressed his nose with her fingers, beaming and wetting her lips. He had the awful sensation that at that very instant Dreyer would suddenly step from behind a curtain: the jester turned executioner.

"Eat, drink, my lord. We are *chez nous*," said Martha, laughing.

She was wearing a black tulle dress, her lips were painted, her green earrings aflame, and her hair, divided by the mathematically pure line of its parting, glistened more than ever with the melanite lustre that was one of the jewels of her beauty. A low lamp with an orange shade cast a voluptuous light on the table. Franz, his worshipful glasses glinting at Martha, sucked on a leg of cold chicken. She leaned toward him, took the glossy-headed, half-bared bone out of his hand and, laughing with eyes alone, began gnawing at it with relish, holding it daintily, her little finger cocked, her lashes beating, her lips growing fuller and brighter. "You are ravishing," Franz whispered. "I adore you."

"If only we could sup like this every night, just you and I," said Martha. With a toss of her head she chased a momentary frown and cried in a slightly false tone: "Would you pour me some of that precious cognac, please, and let us drink to our union."

"I don't think I'll have any. I'm afraid I would not learn

to dance afterwards," said Franz, carefully tipping the diminutive decanter.

But what did she care about dancing. . . . She longed to remain in this oval lake of light, basking in the certainty that it would be thus again tomorrow, and the next night, and thus to the end of their lives. My dining room, my earrings, my silver, my Franz.

Suddenly she snatched at her left wrist, to turn the tiny face of her watch, which always contrived to slip around to where a blue vein trifurcated.

"More than an hour late. Something must have happened. Ring the bell, please—there, it's hanging above you."

It irked him that her husband's absence alarmed her. What in hell did it matter if he were late. All the better. She simply had no right to be alarmed.

"Why must I ring?" he said, thrusting his hands into his coat pockets.

Martha opened her eyes wide. "I think I asked you to press that bell button."

Under the long ray of her gaze he gave way as usual, and rang the bell.

"If you have had all you want, we can move to the drawing room. Have some grapes, though. Here, this bunch."

He started upon the grapes, which were large and expensive-looking but not half as good as the vulgar "crams" of his native town. The shadow of the electric bell swinging on its cord moved like a ghostly pendulum across the tablecloth. Frieda came in, looking pale and dazed.

Martha asked: "My husband did not call while I was out, did he?"

Frieda froze still for an instant, then clutched at her temples. "Goodness," she said. "*Herr Direktor* did call about eight—said he was just leaving for home, and to go ahead with supper. I'm so sorry."

"An abscessed tooth," said Martha, "should not have made you insane."

"I'm so sorry," repeated the maid helplessly.

"Completely insane," said Martha.

Frieda remained silent and, blinking with suspicious frequency, started gathering up the used plates.

"Later," snapped Martha.

The maid hurried out, no longer containing her sobs.

"Incredible female," muttered Martha angrily, leaning her elbows on the table and propping her chin between her joined fists. "Didn't she see us sitting down to table? Didn't she bring the omelette herself? Wait a minute—I didn't realize that she had actually *served* it." Martha's glittering finger pointed. "Ring once more, please."

Franz obediently raised his hand.

"No, don't bother," said Martha. "I'll have a good talk with her before she goes to bed."

An extraordinary agitation had seized Martha.

"Unless my watch and that clock are as dotty as she, it is now half past eleven. Uncle is certainly taking his time driving home."

"Something must have delayed him," Franz responded glumly. He was deeply hurt by her agitation.

She turned off the dining-room lights. They went into the parlor. Martha picked up the telephone receiver, listened, then slammed it down again. "It's in order," she said, "I simply don't understand. Maybe, I ought to ring up—"

With his hands clasped behind his back, Franz was walking to and fro about the room. The poor fellow's eyes smarted. He wondered if he had not better leave, slamming the door after him. Martha flipped through her telephone index ("fits neatly under the phone, holds five hundred entries"), and found the home number of her husband's secretary.

Sarah Reich had just fallen asleep, and now the first pill of the night was thrown away.

"That's certainly odd," she replied. "I saw him leave myself. Yes. In the Icarus. It was—wait a minute—yes, about eight—and it is now only midnight. . . . I mean, almost midnight."

"Thanks," said Martha, and the cradle of the telephone jangled.

She went to the window and drew aside the blue curtain. The night was clear. The day before it had started to thaw, then the freeze had set in again. That morning a cripple walking in front of her had slipped on the bare ice. It was frightfully funny to see his wooden stump erect while he sprawled on his stupid back. Without opening her mouth, Martha broke into convulsive laughter. Franz thought she had uttered a sob and went to her side in confusion. She clutched his shoulder, her cheek rubbed against his face.

"Careful—my glasses," mumbled Franz—not for the first time in the course of the last weeks.

"Start the music," she cried, letting him go. "We'll dance, we'll enjoy ourselves. And don't you dare be frightened—I'll speak to you as tenderly as I wish any time I feel like it—do you hear?"

Franz reverentially turned the crank of the large lacquered box that must have cost more money than all the records it would ever consume. When he looked up, Martha was sitting on the sofa gazing at him with a strange morose expression.

"I thought you'd choose a record meanwhile," said Franz.

She turned away. "No, I definitely don't feel like dancing."

Franz heaved a sigh. He had seen her in difficult moods, but this was something special.

He sat down beside her on the sofa. A door shut somewhere. Frieda going to bed? Still listening intently, he kissed Martha, first on the hair, then on the lips. Her teeth were chattering. "Give me my shawl," she said. He picked up the pink woolly shawl from a corner hassock. She consulted her watch.

Franz got up abruptly. "I'm going home," he said.

"You are what?"

"Going home. I have to get up much earlier than old secretaries and fat maids."

"You shall stay," said Martha.

He considered her, reflecting vaguely that there was something behind all this. But what?

"You know what I have just remembered?" Martha said suddenly, as he plucked at his trouser knees and sat down. "I remembered that rude policeman writing his report. Give me your little red book. And a pencil. There," she continued, getting up and standing straight and stiff. "That's how he held the notebook in front of him. Trembled with fury, and wrote in it."

"What policeman? What are you talking about?"

"That's right. You weren't there. I've got used to including you, retroactively, if you know what I mean, in everything that ever happened."

"Stop it," said Franz. "You frighten me."

"I don't care if you're frightened. In fact I don't care if— Forgive me, darling. I'm talking nonsense. I'm just over-eager, I suppose."

She settled down on the sofa again, with the address book in her lap. She doodled some lines on a page. Then wrote her family name, and slowly crossed it out. She looked at him askance, once more wrote Dreyer in large characters, slitted her eyes, and started blacking it out. The pencil tip broke. She tossed the book and the pencil to him, and got up.

The clock tocked rather than ticked, the tock clicked and clocked. Martha stood before him as if trying to hypnotize him, to transfer some simple thought to his young dull brain.

The front door banged in the unbearable silence, and Tom's rejoicing voice burst forth.

"My spells don't work," said Martha, and a bizarre spasm distorted her beautiful face.

Dreyer came in not quite as jauntily as he usually did. Nor did he greet Franz with a joke.

"Why so late?" asked Martha. "Why didn't you call?"

"Just happened that way, my love, just happened that way." He attempted a smile but nothing came of it. He stared at his nephew's clothes. The pants were much too narrow, the lapels too shiny.

"Well, it's time for me to be going," cried Franz hoarsely.

He was in such a silly panic that he could not remember afterwards how he said good-by, or put on his overcoat, or reached the street.

"You're not telling the truth," said Martha. "Something has happened. What is it?"

"A boring story, my love. A man has been killed."

"Jokes again, always jokes," moaned Martha.

"Not this time," Dreyer said quietly. "We smashed into a streetcar, at full speed. Number seventy-three. I only lost my hat and took a healthy bump against something. In these cases it's always the driver who comes off worst. The ambulance people were angels. We took him to the hospital while he was still alive. Died there. Real angels. Better don't ask for details."

In the dining room they sat facing each other across the table. Dreyer was finishing what remained of the cold chicken. Martha, her face pale and glossy, with drops of sweat over her lip where the tiny black hairs showed, stared with her fingers pressed to her temples at the white, white, intolerably white tablecloth.

7

When the inevitable explosion (somehow sensed as inevitable just before it occurred) was on the point of interrupting an absorbing although incoherent conversation with an unshaven Magyar or Basque about treating surgically, with buckets of blood, a seal's tail to enable the seal to walk upright, Dreyer abruptly returned to the mortality of a winter morning, and with desperate haste, as if he were dealing with an infernal machine, stopped the alarm clock that was about to ring.

Martha's bed was already empty. A bad tingle in his left arm connected like an electric buzzer the previous day with the present one. Along the corridor, sobbing loudly, shuffled soft-hearted Frieda. With a sigh he examined the huge violet bruise on his thick shoulder.

While lying in the tub, he heard Martha perform in the next room the panting, crunching, flopping exercises that were in fashion that year. He had a quick breakfast, lit a cigar, smiled with pain as he put on his overcoat, and went out.

The gardener (who was also the watchman) was standing by the fence, and Dreyer thought it might be well, even at this late date, to solve by means of a direct question the mystery that had preoccupied him for so long.

"A calamity, a real calamity," observed the gardener gravely. "And to think that back in his village he has left a comparatively young father and four little sisters. A skid on the ice, and *kaputt*. He had hoped so much to drive a big truck some day."

"Yes," nodded Dreyer. "Cracked his skull, his rib cage—"

"A good merry chap," said the gardener with feeling. "And now he is dead."

"Listen," began Dreyer, "you did not happen to notice— You see, I have a strong suspicion—"

He faltered. A trifle—the tense of a verb—stopped him. Instead of asking "does he drink?" it would have to be "did he drink?" This shift of tense caused a wobble in logic.

"... as I was saying, have you noticed—there is something wrong with the latch of the big parlor window. I mean, the catch does not work properly; anybody could get in from the outside."

"*Finis*," he mused, as he sat in a taxi with his hand in the strap. "The end of a life, the end of a joke. I shall sell Icarus without repairing it. She does not want another car, and I think she is right. It's best to wait awhile till Fate forgets."

The reason Martha did not want a car was less metaphysical. It might seem a bit strange and suspicious not to use one's own car to go two or three times a week in the late afternoon to lessons in rhythmic inclinations and gesticulations ("Flora, accept these lilies" or "Let us unfold our veils in the wind"), and the reason she could not use it was that she would have to bribe her chauffeur to be silent about her real destination. Therefore she had to resort to other means of transportation, of the most varied kind, including even the subway, which brought one very conveniently from any part of the city (and a roundabout route was essential though it took only fifteen minutes to walk the distance) to a certain street corner where a rather fantastic house was being slowly built. She casually mentioned to Dreyer that she loved taking a bus or a tram whenever she had a chance because it was a shame not to take advantage of the cheap, exhilaratingly cheap, methods of transportation put at one's disposal by a generous city. He said he was a generous citizen who preferred a taxi or a private car. By taking these precautions, Martha believed that nobody would ever guess that she transposed or curtailed or missed altogether those delightful contortions and scattering of invisible flowers in the delightful company of other barefooted ladies in more or less comical tunics.

On the day that businessman Dreyer, owner of the Dandy department store, and his chauffeur briefly appeared in the city news section of her newspaper, Martha arrived a little earlier than usual. Franz was not yet back from work. She sat down on the couch, took off her hat, slowly removed her gloves. That day her face was particularly pale. She wore her high-neck beige dress with little buttons in front. When Franz's familiar footsteps sounded in the corridor and he entered (with that abrupt unceremoniousness with which we enter our own room, assuming that it is empty), she did not smile. Franz emitted an exclamation of pleased surprise and without taking off his hat began to shower Martha's neck and ear with rapid kisses.

"You know about it already?" she asked, and her eyes had the strange expression he had hoped never to see again.

"You bet," he answered and, getting up from the couch, shed his raincoat and striped scarf. "Everybody was discussing it at the store. They asked me all kinds of questions. I was really scared when he came in looking so grim yesterday. What a dreadful thing."

"What's dreadful, Franz?"

He was already coatless and collarless, and was noisily washing his hands.

"Well, all that jagged glass hitting you in the face, that crunch of metal and bones, and blood, and blackness. I don't know why but I picture such things so clearly. Makes me want to vomit."

"That is just nerves, Franz, nerves. Come here."

He sat down close to her and, trying not to notice that she was absorbed in remote dreary thoughts of her own, softly asked:

"No pompons today?"

She did not hear the sweet euphemism, or did not seem to hear it.

"Franz," she said, stroking and restraining his hand, "do you realize what a miracle it was? I had a presentiment yesterday which did not work."

"There we go again," he thought, "how long will she bore me with her concern for him?"

He turned away and attempted to whistle, but no sound came out and he remained brooding with puckered lips.

"What's the matter with you, Franz? Stop acting like a fool. I'm closed for repairs today" (another sweet euphemism).

She drew him to her by the neck; he would not yield but her diamond-like gaze slashed him, and he went all limp and whimpery, the way a child's balloon collapses with a pitiful squeak. Tears of resentment fogged his glasses. He pressed his head to her shoulder: "I can't go on like this," he whined. "Already last night I wondered if your feeling for me was really serious. Worrying about that old uncle of mine! It means you care for him! Oh, it's so painful—"

Martha blinked, then understood his mistake. "So that's what it is," she drawled with a laugh. "Oh, you poor dear."

She took his head in her hands, looked intently and sternly into his eyes, and then slowly, with her mouth half open, as if she were about to give him a gentle bite, drew close to his face, and took possession of his lips.

"Shame on you," she said, releasing him slowly, "shame on you," she repeated with a nod. "I never thought you were that silly. No, just a minute—I want you to understand how silly you are. No, wait. You can't touch me but I can certainly touch you, and nibble you, and even swallow you whole if I want."

"Listen," she said a little while later, after that stunt, quite new to Franz, had been brought to a satisfactory close. "Listen, Franz, how wonderful it would be if I didn't have to go today. Today, or tomorrow, or ever. Of course, we could not live in a tiny room like this."

"We would rent a larger, brighter room," said Franz with assurance.

"Yes. Let's dream a little. Larger and much brighter. Maybe even two rooms, what do you think? Or perhaps three? And of course a kitchen."

"And lots of beautiful knives," said Franz, "meat cleavers, and cheese cutters, and a roast pork slicer, but you would not do any cooking. You have such precious nails."

"Yes, naturally, we'd have a cook. What did we decide—three rooms?"

"No, four," said Franz after a moment's thought. "Bedroom, drawing room, sitting room, dining room."

"Four. Fine. A regular four-room apartment. With kitchen. With bath. And we'll have the bedroom all done in white, won't we? And the other rooms blue. And there'll be a reception room with lots and lots of flowers. And an extra room upstairs, just in case, for guests, say. . . . For a wee little guest, maybe."

"What do you mean—'upstairs'?"

"Why, of course—it will be a villa."

"Ah, I see," nodded Franz.

"Let's continue, darling. A detached villa, then. With a pretty entrance hall. We enter. Rugs, pictures, silverware, embroidered sheets. Right? And a garden, fruit trees. Magnolias. Is that so, Franz?"

He sighed. "All this will come only in ten years, or more. It will be a long time before I earn sufficiently for you to divorce him."

Martha fell silent as if she were not in the room. Franz turned to her with a smile, ready to play on, but the smile faded: she was looking at him with narrowed eyes, biting her lip.

"Ten years," she said bitterly. "You little fool! You really want to wait ten years?"

"That's how it looks to me," Franz replied. "I don't know. Maybe, if I'm very lucky . . . but, for instance, take Mr. Piffke; he's been with the store right from the start, and that's you know how many years. But he lives very modestly. He doesn't make more than four hundred fifty a month. His wife works too. They have a tiny apartment full of boxes and things."

"Thank God you understand," said Martha. "You see, sweetheart, one cannot deposit dreams at the bank. They aren't dependable securities, and the dividends they bring are nothing."

"Then what shall we do?" said frightened Franz. "You know I'm ready to marry you immediately. I can't exist without you. Without you I'm like an empty sleeve. But I can't even afford one of those nice new floormats we sell at the store, let alone carpets. And then, of course, I'd have to look for another job—and I don't know anything (wrinkling his face), I have no experience in anything. That means learning all over again. We'd have to live in a damp, shabby little room, saving on food and clothes."

"Yes, there would be no longer any uncle to help," said Martha dryly. "No uncle at all."

"The whole idea is unthinkable," said Franz.

"Absolutely unthinkable," said Martha.

"Why are you angry with me?" he asked after a moment's silence. "As if I were responsible or something. It's really not my fault. Well, let's dream on, if you want. Only don't get angry. I have seventeen suits, like Uncle— Want me to describe them for you?"

"In ten years," she said with a laugh, "in ten years, my dear, men's fashions will have changed substantially."

"There—you are angry again."

"Yes, I'm angry; not with you, though, but with Fate. You see, Franz—no, you wouldn't understand."

"I'll understand," said Franz.

"All right then. You see, people generally make all kinds of plans, very good plans, but completely fail to consider one possibility: death. As if no one could ever die. Oh, don't look at me as if I were saying something indecent."

She now had exactly the same odd expression as last night when she tried to impersonate a policeman.

"It's time for me to go," said Martha with a frown. She got up and looked at herself in the mirror.

"Christmas trees are already sold in the streets," she said, raising her elbows as she put on her hat. "I want to buy a tree, a huge very expensive fir tree, and lots of presents to go under it. Please, give me four hundred and twenty marks. I'm out of pocket."

"And you're also very nasty," sighed Franz.

He accompanied her down the dark stairs. He walked her to the square. The builders had started on the facade of the new cinema. The sidewalk was very slippery, the glare ice glistened under the street lamps.

"You know something, treasure?" she said when bidding him good-by at the corner. "I might have been in deep mourning today. And very becoming it would have been. It's just by chance that I'm not in mourning. Ponder that, my little nephew."

Exactly what she wanted happened then: Franz looked at her, opened his mouth, and suddenly burst out laughing. She rocked with laughter, too. A gentleman with a fox terrier, who was waiting near by for the dog to make up its mind in regard to a lamppost, glanced at the merry couple with approval and envy. "In mourning," said Franz, choking with laughter. She nodded, laughing. "In mourning," said Franz, stifling a rich guffaw in the palm of his hand. The man with the fox terrier shook his head and moved on. "I adore you," uttered Franz in a weak voice, and for quite a while gazed after her with moist eyes.

However, as soon as she turned away to go home Martha's face again grew stern. Franz meanwhile wiped his glasses with his handkerchief and ambled off, continuing to chuckle to himself. "Yes, it really was a matter of chance. If only the owner of the car had sat beside the chauffeur. Just supposing he'd gone and sat there. There she would be today—a widow. A rich widow, an adorable mistress, a wonderful wife. How drolly she put it: yours is honey; his, poison. And then again, who needs an elaborate crack-up. After all, car accidents are not necessarily fatal; much too often one gets away with bruises, a fracture, lacerations, one mustn't make too complicated demands on chance: exactly that way, please, make the brains squirt out. There are other possibilities: illnesses, for example. Perhaps he has a bad heart and does not know it. And look at all the influenza people who croak. Then we'd really start living. The store would go on doing business. The money would roll in. But then more likely he'll outlive his wife and make it all the way to the twenty-first century. Why, there was something in the papers about a Turk who was a hundred and fifty years old, and still produced children, the filthy old brute."

Thus he mused, vaguely and crudely, unaware that his thoughts were spinning along from the push given them by Martha. The thought of marriage had also come from her. Oh, but it was a good thought. If he derived such pleasure from Martha's satisfying him twice in one hour three or four times a week, what varied ecstasies would she grant him if she were available twenty-four hours a day! He employed this method of calculating happiness quite guilelessly, the way a greedy child imagines a country with chocolate-cream mud and ice-cream snow.

In those days—which as a very old and very sick man, guilty of worse sins than avunculicide, he remembered with a grin of contempt—young Franz was oblivious to the corrosive probity of his pleasant daydreams about Dreyer's dropping dead. He had plunged into a region of delirium, blithely and light-heartedly. His subsequent meetings with Martha appeared to be as natural and tender as all the previous ones but, just as that modest little room, with its unpretentious old furniture and its naively dark corridor, had for master a person, or persons, incurably though not obviously insane, there now lurked in those meetings something strange—a little eerie and shameful at first, but already enthralling, already all-powerful. Whatever Martha said, however charmingly she smiled, Franz sensed an irresistible insinuation in her every word and glance. They were like heirs sitting in a dim-lit parlor while in the bedroom doomed Plutus pleads with the doctor and curses the priest; they might talk about trifles, about the approach of Christmas, about the intense activity of skis and wool at the emporium; one might talk about anything although perhaps a little more soberly than before—for one's hearing is strained, one's eyes have a changeable gleam; a secret impatience allows one no peace as one waits and waits for the grim physician to come out on tiptoe, with an eloquent sigh, and lo— through the crack of the door one glimpses the long back of the cleric, representative of a boundlessly charitable Church, in the act of bending over the white, white bed.

Theirs was a pointless vigil. Martha knew perfectly well that he never seemed to have even so much as a toothache or a cold. Therefore it was particularly irritating to her when just before the holidays she herself contracted a chill; the poor girl developed a dry cough, a tease and a wheeze in the bronchia, night sweats, and spent the day in a kind of dull trance, dazed by the so-called *Grippe*, heavy-headed and with ears abuzz. When Christmas came she felt no better. That evening, nevertheless, she put on a sheer flame-colored dress, very low cut at the back; and deafened by aspirin, trying to dispell her illness by will power, supervised the preparation of the punch, the laying of the table, the ruddy smoky activity of the cook.

In the parlor, its silvery crown touching the ceiling, all decked out in flimsy tinselry, all studded with still unlit red and blue bulbs, a fresh luxuriant fir tree stood, indifferent to its buffoonish array. In an uncozy nook between the parlor and the entry, a bright and rather bare place, termed for some reason a reception room, where among the wicker furniture grew and bloomed potted plants—cyclamens, seven dwarf cactuses, a peperomia with painted leaves—and where the tangerine glow of an electric fireplace could not beat the draft from a plate-glass window, Dreyer in evening dress sat reading an English book while waiting for his guests. The scene was laid on the Island of Capri. He moved his lips as he read and peeked pretty often into a fat dictionary which kept shuttling between his lap and a glass-topped table. Not knowing what to do with herself during this prolonged lull before the first ring, Martha sat down at a little distance from him on a settee and lifted her foot off the floor, examining from every angle her pointed shoe. The stillness was intolerable. Dreyer accidentally dropped the dictionary and, making his generously starched shirt crackle, retrieved it without taking his eyes off his book. What could she do with that oppression, that tightness in the chest? Coughing alone could not relieve it; there was only one thing that could make the whole world well: the sudden and total disappearance of that self-satisfied bulky man with the leonine brows and freckled hands. The acuteness of her hatred reached such a pitch of perception that for a moment she had the illusion that his chair was empty. But his cuff link described a flashing arc as he shut the dictionary, and he said, smiling at her consolingly: "Goodness, what a cold you have. I can hear a veritable orchestra of wheezes tuning up in you."

"Spare me your metaphors and put your book away," said Martha. "The guests will be here any moment. And that dictionary. There's nothing more untidy than a dictionary on a chair."

"*All right, my treasury,*" he answered in English, and

walked away with his books, mentally lamenting his unsure pronunciation and meager though exact vocabulary.

The chair by the glowing grate now stood empty, but that did not help. With her whole being she experienced his presence, there, behind the door, in the next room, and the next, and the next; the house was suffocating from him; the clocks ticked with an effort and the cold folded napkins stood stifling on the festive table with a strangled rose in each individual vase—but how to cough him up, how to breathe freely again? It now seemed to her that it had always been thus, that she had hated him hopelessly since the first days and nights of their marriage when he kept pawing and licking her like an animal, in a locked hotel room in white Salsborg. He now stood in her path, in her plain, straight path, like a solid obstacle, that ought somehow to be removed to let her resume her plain straight existence. How dared he enforce upon her the complications of adultery? How dared he stand in the queue before her? Our cruellest enemy is less hateful than the burley stranger whose placid back keeps us from squeezing through to a ticket window or to the counter of a sausage shop. She walked to and fro, she drummed on a window. She tore off a diseased cyclamen leaf, she felt she would suffocate any moment. At that instant the doorbell sounded. Martha checked her hairdo and walked quickly—not to the front door but back to the door of the drawing room in order to make an elegant entrance from afar to meet her guests.

During the next half hour the bell rang again and again. First to arrive were the inevitable Walds in their Debler limousine; then came Franz shivering from the cold; then, almost simultaneously, the count with a bouquet of mediocre pinks and a paper manufacturer with his wife; then—

two loud, half-naked, ill-groomed girls whose late father had been their host's partner in happier days; then—the snub-nosed, gaunt, and taciturn director of the Fatum Insurance Company; and a rosy-cheeked civil engineer in triplicate—that is, with a sister and a son comically resembling him. All this company gradually warmed up and coalesced until it formed a single many-limbed but otherwise not over-complex creature that made mirthful noise, and drank, and whirled. Only Martha and Franz were unable to identify themselves, as they should have by all the laws of a hearty holiday, with this animated, flushed, palpitating mass. She was pleased to note how unresponsive Franz was to the practically naked charms of those two practically identical vulgar young things with revoltingly thin arms, and snaky backs, and insufficiently spanked little popos. The injustice of life—in ten years' time they would be still a little younger than I am now, all three of them as a matter of fact.

Every now and then her eyes and those of Franz would meet, but even without looking he and she always clearly sensed the changing correlation of their respective where-abouts: while he walked diagonally across the parlor with a glass of punch for Ida or Isolda—no, for old Mrs. Wald—Martha was putting a rustling paper hat on bald Willy at the other end of the room; as Franz sat down and started listen-ing to what the engineer's sister, pink-cheeked and plain, had to say, Martha combined the oblique and the straight line by going from Willy to the door, and then to the din-ing-room table laden with hors-d'oeuvres. Franz lit a ciga-rette, Martha put a mandarin on a plate. Thus a chess player playing blind feels his trapped bishop and his opponent's versatile queen move in relentless relation to each other. There was a vaguely regular rhythm established in those coordinations. And not for an instant was it interrupted. She and especially Franz felt the existence of this invisible geometric figure; they were two points moving through it, and the interrelation between those two points could be plotted at any given moment; and though they seemed to move independently they were nonetheless securely bound by the invisible, inexorable lines of that figure.

The parquet was already littered with motley paper trash; already someone had broken a glass and stood speechless with sticky fingers outspread. Willy Wald, already high, wearing a golden hat and garlanded with paper ribbons, his innocent blue eyes opened wide, was recounting to the gruff old count his recent trip to Russia, ardently extolling the Kremlin, the caviar, the commissars. Presently Dreyer, coatless, flushed, still holding a chef's knife and wearing a chef's cap, took Willy aside and began whispering something to him, while the rosy engineer went on telling the other guests about three masked individuals who, one Christmas night, had broken in and robbed the whole company. The phonograph broke into song in the adjoining boudoir. Dreyer started to dance with one of the pretty sisters, and then caught up the other, and the girls giggled and curved their supple bare backs as he tried to dance with both together. Franz stood by the window drapery, regretting that he still had not had time to learn to dance. He saw Martha's white hand on somebody's black shoulder, then her profile, then the birthmark under her left shoulder blade and somebody's thumb upon it, then the madonna profile again, and again the raisin in the cream; and her silk-sheening legs which the hem of her short skirt revealed up to the knee moved hither and thither, and seemed (if one looked at them only) to belong to a woman who did not know what to do with herself from restlessness and anticipation: she steps, now slowly, now quickly, this way and that, turns abruptly, steps again in her excruciating impatience. Martha danced auto-matically, feeling not so much the rhythm of the music as the syncopic changes between her and Franz, who was standing by the drapery with folded arms and moving eyes. She noticed Dreyer reach through the drapery; he must have opened the window a little, for it grew cooler in the room. As she danced, she kept checking Franz's position: he was there, the dear sentinel; she searched for her husband with her eyes; he had left the room and she told herself that the sudden coolness and well-being were due precisely to his absence. On gliding closer to Franz she bathed him in such a familiar meaningful look that he lost countenance and smiled at the engineer whose face was presented to him by the whim of a whirl. Again and again the phonograph was wound, and among many pairs of ordinary legs flashed those strong, graceful, ravishing legs, and Franz, dizzy from the wine and the gyrations of the dancers, became aware of a certain terpsichorean tumult in his poor head as if all his thoughts were learning to foxtrot.

Then something happened. In mid-dance Isolda cried: "Oh, look! The drape!"

Everyone looked, and, indeed, the window curtain stirred strangely, altered its folds, and swelled slowly. Simultane-ously the lights went out. In the darkness an oval light began to move about the room, the drapery parted, and in the unsteady glimmer, a masked man suddenly appeared, dressed in an old military coat and carrying a menacing flashlight in his fist. Ida gave a piercing scream. The engineer's voice calmly pronounced in the dark: "I suspect that's our genial host." Then, after a curious pause, filled by the phonograph which had gone on dutifully playing in the dark, there sounded Martha's tragic voice. She gave such a howl of warning that the two girls and the old count surged back toward the door (blocked by merry Willy). The masked figure emitted a hoarse sound and, training the light on Martha, moved forward. It is possible that the girls were genuinely frightened. It is also possible that one or two of the men were beginning to doubt its being a prank. Martha, who went on crying for help, noticed with cold exultation that the engineer standing beside her had reached back under his dinner jacket and had produced something from his hip pocket. She realized what her screams meant, what prompted them, and what they should cause to happen; and, secure in her performance, she screamed still louder, urging, hallooing.

Franz could not bear it any longer. He stood nearest of all to the intruder, had recognized him at once by his tailor-made tuxedo trousers, and now his nimble fingers ripped the mask off the intruder's face. Meanwhile Mr. Fatum had finally overcome panting Willy and switched on the lights. In the center of the room, dressed in a combination of apache scarf and soldier's coat, stood Dreyer roaring with laughter, now swaying, now squatting, all red and tousled, and pointing his finger at Martha. Quickly deciding how she should now resolve her feigned terror, she turned her back upon her husband, re-arranged the strap on one bare shoulder, and calmly went off to the faltering phonograph. He rushed after her and, still laughing, hugged and kissed her. "Oh, I knew it was you all along," she said—which, of course, was quite true.

Franz had been trying for some time to fight off the welling of nausea but now he was going to be sick, and he hurriedly left the room. Behind him the hubbub continued; they were all laughing and shouting, probably crowding around Dreyer, squeezing him, squeezing him, squeezing both him and Martha, who wriggled. With his handkerchief pressed to his lips, Franz made for the front hall, and wrenched open the door of the toilet. Old Mrs. Wald came flying out like a bomb and disappeared behind the bend of the wall. "My God, my God," he muttered, doubled over. He emitted horrible sounds, recognizing in the intermittent torrent a medley of food and drink the way a sinner in hell retastes the hash of his life. Breathing heavily, squeamishly wiping his mouth with a bit of toilet paper, he waited for a moment, and pulled the chain. On his way back he paused in the entrance hall and listened. Through an open door a mirror reflected the ominously blazing Christmas tree. The phonograph was singing again. Suddenly he saw Martha.

She went up to him quickly, looking over her shoulder like a conspirator in a play. They were alone in the brightly lit hall, and from beyond the door came noise, laughter, the squeals of a helpless pig, the quawks of a tortured turkey.

"No luck," said Martha. "I'm sorry, dear."

Her piercing eyes were at once in front of him and all around him. Then she started to cough, clutched at her side and dropped in a chair.

He asked: "What do you mean—no luck?"

"It cannot go on like this," muttered Martha between fits of coughing. "It simply cannot. Why, look at yourself— you're as pale as death."

The noise in the house was swelling and drawing nearer; it seemed as though that enormous tree were bellowing with all its lights.

" . . . as death," said Martha.

Franz felt another onset of nausea; the voices surged forward; sweaty Dreyer rushed past, escaping from Wald and the engineer, and after them came the others guffawing and gibbering, and Tom, locked up in the garage, was barking his head off. And the noise of the hunt seemed to pursue

Franz as he vomited in the deserted street and staggered home. At the corner of the square the scaffolding that cocooned the future Kino-Palazzo was adorned on the very top with a bright Christmas tree. The latter could be also seen, but only as a tiny colored blur in the starry sky from the Dreyers' bedroom window.

"Either of the two would make a marvellous little wife for good old Franz," said Dreyer as he undressed.

"That's what you think," said Martha, glaring into her dressing-table mirror.

"Ida, of course, is the more beautiful," continued drunken Dreyer, "but Isolda with that fluffy pale hair and that way of gasping she has while one is telling her something comical—"

"Why don't you sample her? Or both together?"

"I wonder," mused Dreyer as he took off his drawers. He laughed and added: "My love, what about you tonight? After all, it is Christmas."

"Not after your idiotic joke," said Martha, "and if you pester me with your lust I'll take my pillow to the guest room."

"I wonder," repeated Dreyer as he got into bed and laughed again. He had never tried them together. Might be fun! Separately he had had them only on two occasions: Ida three summers ago quite unexpectedly in the woods of Spandau during a picnic; and Isolda a little later in a Dresden hotel. Hopelessly bad stenographers, both of them.

Franz had never gone to bed yet at half past four in the morning. He woke up in the afternoon feeling hungry, healthy, and happy. He remembered with pleasure snatching that mask off. The roaring darkness that had pursued him like a nightmare had been transformed, now that he had surrendered himself to it, into a hum of euphoria.

He dined at the nearby tavern and went back home to wait for Martha. At ten minutes past seven she had not come. At twenty minutes to eight he knew she was not coming. Should he wait till tomorrow? He dared not ring her up: Martha had forbidden him and herself to telephone lest it became a sweet habit which in its turn might lead to the wrong ears' overhearing a careless caressive phrase. The urge to tell her how strong and well he felt, despite all that wine and venison, and music, and terror, was even stronger than his desire to know if her cold was better.

As he reached their street, an empty taxi overtook him and pulled up at the villa. He decided his visit was ill-timed—they were probably going out. He paused at the fence of the garden expecting them to emerge, she in her lovely furs, he in his camelhair coat. Then, changing his mind again, Franz hurried toward the porch.

The front door was ajar. Frieda was pulling half-strangled Tom upstairs by his collar. In the entrance hall Franz saw an opulent suitcase of real leather and a splendid pair of hickory skis of a type they did not have at the store. In the parlor husband and wife stood facing each other. He was talking rapidly, and she was smiling like an angel and nodding in silence.

"Ah, Franz, there you are," he said, turning, and caught his nephew by his stuffed shoulder. "You've come just at the right moment. I'm off for three weeks or so."

"What are those skis doing there?" asked Franz, and realized with surprise that Dreyer had ceased to frighten him.

"Mine. I'm going to Davos. And take this" (five dollars). He kissed his wife on the cheek. "Nurse your cold, dear. Have a good time over the holidays. Tell Franz to take you to the theater. Don't be cross with me, darling, for leaving you behind. Snow is for men and single girls. You can't change that."

"You'll be late for your train," said Martha, slitting sweet eyes at him.

He glanced at his golden watch, mimicked panic, and grasped his valise. The taxi driver helped with the skis. Uncle, aunt and nephew crossed the garden. After all that frost a drizzle had set in! Hatless and wearing her moleskin coat, Martha strolled to the wicket with an indolent swing of the hips, her hands invisibly clasped in her joined coat-sleeves. It took quite a long time to arrange the long skis on the roof of the taxi. At last the door slammed. The taxi drove off. Franz mechanically noted its license number: 22221. This unexpected "1" seemed odd after so many "2"s. They walked slowly back toward the house along the crunching path.

"It's thawing again," said Martha. "Today my cough is much less harsh."

Franz thought for a moment and said: "Yes. But there are still some cold days ahead."

"Possibly," said Martha.

When they entered the empty house, Franz had the impression they had returned from a funeral.

8

She began teaching him obstinately and fervidly.

After the first embarrassments, stumblings, and perplexities, he gradually began to understand what she was communicating to him, doing so with almost no words of explanation, almost entirely through pantomime. He gave his full attention both to her and to the ululating sound which, now rising, now falling, accompanied him constantly; and already he perceived, in that sound, rhythmic demands, a compelling meaning, regular breaks and beats. What Martha wanted of him was proving to be so simple. As soon as he had assimilated something, she would nod silently, looking down the while with an intent smile, as though following the motions and growth of an already distinct shadow. His awkwardness, that feeling of having a limp and a hump, which tormented him in the beginning—all this soon disappeared; instead, the erect poise, the specious grace and pace she was teaching him enslaved him totally: now he could no longer disobey the sound whose mystery he had solved. Vertigo became a habitual and pleasurable state, an automaton's somnambulic languor, the law of his existence; now Martha would gently exult, and press her temple against his, knowing that they were at one, that he would do the proper thing. While teaching him she restrained her impatience, the impatience he had once noticed in the flash and flicker of her elegant legs. Now she stood before him and, holding up her pleated skirt between finger and thumb, she repeated the steps in slow motion so that he might see for himself the magnified turn of toe and heel. He would attempt a scooping caress but she would slap his hand away and go on with the lesson. And when, under the pressure of her strong palm, he learned how to turn and spin; when his steps had finally fallen in with hers; when a glance at the mirror told her that the clumsy lesson had become a harmonious dance; then she increased the pace, gave her excitement its head, and her rapid cries expressed fierce satisfaction with his obedient piston slide.

He came to know the reeling expanse of parquetry in huge halls surrounded by loges; he leaned his elbow on the faded plush of their parapet; he wiped her powder off his shoulder; he saw himself and her in surfeited mirrors; he paid predatory waiters out of her black silk purse; his mackintosh and her beloved moleskin coat embraced for hours on end in the darkness of heavily laden hangers under the guard of sleepy cloakroom girls; and the sonorous names of all the fashionable ballrooms and dancing cafés—tropical, crystal, royal—became as familiar to him as the names of the streets of the little town where he had dwelt in a previous life. And presently they would be sitting out the next dance, still panting from amorous exertions, side by side on the drab couch in his dingy room.

"Happy New Year," said Martha, "our year. Write to your mother, whom I certainly would like to know, that you are having a splendid time. Think how surprised she will be later . . . afterwards . . . when I shall meet her."

[151]

He asked: "When? Have you fixed a deadline?"

"As soon as possible. The sooner the better."

"Oh, we mustn't dawdle."

She leaned back on the cushions, her hands behind her head. "A month—perhaps two. We have to plan very carefully, my dear love."

"I'd go mad without you," said Franz. "Everything upsets me—this wallpaper, the people in the street, my landlord. His wife never shows herself. It's so strange."

"You must be calmer. Otherwise nothing will work out. Come here. . . ."

"I know it will turn out wonderfully," he said, pressing against her. "Only we must make sure of everything. The smallest mistake. . . ."

"Oh, how can you doubt, my strong, stout Franz!"

"No, of course not. God, no. Oh, my God, no. It's just that we have to find a sure method."

"Fast, darling, much faster—don't you hear the rhythm? . . ."

They were no longer coupling on the couch but foxtrotting among gleaming white tables on the bright-lit floor of a café. The orchestra was playing and gasping for breath. There was among the dancers a tall American Negro who smiled tolerantly as one passionate pair bumped into him and his blonde partner.

"We'll find it, we must find it," continued Martha in a rapid patter in time to the music; "after all, we are within our rights."

He saw her long sweet burning eye, and the geranium lobe of her little ear from beneath her sleek bandeau. If only he could glide thus forever, an eternal piston rod in a vacuum of delight, and never, never part from her. . . . But there still existed the store, where he bowed and turned like a jolly doll, and there still were the nights when like a dead doll he lay supine on his bed not knowing whether he was asleep or awake, and who was that, shuffling and two-stepping, and whispering in the corridor, and why was the alarm clock jazzing in his ear? But let us say we are awake, and here comes bushy-browed old Enricht bringing two cups of coffee—why two? And how depressing those torn silk socks on the floor.

One such blurry morning, a Sunday, when he and Martha in her beige dress were walking decorously about the snow-powdered garden, she wordlessly showed him a snapshot she had just received from Davos. It showed a smiling Dreyer, in a Scandinavian ski suit, clutching his poles; his skis were beautifully parallel, and all around was bright snow, and on the snow one could distinguish the photographer's narrow-shouldered shadow.

When the photographer (a fellow-skier and teacher of English, Mr. Vivian Badlook) had clicked the shutter and straightened up, Dreyer, still beaming, moved his left ski forward; however, as he was standing on a slight incline, the ski went further than he had intended, and with a great flourish of ski poles he tumbled heavily on his back while both girls shot past shrieking with laughter. For a while he could not get the damned skis uncrossed, and his arm kept going into the snow up to the elbow. By the time he got up, disfigured by the snow, and put on his snow-crusted mittens, and cautiously began to glide down, his face bore a solemn expression. He had dreamed of performing all kinds of Christianias and telemarks, flying downhill, turning sharply in a cloud of snow—but apparently God had not willed it. In the snapshot, though, he looked like a real skier, and he admired it before slipping it into the envelope. But that morning as he stood by the window in his yellow pajamas and looked at the green larches and the cobalt sky he reflected that he had been there two weeks, and yet his skiing and his English were even worse than the previous winter. From the snow-blue road came the jingle of sleighbells; Isolda and Ida were giggling in the bathroom; but enough was enough. He remembered with a pang of pleasure the inventor, who must already be at work in the laboratory set up for him; he also remembered a number of other entertaining projects connected with the expansion of the Dandy store; he pondered all this, took a look at the snowy slope crisscrossed with shiny ski tracks, and decided to depart for home ahead of time leaving his girl friends to their own devices, which were not negligible; and there was another amusing thought that he deliberately kept in the back of his mind: it would be fun to come home unexpectedly, and catch Martha's soul unawares, and see whether she would let escape a radiant smile of surprise or meet him with her usual ironic morosity as she certainly would if warned of his arrival. Despite his keen sense of humor, Dreyer was too naively self-centered to realize how thoroughly those sudden returns had been exploited in ribald tales.

Franz ripped the photo into little bits which the wind carried across the wet lawn.

"Silly," said Martha, "why did you do that? He's sure to ask me if I pasted it in the album."

"Some day I'll tear up the album too," said Franz.

An eager Tom had come running toward them: he hoped Franz might have thrown a ball or a pebble but a rapid search revealed nothing.

A couple of days later Frieda was allowed to spend the weekend with the family of her brother, a fireman in Potsdam and the brightest Rembrandtesque gleam in her gloomy light. Tom was compelled to spend more time than usual in the gardener's quarters next to the carless garage. Martha and Franz, yielding to the agonizing desire to assert themselves, to be free, to enjoy their freedom, decided, if only for one evening, to live as they craved to live: it was to be a dress rehearsal of future happiness.

"Today you are master here," she said. "Here's your study, here's your armchair, here if you want is the paper: the market has rallied."

He flung off his jacket and sauntered through all the rooms as if reviewing them upon returning to his own comfortable house from a long and difficult journey.

"Everything in order? Is my lord happy?"

He put his arm around her shoulder and they stood side by side before the mirror. He was poorly shaven that evening, and instead of a waistcoat had put on a rather casual dark-red sweater; there was something homy and quiet about Martha too. Her recently washed hair did not lie smoothly, and she wore a woollen jumper that was unbecoming but somehow right.

"Mr. and Mrs. Bubendorf. You know, once we were standing like this, and I was sure you'd kiss me for the first time, but you didn't."

"I'm now an inch taller," he said with a laugh. "Look, we are almost the same height."

He sank into the leather armchair, and she sat in his lap, and the fact that she had gained weight and was quite bottom heavy made things all the more cozy.

"I love your ear," he said, lifting up a strand of hair with a nose-wrinkling horse-nuzzle.

A clock began chiming gently and tunefully in the next room. Franz laughed softly.

"Imagine if he were suddenly to come in now—just like that."

"Who?" asked Martha. "I don't understand whom you're speaking about."

"I mean him. If he should come home all at once. He has such a stealthy way of opening doors."

"Oh, you are speaking of my late husband, oh, I see," said Martha in a smoky voice. "No, my deceased was always a man of precision. He would let me know—no, no, Franz, not now, after supper, perhaps. I think he meant to be an example to his little wife, who otherwise might visit him—I said no—without warning in that little room with the couch he has at the back of his office."

Silence. Matrimonial well-being.

"The deceased," chuckled Franz, "the deceased."

"Do you remember him well?" murmured Martha, rubbing her nose against his neck.

"Vaguely. And you?"

"The red fur on his belly and—"

In atrocious, disparaging and quite inaccurate terms she described the dead man's private parts.

"Pah," said Franz. "Don't make me throw up."

"Franz," she said, her eyes beaming, "no one will ever find out!"

Well accustomed by now to the idea, by now quite tame and bloodthirsty, he nodded in silence. A certain numbness was invading his lower limbs.

"We did it so simply, so neatly," said Martha, slitting her eyes as if in dim recollection, "not the merest shadow of suspicion. Nothing. And why, sir? Because destiny is on our side. It could not have been otherwise. Remember the funeral? Piffke's tulips? Isolda's and Ida's violets bought from a street beggar?"

He mutely acquiesced again.

"It was during the final thaw. We had forsythias in the

bay window. Remember? I was still coughing but it was already a soft wet delicious cough. Ah, getting rid of the last thick gob."

Franz winced. Another pause.

"You know, my knees are getting sort of tired. No, wait, don't get up. Just move over a little. That's right."

"My treasure, my all," she cried, "my darling husband. I never imagined there could be such a marriage as ours."

He passed his lips along her warm neck and said:

"Isn't it time for us to lie down for a bit, eh?"

"What about some cold cuts and beer? No? Okay, we shall eat afterwards."

She rose, leaning hard on him as she did so. Then she stretched herself.

"Let's go up," she said with a contented yawn, "to our bedroom."

"Is that all right?" asked Franz. "I thought we'd do it here."

"Of course not. Oh, come on, get up. It's already past ten."

"You know. . . . I'm still a little scared of the deceased," said Franz, biting his lip.

"Oh, he won't be coming for a week yet. That's as sure as death. What's there to be scared of? Little fool! Or don't you want me?"

"Oh, I do," said Franz, "but you must cover his bed, I don't want to see it. It would put me off."

She turned off the lights in the parlor and he followed her up an inner staircase that was short and creaky; then they passed through a baby-blue corridor.

"Why on earth are you walking on tiptoe?" exclaimed Martha with a loud laugh. "Can't you understand—we're married, married!"

She showed him the mangle room which she used for her Hindu-kitsch exercises, her dressing room, his and her bathroom, and finally their bedroom.

"The deceased used to sleep on that bed there," she said. "But of course the sheets have been changed. Let me put this tiger rug over it. So. Would you like to wash or something?"

"No, I'll wait for you here," said Franz, examining a soft doll on the night table.

"All right. Undress quick and hop into my bed. I have a great need."

She left the door ajar. Her pleated skirt and jumper were already lying on a chair. From the toilet across the corridor came the steady thick rapid sound of his sister making water. It stopped. Martha passed into the bathroom.

He suddenly felt that in this cold, inimical, unbearably white room where everything reminded him of the dead man, he was unable to undress, let alone make love. With revulsion and fear he gazed at the next bed.

Then he strained his ears. He thought he heard a door slam downstairs followed by creeping steps. He darted to the corridor. Simultaneously Martha came out of the bathroom stark naked.

"Something's happened," he said in a spitting whisper. "We're not alone any more. Listen to that noise."

Martha frowned. Wrapping herself in a negligee, she went down the corridor and stopped with her head bent sidewise.

"I'm telling you! . . . I've heard."

"I too had a bizarre feeling," said Martha in a low voice. "I know, darling, you are terribly disappointed, but we'd better not go on with this madness. It won't be long now. You'd better go. I'll come tomorrow as usual."

"But if I meet somebody downstairs?"

"There's no one there, Franz. Here, take my keys. You'll return them tomorrow."

She accompanied him as far as the main staircase, still listening. Now she was as puzzled and upset as he.

Oh! Down in the hall harsh bangs resounded. Franz stopped, clutching at the banister, but she gave a laugh of relief.

"I know what it is," she said. "That's the downstairs toilet. It sometimes bangs at night if there is a big wind, and if you don't close it well."

"I'll admit I was a little frightened," said Franz.

"All the same, you'd better go, darling. We mustn't take risks. Close that door in passing, will you."

He embraced her. She let herself be kissed on the bare shoulder, drawing back herself the lace of her negligee to grant him that farewell treat. She remained standing on the landing of the theatrically illumined blue staircase until with a winky-winky he was gone.

A strong clean wind hit him in the face. The gravel path crunched pleasantly and securely beneath his feet. Franz inhaled deeply; then he cursed. She was so sinful and beautiful! He felt a man again. Why was he such a coward? To think that a specter, a cadaver, had turned him out of the house where he, Franz, was the real master! Muttering as he went (something that happened to him rather often of late), he walked swiftly along the dark sidewalk, and then without looking right or left began diagonally crossing the street at the place where he always crossed it on his way home.

A taxicab's horn, nasal and nasty, made him jump back. Still muttering, Franz turned the corner. Meanwhile the taxi braked and uncertainly pulled up to the curb. The driver got out and opened the door. "What number, did you say?" he asked. No answer. The driver, reaching into the darkness, shook his fare by the shoulder. Finally the latter opened his eyes, leaned forward. "Number five," he replied to the driver's question. "You're a little off."

The bedroom window glowed. Martha was arranging her hair for the night. Suddenly she froze, still with raised elbows. Now she heard quite distinctly a loud clatter as if something had fallen. She darted toward the stairs. From the front hall came peels of laughter—familiar laughter, alas. He was laughing because, having turned awkwardly with the long skis on his shoulder, he had dropped one of them while knocking off with the other the white brush which flew up like a bird from the looking-glass shelf, after which he had tripped over his own suitcase.

"*I am the voyageur,*" he cried in his best English. "*I half returned from shee-ing!*"

The next instant he knew perfect happiness. There was a magnificent smile on Martha's face. Oh, no doubt, he was pretty to look at, tanned, trimmed by gravity, shedder of at least five pounds (as if Martha and Franz had already started to demolish him), but she was looking not at him: she was looking somewhere over his head, welcoming not him, but wise fate that had so simply and honestly averted a crude, ridiculous, dreadfully overworked disaster.

"A miracle saved us," she later told Franz (for people talk very lightly of miracles), "but let this be a lesson. You can see for yourself: it's impossible to wait any longer. Lucky once, lucky twice, and then—caught. And what can we expect then? Let us suppose he gives me a divorce. Let us even suppose I catch him with a stenographer. He does not have to support me, if I remarry. What next? I'm just as poor as you. My relatives in Hamburg are not going to help me."

Franz shrugged.

"I wonder if you understand," she said, "that his widow inherits a fortune."

"Why do you tell me this? We have discussed it sufficiently. I know perfectly well that there's only one solution."

Then, as she peered through the slippery glint of his glasses deep into the mire of his greenish eyes, she knew that she had achieved her end, that he had been fully prepared, was completely ripe, and that the time had come to act. She was right. Franz no longer had a will of his own; the best he could do was to refract her will in his own way. The easy fulfillment of two merged dreams had become familiar to him, owing to a very simple interplay of sensations. By now Dreyer had already been several times murdered and buried. Not a future happiness, but a future recollection had been rehearsed on a bare stage, before a dark and empty house. With stunning unexpectedness, the corpse had returned out of nowhere, had walked in like an animated snowman, had begun talking as if he were alive. But what of it? It would be easy now and not at all frightening to cope with this sham existence, to make the corpse a corpse once more, and this time for good.

The discussion of methods of murder became with them an everyday matter. No uneasiness, no shame accompanied it; neither did they experience the dark thrill gamblers know, or the comfortable horror a family man enjoys when reading about the destruction of another family, with gory details, in a family newspaper. The words "bullet" and "poison" began to sound about as normal as "bouillon" or "pullet," as ordinary as a doctor's bill or pill. The process of killing a man could be considered as calmly as the recipes in a cookbook, and no doubt Martha first of all thought of poison because of a woman's innate domestic bent, an instinctive knowledge of spices and herbs, of the healthful and the harmful.

From a second-rate encyclopedia they learned about all sorts of dismal Lucrezias and Locustas. A hollow-diamond ring, filled with rainbow venom, tormented Franz's imagination. He would dream at night of a treacherous handshake. Half-awake, he would recoil and not dare to move: somewhere under him, on the sheet, the prickly ring had just rolled, and he was terrified it might sting him. But in the daytime, by Martha's serene light, all was simple again. Tofana, a Sicilian girl, who dispatched 639 people, sold her "aqua" in vials mislabelled with the innocent image of a saint. The Earl of Leicester had a mellower method: his victim would blissfully sneeze after a pinch of lethal snuff. Martha would impatiently shut the P-R volume and search in another. They learned, with complete indifference, that toxemia caused anemia and that Roman law saw in deliberate toxication a blend of murder and betrayal. "Deep thinkers," remarked Martha with a snarling laugh, sharply turning the page. Still she could not get to the heart of the matter. A sardonic "See" sent her to something called "alkaloids." Another "See" led to the fang of a centipede, magnified, if you please. Franz, unaccustomed to big encyclopedias, breathed heavily as he looked over her shoulder. Climbing through the barbed wire of formulae, they read for a long time about the uses of morphine, until having reached in some tortuous way a special case of pneumonia cruposa, Martha suddenly understood that the toxin in question belonged to a domesticated variety. Turning to another letter, they discovered that strychnine caused spasms in frogs and laughing fits in some islanders. Martha was beginning to fume. She kept brutally yanking out the thick tomes and squeezing them back any which way in the bookcase. There were fleeting glimpses of colored plates: military decorations, Etruscan vases, gaudy butterflies. . . . "Here, this is more like it," said Martha, and she read in a low solemn voice: "vomiting, a feeling of dejection, a singing in the ears —don't wheeze like that, please—a sensation of itching and burning over the entire surface of the skin, the pupils narrowed to the size of a pinhead, the testicles become like oranges. . . ." Franz remembered how as an adolescent he had looked up "onanism" in a much smaller encyclopedia at school, and remained terrified and chaste for almost a week.

"Chucks," said Martha, "that's all medical rot. Who wants to know about cures or about traces of arsenic found in a stinking dead ass. I suppose we need some special works. There is a treatise mentioned here in parentheses, but it is a work written in the sixteenth century in Latin. Why people should use Latin is beyond me. Pull yourself together, Franz —he's here."

She unhurriedly put the volume back and unhurriedly closed the glass doors of the cabinet. From the ancient world of the dead came Dreyer, whistling as he approached with the bouncing dog. But she did not give up the idea of poison. In the morning, alone, she again scanned the evasive articles in the encyclopedia, trying to find that plain, unhistorical, unspectacular, matter-of-fact potion or powder that she so clearly imagined. By accident at the end of one paragraph, she came upon a brief bibliography of plausible-looking modern works. She sought Franz's advice as to whether they ought to obtain one of them. He gave her a blank look but said that if it were necessary he would go and buy it. But she was afraid to let him go alone. They might tell him that the book had to be ordered or it would turn out to consist of ten volumes costing twenty-five marks each. He might get flustered, foolishly leave his address. If she were to accompany him he would of course behave splendidly—naturally and casually as if he were a student of medicine or chemistry—but it was dangerous to go together, and that was why public libraries were taboo. And once you get involved in the book racket and begin running from shop to shop, the devil knows what kind of nonsense might ensue. In her mind she now reviewed the little she had known before and the little she had dug up about poisoners' techniques. Two things she had gleaned: first, that every poison has its echo—an antidote; and, secondly, that a sudden death led to an inquisitive zestful autopsy. However, for quite some time longer, with the obedient cooperation of Franz (who once quite on his own, the dutiful darling, bought at a street stall *The True Story of the Marquise de Brinvilliers*), Martha continued to toy with the idea. The most attractive poison seemed to be cyanide. It had a brisk something about it with no romantic trimmings: an ordinary mouse that has swallowed an insignificant fraction of one gram falls dead before it can run thirty inches. She saw the stuff as a pinch of colorless powder which could be dropped unnoticed with a lump of sugar into a cup of tea. "It says here that in certain cases cyanide cannot be traced in the cadaver. What certain cases? Tell us! Oh, it would be simple," she said to Franz. "We'd have tea together in the evening with those delicious little éclairs Menzel makes, and he'd swallow his sweet tea and cream—you know the quick way he does it—and suddenly—poof!"

"Well, let's get that powder," he replied. "I would get it if I had any idea how and where. Should I go to a pharmacy, or what?"

"I don't know either," said Martha, "I've read in a detective story about shady little cafés where one gets in touch with sellers of cocaine. But that's a long way to the stuff we need. Poisons are out, I'm afraid, unless of course we managed to bribe a doctor so that he would not dissect him, but that's too risky. Somehow I was absolutely certain they existed, those absolutely safe poisons. How stupid they don't. What a pity, Franz, you're not studying medicine; you could find out, you could decide then."

"I'm ready to do anything," he said in a strained voice, for at that moment he was bending and pulling off his shoes—they were new and pinched. "I'm game for anything."

"We've wasted a lot of time," sighed Martha. "Of course, I'm no scientist. I'm only a woman."

She carefully folded on a chair the dress she had taken off. The February wind was rattling the windowpane, and she shivered as she stepped out of her panties. In the beginning of the winter she had started putting on warm underwear for her visits to him, but he had hated her incongruous appearance in those oatmeal tights which were almost as long and as tedious to peel off as his own and made her hips and bosom appear like those of a certain particularly offensive, dully rounded dummy in the store opposite the service lift. And after a while she stopped wearing anything but his favorite frills against her gooseflesh.

"One must study poisons for years and years," she said, tidily rolling down her stockings, which she wanted to keep but did not want to tear. "Hopeless, hopeless," she sighed as she loosened the bedcovers (it would be warmer today between sheets, though she knew he preferred the couch) "You will be a chemist of genius with a long white beard when at last we offer him that cup of tea!"

Meanwhile, slowly and meticulously, Franz was draping his jacket over the broad shoulders of a special hanger (filched from the store), after having removed and placed on the table a wallet containing a five-dollar bill, seven marks and six post stamps; a little notebook; a fountain pen;

two pencils; his keys; and a letter to his mother he had forgotten to mail. Ruminative, naked, morose, he sniffed one armpit, and tossed his undervest under the washstand. It landed on the floor next to a rubber basin with Martha's rather depressing paraphernalia. He kicked the vest into a corner—she could wash it for him after tomorrow, with the socks, which were still comparatively clean. Well, to work, old soldier. Because he wore glasses even for love-making, he reminded her of a handsome, hairy young pearl diver ready to pry the live pearl out of its rosy shell as in that Russian ballet they had seen together, or that picture of conches facing the last page in volume M. He took off his wristwatch, listened to it and put it on the night table, near the alarm clock. There was less than half an hour left; they had dwelt too long on the cyanide.

"Darling, hurry up," said Martha from under the blankets.

"God, what a corn I've developed," he grunted, placing his bare foot on the edge of the chair and examining the hard yellow bump on his fifth toe. "And yet it's the right size of shoes. I don't know, maybe my feet are still growing."

"Franz, do come, dear. You can inspect it later."

In due time he did in fact give his corn a thorough examination. Martha, after a brisk ablution, lay down again, replete with physical bliss. The callus was like stone to the touch. He pressed it with his finger, and shook his head. A kind of listless seriousness accompanied all his movements. He pouted, he scratched the crown of his head. Then, with the same listless thoroughness, he began studying the other foot, which seemed smaller and smelled differently. He just could not reconcile in his mind the fact that the size was correct and yet the shoes pinched. There they stood, the rascals, side by side. American type, knobby-nosed, a nice reddish brown. He eyed them suspiciously—they had cost quite a lot even with a *Rabatt*. He slowly unhooked his glasses, breathed on the lenses, his mouth forming a lower-case *o*, and wiped them with a corner of the sheet. Then, just as slowly he put them on.

Martha looked at the clock. Yes, it was time to get dressed and go.

"You absolutely must come to supper tonight," she said, pulling up her stocking and snapping her garters. "I don't mind so much when there are guests but to sit alone with him—I can't bear it any more. . . . And put on your old shoes. Tomorrow you'll go and have these stretched for you. Free, of course. Every day is precious, oh, how precious!"

He was sitting on the bed, clasping his knees and staring at a point of light on the decanter that stood on the washstand. With his round head and prominent ears he seemed so special, so lovable to her. In his attitude, in his fixed gaze, there was the immobility of hypnosis. It crossed her mind that one word from her at this very moment could make him rise and follow her—as he was, as naked as a little boy—down the stairs, through the streets. . . . Her feeling of happiness now attained such a degree of brightness, and she imagined so vividly the regular well-planned, straightforward course of their common existence after the elimination, that she was afraid to disturb Franz's immobility, the immobile image of future happiness. She quickly finished dressing, slipped into her coat, took her hat, threw him a kiss, and was off. In the front hall, before a slightly better mirror than the one in her lover's room, she powdered her nose and put on her hat. How becomingly her cheeks were burning!

The landlord emerged from the toilet and made her a low bow.

"How is your wife feeling?" she asked, looking back as she took hold of the doorknob.

He bowed again.

She reflected that this wizard-like old codger was sure to know something about methods of poisoning people. It would be curious to know what they do, he and that invisible old woman of his. And for a few days longer she could not rid herself of the dream of magic powders instantly dissolving in death's nothingness, even though she knew already that nothing would come of it. A complicated, dangerous, outdated practice! Yes, that was it—outdated. "Whereas in the middle of the last century an average of fifty cases of poisoning were investigated annually, statistics show that in modern time—" Yes, that was the point.

Dreyer raised the cup to his lip. Involuntarily Franz met Martha's eyes. The snow-white table described a slow circle with a crystal vase for hub. Dreyer put his half-empty cup down, and the table stopped revolving.

". . . The light there is not particularly good," he continued. "And it's cold. The resonance is terrific. Every jump is echoed. I think the place used to be a riding school. But of course that's the only way to keep in training. One's serve does not fall apart during the winter. In any event (a final swallow of tea) spring, thank Heavens, is in the air, and it will soon be possible to play out of doors. My new club comes to life in April. And then I'll invite you. Eh, Franz?"

The previous day, at nine in the morning, he had created a minor sensation by appearing in Sports Goods, which he seldom visited during the winter. From behind a stucco column Franz saw him stop to chat with the respectfully bowing Piffke. The salesgirls and Mr. Schwimmer stood at attention. An early customer, who wanted another ball for his dog, was ignored for an instant. "Regards to your cockroaches," said Dreyer to Piffke cryptically and merrily, and came up to the counter behind which in the meantime Franz had slipped and feigned to be occupied with pad and pencil.

"Work, work, my boy," he said with the absentminded geniality with which he always, addressed his nephew, whom he had filed away in his mind long ago under "cretin" with cross references to "milksop" and *sympathisch*." Then he advanced with humorously outstretched hand toward an unresponsive young man of painted wood who had been changed recently into tennis togs. The shopgirls had dubbed him Ronald.

Dreyer stood before the red-sweatered oaf for a long time looking with contempt at his posture and olive face, and thinking with a tender excitement about the task which the happy inventor was struggling with. From the way Ronald held his racket it was obvious he could not hit a single ball—even an abstract ball in his world of wood. Ronald's stomach was sucked in, his face bore an expression of inane self-satisfaction. Dreyer noticed with a shock that Ronald was wearing a tie. Encouraging people to wear ties for tennis!

He turned. Another young man (more or less alive, and even wearing glasses) dutifully listened to the boss's brief instructions.

"By the way, Franz," added Dreyer, "show me the very best rackets."

Franz complied. Touched, Piffke watched with a melting gaze from afar. Dreyer selected an English racket. He gave the amber strings a couple of twangy fillips. He balanced it on the back of his finger to see which was heavier, frame or grip. He swung it in a passable imitation of a good player's backhand drive. It was a comfortable thirteen and a half.

"Keep it in a press," he said to Franz. Emotion clouded the young man's glasses.

"Token of affection, modest gift," said Dreyer in an explanatory patter and, casting an unfriendly last glance at vulgar Ronald, he walked away, with Piffke trotting beside him.

Although strictly speaking it was not at all part of his job, Franz embraced the wooden corpse and started undoing its tie. As he worked at it, he could not help touching the stiff cold neck. Then he undid a tight button. The shirt collar opened. The dead body was a brownish green with darker blotches and paler discolorations. Because of the open collar Ronald's fixed condescending grin became even more caddish and indecent. Ronald had a dark-brown smear under one eye as if he had been punched there. Ronald had a pied chin. Ronald's nostrils were clogged with black dust. Franz tried to recall where he had seen that horrible face before. Yes, of course—long, long ago, in the train. In the same train there had been a beautiful lady wearing a black hat with a little diamond swallow. Cold, fragrant, madonna-like. He tried to resurrect her features in his memory but failed to do so.

9

A purposeful gaiety, a dash of excitement now marked the rains. They no longer drizzled aimlessly; they breathed, they spoke. Violet crystals, like bath salts, were dissolved in rain water. Puddles consisted not of liquid mud but limpid pigments that made beautiful pictures reflecting housefronts, lampposts, fences, blue-and-white sky, a bare instep, a bicycle pedal. Two fat taxi drivers, a garbage collector in his sand-colored apron, a housemaid with golden hair ablaze in the sun, a white baker with glistening rubbers on his bare feet, a bearded old émigré with a dinner pail in his hand, two women with two dogs, and a gray-suited man in a gray borsalino had crowded together on the sidewalk looking up at the corner turret of an apartment house across the street where, conversing shrilly, a score of swallows swarmed. Then the yellow garbage collector rolled his yellow can up to the truck, the chauffeurs returned to their vehicles, the baker hopped back on his bicycle, the pretty servant maid went into a stationery store, the women trailed off behind their dogs, which were beside themselves with new scents; the last to move off was the man in gray, and only the bearded old foreigner with his dinner pail and a Russian-language newspaper remained in a trance gazing up at a roof in remote Tula.

The man in the gray hat walked slowly, squinting because of sudden flashes of zigzag light cast by passing windshields. There was something in the air that produced an amusing feeling of dizziness, alternate waves of warm and cold flowing over his body beneath his silk shirt, a funny levity, an ethereal flutter, a loss of identity, name, profession.

He had just lunched and, theoretically, was supposed to return to his office; on this first day of spring, however, the notion of "office" had quietly evaporated.

Toward him along the sunlit side of the street came a slender bob-haired lady in a karakul coat and a boy of four or five in a blue sailor suit rolling beside her on a tricycle.

"Erica," exclaimed the man, and stopped with outspread arms.

The boy, pedalling energetically, rolled past, but his mother paused, blinking in the sunlight.

She was now more elegant, the features of her mobile, intelligent, bird-like face seemed even more delicate than in the past. But the aura, the flame of her former charm had gone. She was twenty-six at the time they had parted.

"I've seen you twice in eight years," she said, in that familiar, rasping, rapid little voice. "Once you went by in an open car, and once I saw you at the theater—you were with a tall dark lady. That was your wife, wasn't it? I was sitting—"

"That's right, that's right," he said, laughing with pleasure and weighing on his large palm her little hand in its tight white glove. "But you were the last person I expected to meet today, though it is the best day to meet. I thought you went back to Vienna. The play was *King, Queen, Knave*, and now they are making a film out of it. I saw you too. And what about you—are you married?"

She was talking at the same time, so that their dialogue is hard to record. Music paper would be necessary with two clefs. As he was saying: "You were the last person" . . . , she was already continuing: " . . . ten seats or so away from you. You haven't changed, Kurt. Only your mustache is cropped now. Yes, this is my boy. No, I'm not married. Yes, mostly in Austria. Yes, yes, *King, Queen, Knave.*"

"Seven years," said old Kurt. "Let's walk here a little" (guiding the pleased boy's tricycle into a small public garden). "You know, I just saw the first— No, not quite that much—"

" . . . millions! I know you are making millions. I'm getting along all right myself" ("not quite that much," Kurt put in, "but tell me—") " . . . I'm very happy. I had only four lovers after you, but to make up for it, each was richer than the last, and now I'm exceptionally nicely established. He has a consumptive wife, the daughter of a general. She lives abroad. In fact, he has just left to spend a month with her at Davos." ("Goodness, I've been there last Christmas.") "He is elderly and very chic. And he adores me. And you, Kurt, are you happy?"

Kurt smiled and gave a little push to the boy in blue, who had come to a parting of paths: the child looked up at him with round eyes; then, making a tooting noise with his lips, pedalled on.

" . . . no, his father is a young Englishman. And look, his hair is done just like mine, but the color is still redder. If anyone had told me then, when we stood on that stairs—"

He listened to her rapid chatter and recalled a thousand trifles, an old poem she liked to repeat ("I am the page of High Burgundy"), chocolates with liqueur inside ("No, this one is with marzipan again—always marzipan for little Erica —I want one with curaçao or at least kirsch"), the paunchy kings of moonlit stone in the Tiergarten, so dignified on a spring night with the lilacs in gray fluffy bloom under the arc lights, and moving patterns on the white stairs. Such sweet smells, oh, God . . . those two brief happy years when Erica had been his mistress he visualized as an irregular series of such trifles: the picture composed of postage stamps in her front hall; her way of jumping up and down on the sofa or of sitting on her hands, or of suddenly sprinkling his face with rapid little pats, and *La Bohème*, which she adored, the trips to the country when they had fruit wine on a terrace; the brooch she had lost there . . . All these vaporous frivolous pathetic memories came alive within him while Erica was telling him at top speed about her new apartment, her piano, her lover's business.

"Are you happy at least, Kurt?" she asked again.

"Remember—" he said, and sang offkey but with feeling: "*Mi chiamano Mimi . . .*"

"Oh, I'm not Bohemian any more," she laughed with a little shake of her head. "But you are still the same, Kurt: so (she shaped several consecutive words with her no longer maddening mouth, not finding the right one)—so lacking in common sense."

"Such a nitwit," he said, and gave the little boy, expectantly hunched over the handlebars, another push; tried to stroke his curly head, but he was already too far.

"You haven't replied; are you happy?" insisted Erica. "Tell me, please, please."

The poem's lilt kept coming back to him and he quoted:

"Her lips were pale, but when kissed, glowed red,
    And if the end one guesses,
Still I must not tell what I leave unsaid
    About a queen's caresses.

Don't you remember, Erica, you would recite it with curtseys, oh, don't you remember?"

"I certainly don't. But I was asking you, Kurt. Does your wife love you?"

"Well, how should I put it. You see. . . . She is not what you'd call a passionate woman. She does not make love on a bench in the park, or on a balcony like a swallow."

"Is she faithful to you, your queen?"

"*Ihr' blasse Lippe war rot im Kuss. . . .*"

"I bet she deceives you."

"But I'm telling you she's cold and reasonable, and self-controlled. Lovers! She does not know the first letter of adultery."

"You're not the best witness in the world," laughed Erica. "You never knew I deceived you until his fiancée rang you up. Oh, I can just see what you do with your wife. You love her and don't notice her. You love her—oh, ardently—and don't bother about what she's like inside. You kiss her and still don't notice her. You've always been thoughtless, Kurt, and in the long run you'll always be what you've been, the perfectly happy egotist. Oh, I have studied you carefully."

"So have I," he said.

"Thus speaks the page of High Burgundy
    The train of a queen he bears,
Dum-dee-dee her mouth, her mouth dum-dee,
    On the marble pillared stairs."

"You know, Kurt, to be quite frank, there were moments when you made me simply miserable. I would realize that you were merely—skimming along the surface. You seat a person on a little shelf and think she'll keep sitting like that forever. But, you know, she tumbles off, and you think she still is sitting there, and even when she vanishes you don't give a hoot."

"On the contrary, on the contrary," he interrupted, "I'm very observant. The color of your hair was blond and now it is reddish."

As in the past, she gave him a tap of assumed exasperation.

"I've long stopped being cross with you, Kurt. Come and have coffee with me soon. He won't be back till mid-May. We'll have a chat, we'll remember old times."

"Certainly, certainly," he said, feeling suddenly bored, and knowing perfectly well that he would never do it.

She handed him her card (which a couple of minutes later he tore up and crammed into the ashtray of a taxi); she shook his hand many times in parting, still chattering very fast. Funny Erica. . . . That little face, the batting eyelashes, the turned-up nose, the hoarse hurried patter. . . .

The boy on the tricycle also proffered his hand and immediately wheeled away, his knees coming high and fast. Dreyer looked back as he walked and waved his hat several times; then he begged pardon of a clumsy lamppost, put on his hat, and walked on. On the whole—an unnecessary encounter. Now I shall never remember Erica as I remembered her before. Erica number two will always be in the way, so dapper and quite useless, with the useless little Vivian on his tricycle. Now was it right to let her infer that I am not quite happy? In what way am I unhappy? Why talk like that? Why should I want a hot little whore in my house? Perhaps her whole charm lies in the fact that she is so cold. After all, there should be a cold shiver in the sensation of true happiness. She's exactly that chill. Erica with her dyed hair cannot understand that the queen's coldness is the best guarantee, the best loyalty. I should not have answered like that. And besides, everything around, those sparkling puddles—why do bakers wear rubbers without socks, I don't

know—but every day, every instant all this around me
laughs, gleams, begs to be looked at, to be loved. The world
stands like a dog pleading to be played with. Erica has forgotten a thousand little sayings and songs, and that poem,
and Mimi in her pink hat, and the fruit wine, and the spot of
moonlight on the bench that first time. I think I'll make a
date with Isida tomorrow.

Next day Dreyer was particularly cheerful. At the office
he dictated to Miss Reich an absolutely impossible letter to
an old respectable firm. In the evening, in the strangely
lighted workshop where a miracle was slowly coming to life,
he gave the inventor such slaps on the back that the latter
doubled up. He telephoned he would be late for supper, and
when he came home at half past ten, he kidded poor Franz,
examining him on the science of salesmanship, asking him
absurd questions such as: What would you do if my wife
visited your department and before your very eyes stole
Ronald? Franz, to whom humor, and especially Dreyer's
humor, came a little hard, would open his eyes and spread
his hands. This amused Dreyer, who was easily amused.
Martha toyed with a teaspoon, now and then touching a
glass with it and extinguishing the vibration with a cold
finger.

In the course of that month she and Franz had investigated several new methods, and as before, she spoke of this
or that procedure with such austere simplicity that Franz
felt no fear, no discomfort, for a strange rearrangement of
emotions was taking place in him. Dreyer had divided in
two. There was the dangerous irksome Dreyer who walked,
spoke, tormented him, guffawed; and there was a second,
purely schematic, Dreyer, who had become detached from
the first—a stylized playing card, a heraldic design—and it
was this that had to be destroyed. Whatever method of

annihilation was mentioned, it applied precisely to this schematic image. This Dreyer number two was very convenient to manipulate. He was two-dimensional and immobile. He resembled those photographs of close relatives cut out along the outline of the figure and reinforced with cardboard that people, fond of cheap effects, place on their desks. Franz was not conscious of the special substance and stylized appearance of this inanimate personage, and therefore did not pause to wonder why those sinister discussions were so easy and harmless. Actually Martha and he spoke of two different individuals: Martha's subject was deafeningly loud, intolerably vigorous and vivacious; he threatened her with a priapus that had already once inflicted upon her an almost mortal wound, smoothed his obscene mustache with a little silver brush, snored at night with triumphant reverberations; while Franz's man was lifeless and flat, and could be burned or taken apart, or simply thrown away like a torn photograph. This elusive gemination had already begun when Martha rejected poisoning as "an attempt on human life with inadequate means" (a bit of subtle legality treated extensively in the long-suffering encyclopedia), and as something incompatible with matter-of-fact modern mores. She began talking of firearms. Her chilly rationality, combined, alas, with clumsy ignorance, produced rather weird results. Subliminally mustering recruits from the remotest regions of her memory, unknowingly recalling the details of elaborate and nonsensical shootings described in trashy novelettes, and thereby plagiarizing villainy (an act which after all had been avoided only by Cain), Martha proposed the following: first, Franz would acquire a revolver; then ("By the way, I know how to shoot," Franz interjected)—fine, that helped ("Though you know, darling, you still ought to practice a little, somewhere in a quiet lane"). The plan was this:

She would keep Dreyer downstairs until midnight ("How will you manage that?" "Don't interrupt, Franz, a woman knows how"). At midnight, while Dreyer was celebrating her sudden submissiveness with champagne, she would go to the window in the next room, draw back the curtain, and stand there for a while with a sparkling flute glass in her raised hand. That would be the signal. From his post near the garden fence Franz would clearly see her within the fire-bright rectangle. She would leave the window open and rejoin Dreyer on the parlor divan. He would probably be sitting, his clothes in disarray, drinking champagne and eating chocolates. Franz would immediately vault the gate in the dark ("It's easy to do; of course, there are some iron spikes on it but you're such a fine athlete") and, quickly crossing the garden, on tiptoe so as not to leave any telltale foot traces, would enter through the French window she would have left ajar. The door to the parlor would be open. From its threshold he would fire half a dozen times in quick succession, as they do in American movies. For appearance's sake, before vanishing, he would take the dead saloonkeeper's wallet and perhaps the two ancient French silver candlesticks from the mantelpiece. Then he would go the way he had come. Meanwhile she would run upstairs, undress, and go to bed. And that was all.

Franz nodded.

Another way was as follows: She would go to the country alone with Dreyer. The two of them would go for a good tramp. He loved walking. She and Franz would have chosen beforehand a nice lonely spot ("In the woods," said Franz, picturing to himself a dark grove of pines and oaks and that old dungeon on its wooded hill where cobolds had haunted his childhood). He would be waiting behind the tree with the reloaded revolver. When they had again killed him,

Franz would shoot her through the hand ("Yes, that's necessary, darling, it is always done, it must look as if we had been attacked by robbers"). Franz would again take the wallet (which he could return to her later with the candlesticks).

Franz nodded.

These two projects were the basic ones. The others were merely variations on the theme. Believing, with so many novelists, that if the details were correct the plot and characters would take care of themselves, Martha carefully worked out the theme of the burglarized villa and that of the forest robbery (the two unfortunately tended rather to get mixed up). Here Franz turned out to have an unexpected and most fortunate gift: he could imagine with diagrammatic clarity his movements and those of Martha and coordinate them in advance with those concepts of time, space, and matter which had to be taken into account. In this lucid and flexible pattern only one thing remained always stationary, but this fallacy went unnoticed by Martha. The blind spot was the victim. The victim showed no signs of life before being deprived of it. If anything, the corpse which had to be moved and handled before burial seemed more active than its biological predecessor. Franz's thoughts travelled around this fixed point with acrobatic agility. All the necessary movements and their sequence were admirably calculated. The thing called Dreyer at the present time would differ from the future Dreyer only inasmuch as a vertical line differs from a horizontal. A difference of angle and perspective—nothing more. Martha unwittingly encouraged Franz in those abstractions because she always took for granted that Dreyer would be caught unawares and have no time to defend himself. For the rest, she imagined quite vividly and realistically how he would raise his eyebrows on seeing his nephew point a pistol at him, how he would begin to laugh, assuming that the weapon was a toy, and how he would finish his laughter in another world. When, in order to abolish all risk, she placed Dreyer in the position of a piece of merchandise, packaged, tied up and ready to be delivered, she did not realize how much easier this made things for Franz. "Smart boy," she would laugh, kissing him on the cheek, "bright, bright darling." Reacting to her praise, he presented a kind of estimate (which had to be burned afterwards, unfortunately): the number of paces from fence to window; the number of seconds needed to cover that distance; the distance from window to door and from door to armchair (into which Dreyer had been transferred from the couch at a certain point in their planning), and from the revolver hanging as it were in mid-air to the back of the conveniently placed head. And while Dreyer was actually sitting in that armchair and reading the Sunday papers in a shaft of April sunlight, Martha with a glowing comb in her chignon, wearing a new pink tailor-made dress, and coatless Franz, with Tom following them, a black ball in his jaws, would busily pace to and fro in the garden and along the wall of the villa up to the parlor window, and back again to the wicket, counting steps, memorizing them, rehearsing approaches and retreats, and Dreyer, arms akimbo, would come out on the terrace and presently join them in the garden and help discuss in his turn the new arrangement of flagged paths and flowerbeds that she and Franz were so diligently planning.

They continued their planning when alone in the drab beloved little room, with the still unsold big-nippled slave girl above the bed and a brand-new expensive, unwanted tennis racket in its frame. It was time to think of obtaining the weapon. As soon as they got to that stage, a ridiculous obstacle arose. They were both certain that a permit had to be obtained for the purchase of a revolver. Neither Martha nor Franz had the least idea how one obtained such a permit. They would have to make inquiries, go to the police maybe, and that might mean having to write and sign applications. It now became apparent that the acquisition of the tool was something many times vaguer than the image of its use. Martha could not tolerate such a paradox. She eliminated it by seeking out insurmountable difficulties in the execution of the project as well. There was for example the gardener—who acted also as a (bribable? druggable?) watchman—a level-headed husky old rascal who had sharp eyes for intruders and squashed caterpillars with a special juicy squeak and a special horrible twitch of iron-nailed finger and thumb which caused Franz, the first time he witnessed that green garrotte, to cry out like a girl. There was the policeman who frequently passed along the street as though strolling; miscalculations and flaws also turned up in the forest plan: after an excursion to Grunewald, Franz reported that it contained more picnickers than pines. There were lots of other woods in the suburbs, but one had to find a way to get him to go there. And when the fulfillment of these projects receded to its proper place, the question of procuring the weapon no longer seemed so insoluble: there existed probably friendly gun dealers in the northern part of the city who did not bother about permits, and once the gun was there, surely chance was on their side, and would place the target in the right position at the right moment. Thus Martha satisfied in passing her innate sense of correct relationships ("First things first" and "If you want two noses, you should be content with one eye" were her favorite proverbs).

So now the time came to obtain a small dependable revolver. She imagined how Franz—slow, lanky, shy Franz—

would make the rounds of gunshops, how the friendly salesman would suddenly start asking him tricky questions, how
the idiot would remember later Franz's tortoise shell glasses
and the explanatory gestures of his thin, white, innocent
hands, how later, after the gun had been used and buried,
some meddlesome detective would ferret all this out. . . .
Now, if *she* should go and buy it. . . . Perhaps she thought
Tom had the rabies and she wanted to shoot him, and actually
did for practice—women can also learn to shoot well. And
suddenly an extraneous image floated by, stopped, turned,
and floated on like those cute objects that move by themselves in commercial cinema advertisements. She realized
why the image of the revolver had in her mind such a definite form and color, though she knew nothing about guns.
Willy's face emerged from the depth of her memory; he
laughed his fat laugh, and bent low examining something, and
holding back Tom, who thought it was a plaything for him.
She made another effort and remembered that Dreyer was
sitting at his desk and showing Willy—what? a revolver!
Willy had turned it in his hands, laughing, and the dog barked.
She could remember nothing more, but that was sufficient.
And she was amazed and gladdened to see how painstakingly
and providently her mind had conserved for a couple of years
that fleeting but absolutely indispensable image.

It was yet another Sunday. Dreyer and Tom went out for
a little walk. All the windows in the villa were open. Sunlight made itself comfortable in unexpected corners of the
rooms. On the terrace a breeze ruffled the pages of the April
issue (already old) of a magazine with a photograph of the
newly discovered, really lovely arms of Venus. First of all,
Martha thoroughly explored the desk drawers. Among blue
folders containing documents, she found several sticks of
gold-tinted sealing wax, a flashlight, three guldens and one

shilling, an exercise book with English words written in it, his grinning passport (who grins in official circumstances?), a pipe, broken, that she had given him a long long time ago, an old little album of faded snapshots, a recent snapshot of a girl that might have been Isolda Portz had she not worn a smart ski suit in the photo, a box of thumbtacks, pieces of string, a watch crystal, and other trivial junk the accumulation of which always infuriated Martha. Most of these articles, including the copybook and the winter sports advertisement, she deposited in the wastebasket. She thrust back the drawers violently and, leaving the deafened desk, went up to the bedroom. There she rummaged through two white chests-of-drawers, finding among other things a hard ball that bore Tom's toothmarks which God knows how had got into the drawer where her husband's ten pairs of shoes stood in two neat rows. She threw the ball out of the window. She ran downstairs. In passing by a mirror she noticed that the powder had come off her nose and her eyes were positively haggard. Should she see a lung doctor or a heart specialist? Or both? She inspected a few more drawers in various rooms, chiding herself for looking in absurd places, and finally decided that the gun was either in the safe, to which she did not have a key (the Will was there, the treasure, the future!), or else at the office. She tried the accursed desk again. It cringed and stood holding its breath at her menacing approach. The drawers began clacking like slaps on the face. Not here! Not here! Not here! She noticed a brown briefcase in one. She lifted it angrily. Beneath it she saw deep in the drawer a small revolver with a mother-of-pearl handle. Simultaneously her husband's voice came from nearby, and pushing the briefcase back, she quickly closed the drawer.

"Heavenly day," Dreyer was saying in a singsong voice. "Almost like summer."

Morosely, without turning, she said:

"I'm looking for some pills. You had pyramidon in your desk. My head is splitting."

"I don't know. Nobody's head should split on such a lovely day."

He seated himself on the leather arm of a chair and wiped his brow with a handkerchief.

"You know what, my love," he said. "I've got an idea. Listen—what's Franz's telephone number?—I'll call him up, and we'll all drive to the tennis club. Good idea? Charming idea?"

"When do you want to lunch? He is coming for lunch. Why don't you ring somebody else and play after lunch?"

"It's only ten now. We can lunch at half past one. It's a shame to waste such weather. You come too. Okay, okay, okay?"

She consented to come only because she knew how unbearable it would be for Franz to be with him alone. "I'll call him," she said.

The landlord asked who she was, and why she wanted to talk to his lodger. But Martha told him to mind his own business. Franz, taken by surprise, arrived in an ordinary suit, having simply changed to sneakers. Dreyer, puffing with impatience and afraid that at any moment a thunder head might form in the sky, rushed him upstairs and issued him a pair of white flannel pants which he had bought in London a couple of years ago, and which were too tight for him. Standing there, arms akimbo, eyes bulging, head cocked, he watched as Franz changed. The poor boy stank like a goat. And those long drawers on a day like this! Whoever sewed on that monogram was not a professional—at least not a professional seamstress. Franz, numbed with embarrassment, well aware that his underwear was not what it should be, and grotesquely fearful that something about the whole situation might give away the messy secrets of adultery, had trouble with the changing of trousers, as he stepped from foot to foot, hopping and extending one leg, and trying to persuade himself that it was only a bad dream. Dreyer too began stepping from one foot to the other. The awfulness dragged on. The trousers seemed too long and too voluminous, and in the course of that sack race a spasmodic movement landed Franz on the top of a broken luggage rack which had no business to be in the dressing room. Dreyer made vague motions as if he wanted to help. No less nightmarish was the business of buttoning the dummy's fly, which he was told to do himself. After which the fitter with two fingers delicately pulled up the waist, adjusted the side straps, expertly slipped a belt around the wooden waist, and sank on one knee to measure the leg with a tape which he wore as one does a dancing serpent. Finally he gave a chuckle of relief and approval, and dealt Franz a robust slap on the buttocks. The blow kept vibrating for quite a long time in the poor fellow's system whereas his double squeamishly advanced on bent legs, tucking in his bottom. The tingle endured even in the taxi. When they got out Dreyer gave him another exuberant slap, this time with Franz's racket, which he was about to forget in the cab. "*Aber lass doch*," said Martha to her vulgar husband.

On the terra-cotta red courts white figures darted to and fro, while hired children picked up the balls at top speed. All around, a tall wire fencing was hung with green tarpaulin. White tables and wicker armchairs stood in front of the clubhouse. Everything was very clean and sharply defined.

Martha fell into conversation with a blond-legged beautiful pale-eyed woman in a white skirt no bigger than a paper lampshade. They ordered drinks—an ice-cold American coffee-dark concoction. Dreyer went inside to change. Dark Martha and the platinum lady spoke loudly but Franz did not catch a single word. A stray ball bounced past him onto a table, onto a chair, onto the turf. He picked it up and examined it: it was quite new and signed in violet by a firm well represented at the Dandy. Franz put the ball on the table. Two other young women went by with bare arms and legs, putting the red soles of their silk-laced white shoes (Mercury—no, Loveset) down on the lawn quite flat as if walking barefoot. Their eyes were happy, their mouths red. All that was in the past, dreams and desires of a boyhood long gone. They blinded him with a blended smile, mistaking him for somebody. Beside one of the further courts a kind of judge, or guardian of games, sat on a stepladder chair watching the ball cross the net, and like an automaton shaking his head in rhythm—denying, denying, denying, they are not for you. In the black aperture of the door appeared a dazzling white Dreyer. "Let's go," he cried, and with a bouncing step, a fluffy towel around his neck, two rackets under his arm, and a box of new balls in his hand, headed for court number six. Martha said au revoir to the lady and moved to another chair to watch the two players. On the court, with the thoroughness of an executioner preparing the block, Dreyer was already measuring the height of the net with his racket. Franz stood on the side of the court near his mistress, looking up at a passing airplane. With stern tenderness she took note of his dear boyish neck, his shining glasses, his elegant tennis trousers which were a bit too roomy around the hips but otherwise very becoming. Having completed his sinister manipulations, Dreyer jogged heavily to his base line. Franz remained standing in the center of his own rectangle. A scrawny little girl with a blank expression on her freckled face bounced toward him one of the balls from the box. As the ball jumped, it struck him in the groin, he tried to pat it down with his racket but it passed between his legs and she threw him another which eluded him too. This time, however, he ran after it, and finally picked it up from under the feet of a player on the adjacent court, who muffed his shot and glared at him. Zestful Franz ran back with the pocketed ball and assumed his former position. With a tolerant grin Dreyer waved at him to stand further back and ladled out a warm-up underhand serve in tolerably correct style copied from that of the club coach Count Zubov. Franz swung at it and with a beginner's luck returned it by means of a tremendous, though unorthodox, whack that propelled the ball well beyond Dreyer's reach. Martha could not refrain from applauding. Dreyer dealt out another underhand serve. Franz's weapon swished mightily but the ball flew by unscathed and was neatly fielded by the little girl behind him. Then, taking his time, Franz held the ball found in his pocket at arm's length, gauged the altitude, dropped the ball, and attempted to hit it on the rebound. Again nothing happened except that he stepped on the ball and nearly fell. He trotted to the net, where the ball had finally got entangled. Dreyer told him to go well back and continued to send him ball after ball. Franz lunged and whirled but his main stroke remained a swing in a void. The little girl, who was beginning to enjoy herself, kept flitting this way and that, cupping every ball in her tiny hands, and with nonchalant precision rolling it or tossing it back to Dreyer.

"Stop getting in the way," cried Martha to the impudent little catcher, but the child did not hear or did not understand. She had a brass ring on her finger. Might be a dirty little gypsy or something.

The ordeal continued. Finally Franz in the ecstasy of despair did get a crack at the ball, and it soared over the roof of the pavilion.

Dreyer slowly walked up to the net and beckoned to Franz.

"Have I won?" asked Franz, panting.

"No," said Dreyer, "I just want to explain something. We are not playing American baseball or English cricket. This is a game called 'lawn tennis' because it was first played on grass." He invariably mispronounced "lawn" as if rhymed with "down."

Then, slowly and sadly, Dreyer returned to his base line, and the same thing began all over again. Martha could bear it no longer. She shouted from where she sat:

"Enough, enough! You see perfectly well he can't—"

She had wanted to shout "can't play" but a gust of spring wind cut off the ultimate word. Franz intently examined the strings of his racket. A young fellow, also lanky and also wearing glasses, who had been watching the play with predatory irony, stepped forward and bowed, and Dreyer, indicating with his racket to Franz that he could go, joyfully greeted the newcomer, whom he knew to be a strong player.

Franz walked over to Martha and sat down beside her. His face was pale and drawn, and glistened with sweat. She was smiling at him but he wiped his glasses and did not look her way. "Dear," she whispered, trying to catch his eye; she caught it, but he shook his head gloomily, his teeth clenched.

"Everything is all right," she said softly. "It won't happen again. I'll tell you something," she added still more softly. "Listen, I found it."

His gaze slipped away but she firmly recaptured it. ". . . I found it in the desk. You'll simply take it the day before. Understand?"

He blinked. "You'll catch cold like that," she said. "There's a bad wind blowing. Put on your sweater and coat, darling."

"Not so loud," whispered Franz. "Please."

She smiled, looked around, shrugged.

"I must explain to you. . . . No, listen, Franz—I have a completely new plan."

Dreyer had just made a good shot, gently slicing the ball close to the net, and glanced from under his brows at his wife, pleased that she was looking at him.

"You know what," whispered Martha. "Let's go. I must explain everything to you."

Dreyer missed a volley and returned to his base line, shaking his head. Martha called him over. She told him that her headache was worse, and that he should not be late for lunch. Dreyer nodded and went on with the game.

They could not find a taxi but anyway it was only a few minutes of fast walking. They cut across a park where happy lovers were melting in each other's arms on yesteryear's dry leaves. She began explaining on the way.

The plan was delightfully innocent: it was based on his study of English. Occasionally he would ask her to dictate something to him. She knew fewer words than he but her pronunciation was perhaps a little better than his or at least different from his: her "lawn" for example rhymed with "own" and not "down," which was ridiculous, as she had told him many times, the obstinate fool. He used to take down her dictation in an exercise book. Then he would compare what he had written with the text. And it was on such a dictation that everlasting happiness in a private park would depend. They would take a Tauchnitz novel and find a suitable sentence in it, such as "I could not have acted otherwise" or "I am shooting myself because I am tired of life." The rest was clear. "In your presence," she said, "I shall dictate to him the chosen sentence. Of course, he must write it not in a copy-book but on a clean sheet of letter paper. In fact I have already destroyed that copybook. As soon as he has written that down but just before he has lifted his head you'll come up to him very close and a little behind him, as if you wanted to look over his shoulder, and then very carefully—"

10

Almost three months had already elapsed since that unforgettable day when the Inventor (by now capitalized in Dreyer's mind) had produced the first samples of his automannequins, as he called them. Because of the strong naked lighting, his workshop resembled a medical laboratory, and indeed it had been exactly that in the past. Demonstrations were conducted in a large bare room that had been once a repository for dead bodies and parts of such bodies, which ribald students (some of them, though not all, respectable old surgeons today) frequently used to place in various attitudes and reciprocal positions suggestive of strange orgies. The Inventor and Dreyer stood in a corner of the room and watched in silence.

In the center of the brightly illuminated floor, a plump little figure about a foot and a half tall, tightly bundled in brown sackcloth that left exposed only a pair of short blood-red legs made of some substance resembling rubber and shod in baby boots with buttons, walked back and forth with a very natural human-like motion, swaggering a wee bit and turning at every tenth step with a built-in little cry between "hep" and "help" meant to disguise the slight creak of its mechanism. Dreyer, hands clasped on his stomach, watched with soft emotion, as a sentimental visitor watches a child—perhaps his own little bastard—to whose first toddle he is being treated by a proud mother. The Inventor, who had let his beard grow and now looked like an Oriental priest in mufti, kept tapping his foot lightly in time to the movements of the little figure. "Goodness," said Dreyer suddenly in a high-pitched voice, as if he were ready to burst into tears of tenderness. The hooded gnome did in fact walk about very catchingly. That brown cloth was there only for decency's sake. Afterwards, when the mechanism had died, the Inventor unwrapped his prototypical automannequin and laid bare its works: a delicate system of joints and muscles, and three small but remarkably heavy batteries. One thing about this invention could be discerned even in this first crude model; what impressed one was not so much those electrical ganglia and the rhythmic transmission of current as the springy, somewhat stylized, but wonderfully lifelike gait of the mechanical infant. Paradoxically, it paced the floor more like a meditating mathematician than a babe in the wood. The secret of this motion lay in the flexibility of voskin—the very special stuff with which the Inventor had replaced live bones and live flesh. The two pseudopodia of this original voskiddy seemed alive not because it moved them (a mechanized "strollie" or *zhivulya* are after all no rarity, they breed like rabbits on sidewalks around Easter or Christmas) but rather because the material itself, animated by a so-called galvanobiotic current, remained active all the time—rippling, tensing, slackening as if organically alive or even conscious, a double ripple grading into triple dapple with the smoothness of reflections in water. It walked without jerking—this was the wonder of it. And it was this that Dreyer appreciated most while reacting rather indifferently to the technical mystery, imparted to him first in code, then in coded explanation of the code, by the cagy Inventor.

"What is its sex? Can you tell me?" asked Dreyer as the brown little figure stopped before him.

"Not differentiated yet," answered the Inventor. "But in a month or two there will be two males and one female over five feet high."

In other words, the infant had to grow up. It was necessary to create not only a semblance of human legs, but also the semblance of a graceful human body and expressive face. The Inventor, however, was neither an artist nor an anatomist. Dreyer therefore found him two helpers: an old sculptor whose work was so lifelike that he managed to convey the impression of acute chorea, for example, or, say, the beginning of a sneeze; and a professor of physiology who, in trying to explain the well-known capacity of waking up at a self-imposed hour, had written a long treatise which explained nothing but contained the first description of the "self-awareness" of muscles with beautiful illustrations in color. The workshop soon began to look as if those medical students had again been horsing about with dismembered cadavers. The professor of anatomy and the fantastic sculptor assisted the Inventor very successfully. One was lean, pale, nervous, with long hair combed back and a huge Adam's apple; the other was sedate and bald, and wore a high starched collar. Their appearance afforded Dreyer a source of endless delight, since the first was the professor, and the second, the artist.

He could now clearly imagine the full-grown, perfect, elegantly dressed automannequins walking back and forth in a huge bay window of the emporium, among potted plants, discreetly disappearing to change their clothes behind the scenes, and stalking in again to the delight of the populace.

It was a poetical vision and no doubt a lucrative enterprise. In mid-May he bought the patent rights from the Inventor at a comparatively low price and now he was debating—what would be better—to create a sensation on the Kurfürstendamm by putting those figures literally into circulation or to sell the invention to a foreign syndicate: the former was richer fun, the latter, safer profit.

As happens in the lives of many businessmen, he began to feel in that spring of 1928 that his affairs somehow or other were assuming a certain independent existence. The part of his funds that was in a state of constant fruitful gyration moved by momentum, and moved too rapidly; he seemed to be losing control over his wealth, seemed no longer able to stop this great golden wheel at will. Half of his fortune was reasonably safe; but the other, which he had created in a year of freakish luck—at a time when luck, a light touch, and his special kind of imagination were needed—had now become too lively, too mobile. An optimist by nature, he hoped that this was but a temporary loss of control and did not for an instant suppose that the increased spin might transform the wheel of fortune into the shimmer of its gyration, and that if he stopped the wheel with his hand, it would prove to have been nothing but its own golden ghost. But Martha, who now more than ever loathed her husband's whimsical levity (even though it had once helped him to become rich), could not help feeling that he might dance his way into some financial disaster before she was able to remove him and halt the lighthearted spin herself.

The store was doing good business but the profits did not accumulate as solidly as they should have. The stock market had recently given a sudden shiver; he had gambled on it and lost, and now was gambling again. In all this Martha saw a doomful admonition. She might have been willing to grant him a reprieve for some solid deal, for she admitted that she "trusted his scent"; but that juggling with shares was too risky. Why procrastinate when every passing month might mean a further dwindling of wealth?

On that sunny and terrible morning, as soon as she and Franz returned from the tennis club, she led him to the study to show him the revolver. From the threshold she indicated with a rapid glance and a barely perceptible motion of the shoulder the desk at the far end of the room. There, in a drawer, lay the instrument of their happiness.

"In a moment you'll see it," whispered Martha and glided toward the desk. But at that instant Tom entered the room with a bold buoyant step. "Get that dog out of here," said Franz. "I can't do anything with the dog here." "Out!" cried Martha. Tom laid back his ears, extended his gentle gray muzzle, and slunk behind a chair. "Oh, get him out," said Franz through clenched teeth with a convulsive shudder. Martha clapped her hands. Tom slipped beneath the chair and emerged on the other side. She gestured threateningly. Tom jumped back in time and, licking his chops with a hurt expression, trotted toward the door. On the threshold he looked back, one front paw raised. Martha, however, was coming at him. He submitted to the inevitable. She slammed the door shut. An obliging draft promptly banged the windowpane. "All right now, let's hurry," she said crossly. "Why are you sulking there? Come here."

She quickly yanked open the drawer. She lifted the brown briefcase. Under it, a gleaming object showed. Franz mechanically extended his hand and took it. He turned it this way and that.

"Are you sure—" he began apathetically.

He heard Martha snort, and looked up. She uttered a dry laugh and walked away.

[196]

"Put it back," she said, standing at the window and drumming on the pane. No wonder Willy had laughed.

"I said put it back. You see perfectly well it's a cigar lighter."

"Yes, of course. But really quite like a little revolver. Very fancy, isn't it? I think I saw a couple of them at the store." Noiselessly, he shut the drawer.

That day Martha realized a saddening thing. Until then she had thought she was acting no less judiciously than she had acted or wanted to act all her life. Now she saw that some kind of atrocious dreamland was encroaching upon her charts. A beginner's self-confidence might be pardonable— but that pardonable phase had come and gone. All right— she should never have accepted to marry that clown with the foul-smelling monkey in his arms; all right—she should not have been impressed by his money, she should not have hoped in her youthful naivete to make an ordinary, dignified, obedient husband out of that joker. But at least she had arranged her life the way she wished. Almost eight years of grim struggle. He wanted to take her to Ceylon or Florida, if you please, instead of buying this elegant villa. She needed a sedentary husband. A subdued and grave husband. She needed a dead husband.

There were several days when she retired as it were into the remotest deserts of her spirit to review her blunders and collect her forces so as to return purified to the task, and thenceforth commit none of the former errors. Elaborate combinations, complicated details, phony weapons—all this was to be abandoned. From now on the motto would be: simplicity and routine. The sought-for method must be absolutely natural, absolutely pure. Intermediaries please abstain. Poison was a procuress; the pistol, a pimp. Each might betray her. One must stop buying novelettes about the

Borgias. One cannot kill a man with a cigar lighter as some had apparently thought she had thought.

Franz shook his head or nodded it, according to this or that turn of her earnest speech. The little room was brimming with sunlight. He was sitting on the window ledge. The panes were thrown open and secured with wedges of wood. In spite of its being a holiday, the builders were stubbornly at work, clinking and knocking higher and higher. A girl's voice cried something from a window below, and another girl's voice, still more angelic, responded from a balcony on the opposite side of the street. This was the season of guitar music on the river at home, of rafts gently singing in the shadow of the willows.

His back began to feel hot. He slid off the window ledge onto the floor. With her legs tightly crossed, showing a strip of fat thigh under her skirt, Martha sat sideways at the table. In the inexorable light her skin looked coarser and her face seemed broader, perhaps because her chin was propped on her fist. The corners of her damp lips were lowered, her eyes looked upward. A complete stranger within Franz's consciousness observed in passing that she rather resembled a toad. Martha moved her head. Reality returned. And once again everything became oppressive, dark, and relentless.

". . . strangle him," she muttered. "If we could simply strangle him. With our bare hands."

The great Dr. Hertz had told her a couple of years before that her cardiogram showed a remarkable, not necessarily dangerous, but certainly incurable abnormality which he had seen only in one other woman, a Hohenzollern, who was still alive at almost forty, and now it seemed to Martha that her heart would burst, unable to withstand the feeling of hatred that Dreyer's every move and sound aroused in her. Sometimes at night, when he approached her with a tender little laugh, she felt an urge to dig her hands into his neck and squeeze, squeeze with all her might. And vice versa, when on a recent occasion she had made him promise not to sell the best of his three apartment houses for the ridiculous price he was offered by Willy, and in generous compensation had offered him of her own accord a brief caress, his unexpected lack of manly response had revolted her as much as his advances. She realized how difficult it was in these circumstances to reason logically, to develop simple, smooth, elegant plans, when everything within her was screaming and raging. Yet if she must survive something had to be done. Dreyer was spreading out monstrously before her, like a conflagration in a cinema picture. Human life, like fire, was dangerous and difficult to extinguish; but, as in the case of fire, there must be, there simply must be, some universally accepted, natural method of quenching a man's fierce life. Enormous, tawny-haired, tanned from tennis; wearing bright yellow pajamas, redly yawning; radiating heat and health, and making the various grunting noises that a man who cannot control his gross physicality makes when waking up and stretching, Dreyer filled the whole bedroom, the whole house, the whole world.

More and more often, and with a recklessness she no longer noticed, Martha escaped from that triumphant presence to her lover's room, arriving even at hours when he was still at the store and the vibrant sounds of construction in the sky were not yet replaced by nearby radios, and would darn a sock, her black brows sternly drawn together as she awaited his return with confident and legitimate tenderness. Without his obedient lips and young body she could not live more than a single day. At that instant in their meeting when still feeling the receding ripples of pleasure she would open her eyes, it seemed strange to her that Dreyer had not been destroyed by her lover's thrusts. She would soon try to entice sluggish Franz anew, and having succeeded not without trouble (that job at the store exhausted the poor pet!), she would feel again that Dreyer was perishing, that each frantic stroke wounded him more deeply, and finally, that he collapsed in terrible pain, howling, discharging his intestinal fluids, and dissolving in the unbearable splendor of her joy.

Yet, as if nothing had happened, he would revive, walk noisily through all the rooms and, cheerful and hungry, sit opposite her at meals, folding a slice of ham, spearing it with an energetic fork, and making a circular motion with his mustache as he chewed.

"Help me, Franz, oh, help me," she would murmur sometimes, shaking him by the shoulders.

His eyes were totally submissive behind their well-wiped lenses. However, he could not think of anything. His imagination was at her command; it was ready to work for her, but it was she who had to give his fancy its impulse and food. Outwardly he had changed a great deal during these last months: he had lost weight, his protruding cheekbones made him look more than ever like a hungry Hindu, a curious debility blurred his movements as if he were existing only because existing was the proper thing to do; but one did it unwillingly and would have been glad to return at any moment to a state of animal stupor. His day ran its course automatically but his nights were formless and full of terror. He took sleeping pills. The morning jolt of his alarm clock was like a coin dropped into a vending machine. He would rise; shuffle to the smelly toilet (a little dark hell in its own right), shuffle back, wash his hands, brush his teeth, shave, wipe the soap from his ears, dress, walk to the subway station, get on a non-smoking car, read the same old advertisement ditty overhead, and to the rhythm of its crude trochee reach his destination, climb the stone staircase, squint at the mottled pansies in the bright sun on a large flowerbed in front of the exit, cross the street, and do everything in the store that he was supposed to do. Returning home in the same way, he would do once again all that was expected of him. After her departure, he would read the newspaper for a quarter of an hour or so because it was customary to read newspapers. Then he would walk over to his uncle's villa. At supper he would sometimes repeat what he had read in the paper, reproducing every other sentence verbatim but strangely jumbling the facts in between, so that Dreyer had fun egging him on and then correcting him. Around eleven he would leave. He would make his way home always along the same sidewalks. A quarter of an hour later he would be undressing. The light would go out.

His thoughts were characterized by the same monotony as his actions, and their order corresponded to the order of his day. Why has he stopped the coffee? Can't flush if the chain comes off every time. Dull blade. Piffke shaves with his collar on in the public washroom. These white shorts are not practical. Today is the ninth—no, the tenth—no, the eleventh of June. She's again on the balcony. Bare arms, parched geraniums. Train more crowded every morning. Clean your teeth with Dentophile, every minute you will smile. They are fools who offer their seats to big strong women. Clean your teeth with Dentophile, clean your minute with your smile. Out we file.

And behind these regular everyday thoughts, as behind words written on glass, lay darkness, a darkness into which one ought not to peer. One was treated, however, to strange glimpses. Once it seemed to him that a police official, smelling strongly of cheese, with a briefcase under his arm, kept looking at him with suspicion from the opposite seat. His mother's letters contained terrifying insinuations: she maintained for example that he misspelled words or left them unfinished. At the store, the face of a rubber sea lion, intended for the amusement of bathers, began to resemble the face of Dreyer, and Franz was glad when a Mrs. Steller, Robbe Avenue 1, had him pack it and send it to her. Catching a whiff of blooming lindens, he would remember nostalgically the schoolyard in his hometown where they touched the bark of a lime in a game of tag. Once a young girl with bouncing breasts, in a short red frock, almost ran into him; she carried a bunch of keys in her hand, and he fancied he recognized in her a janitor's daughter he had longed for, many ages ago. These were mere ephemeral glints of consciousness; he would instantly revert to semi-existence.

Then at night, in his drugged sleep, something more significant would burst through. Together with naked Martha, he would be sawing off the head of Piffke in a public toilet, even though in the first place he was undistinguishable from the Dreyers' dead chauffeur, and in the second, was called Dreyer in the language of dreams. Horror and helpless revulsion merged in those nightmares with a certain nonterrestrial sensation, known to those who have just died, or have suddenly gone insane after deciphering the meaning of everything. Thus, in one dream, Dreyer stood on a ladder slowly winding a red phonograph, and Franz knew that in a moment the phonograph would bark the word that solved the universe after which the act of existing would become a futile, childish game like putting one's foot on every flag edge at every step. The phonograph would croon a familiar song about a sad Negro and the Negro's love, but by Dreyer's expression and shifty eyes Franz would understand that it was all a ruse, that he was being cleverly fooled, that within the song lurked the very word that must not be heard, and he would wake up screaming, and could not identify a pale square in the distance until it became a pale window in the dark, and then he would drop his head on the pillow again. All at once Martha, her face dreadful— waxy, glossy, heavy-jowled, with the wrinkles of age and gray hair—would run in, grab him by the wrist, and drag him onto a balcony suspended high above the street, and on the pavement below stood a policeman holding something in front of him, and slowly growing until his face reached the balcony and, holding a newspaper, in a loud voice he read Franz's death sentence to him.

His colleagues in the sports department, athletic Schwimmer and his effeminate Swedish friend (who now sold bathing suits), happened one day to notice his pallor and advised him to sunbathe on the banks of the Grunewald lake on Sundays. But an icy indolence hung upon Franz, and besides, an hour of leisure meant an hour with Martha. As for her, she mistook his moodiness for the malady from which she herself suffered, the white-hot fever of incessant murderous thought. It gladdened her when, in Dreyer's presence, upon meeting her gaze, Franz would sometimes start clenching and unclenching his hands, breaking matches, or fiddling with the saltcellar. She believed that her death rays ran clear through him, and that she had only to stab him with that beam of light, and then a tense particle of his soul where the imprisoned image of death lay hidden would explode and make a gigantic Franz stamp on the crawling hornet. Conversely, she was irritated when Franz complained. She would shrug her shoulders as she listened to his muttering.

"Don't you understand—he is insane," Franz would repeat. "I know he's insane."

"Nonsense, not insane, a little peculiar. This is even an advantage. Stop twitching, please."

"But it's horrible," Franz insisted. "He has stopped bringing me coffee, I don't know when, and then he suddenly appeared with a bowl of red beef tea."

"Oh, stop. Who cares? He is quite harmless. He has a sick wife."

Franz kept shaking his head. "One never sees her. I've rattled the door thousands of times to get him out of the toilet but it's always he, not she. I don't like it."

"Silly. Why, I tell you, that's an advantage. Nobody snoops on us. It's my impression that we are very lucky in this respect."

"God knows what goes on in that room of theirs," sighed Franz. "Such strange noises come from there sometimes. Not laughter, rather the clucking of a hen."

"That will do," said Martha quietly.

He stopped speaking, sitting naked on the edge of the bed and staring at the floor.

"Oh, darling, darling," she said cheerlessly and impetuously. "Does this matter? Don't you feel the days are going by while we keep aimlessly discussing things, not knowing where to begin? Don't you see, this way we'll drive ourselves to the point where one fine day we'll simply pounce on him, tear him apart? . . . We can't go on like that. We've got to think of something. And you know lately he's been so terribly alive. Is he stronger than we? Is he more alive than this, and this, and *this?*"

But she was right, oh, she was right! The old boy was aflame with rich life. He was young, his backhand was now as good as his forehand, his digestion was a dream, he would go to Brazil or Zanzibar next winter. Isolda was expensive and unfaithful but every once in a while he purged himself erotically with her in the pretty little flat he had rented for both of the sisters (Ida however had soon been whisked away to Dresden by a jealous lover); at a party given by the Commercial Consul of Luxembourg, tall Martha with her black silks, lovely shoulders and emerald ear pendants, had eclipsed all the other ladies. He had decided to conceal from her, until the proper moment, his special project, although it was true that on three or four occasions he had hinted at a new extraordinary undertaking. But then again how would he go about explaining to her what absorbed him. It was impossible. She would dismiss it as an inane whim. Mechanical mannequins indeed! What next, Pygmalion? You, Galatea. No, that was a hopeless line. She would say: "You're spending your time on rubbish." Yes, but what marvellous rubbish. He smiled at the thought that she too had her eccentricities. The iced rose water applied to her face at bed time. Those Hindukitsch gymnastics nearly every day. He ran his cane clatteringly along the pales of a fence. They were walking along the sunlit side of the street. His companion, the black-bearded Inventor, kept hinting that it might not be a bad idea to cross over to the other, shady, sidewalk. But Dreyer did not listen. If he enjoyed the sun, others were bound to enjoy it too. "It's still quite a long way," sighed his companion. "Are you quite sure you want to walk?" "With your permission," said Dreyer absentmindedly, and quickened his pace. What fun it was to be alive. At that moment, for example, this black-bearded genius was taking him to see something most amusing. If he were to stop a passer-by and ask him, "Try to guess, friend, what I'm on my way to see, and *why* I must see it?" The passer-by would never be able to answer. And, as if that were not enough, all those people in the street scurrying by, waiting at streetcar stops: what a bunch of secrets, astonishing professions, incredible recollections. That fellow, for instance, with the cane and the very English yellow mustache: who knows, perhaps during the war he had been assigned the dreary and preposterous task of transmuting for national use sundry elements of captured enemy uniforms; but after two years of it, the material had begun to dwindle, and he was sent to the front where he enjoyed the exhilaration of at least one good battle among the ruins of a village, once renowned for its hops and hogs, and then hostilities were suspended, and a last soldier was killed by a sack of declaration-of-peace leaflets dropped from an airplane. But why assign one's own memories to strangers? That old man there on the bench had been in his youth—oh, I don't know—perhaps, a celebrated acrobat; or that black-bearded foreigner, rather a dull companion between us be it said, had perhaps made a spectacular invention. Nothing was known, and anything was possible.

"To the right," said the dull companion, breathing heavily. "That building over there with the statues."

In an annex to the courthouse, the police had staged an exhibition of crime. One respectable burgher, who suddenly, for no good reason, had dismembered a neighbor's child, was found to have in his apartment an artificial woman. She could walk, wring her hands, and make water, and was now in that police museum. Impelled by professional anxiety, the Inventor wanted to take a look at her. They were led to her by a retired gendarme whom Dreyer bribed to make the mechanism work. The poor woman turned out to be rather crudely made, and the mysterious substance of which the papers had spoken was, thank God, only gutta-percha. Her power to move was also exaggerated. A clockwork device permitted her to close her glass eyes and spread her legs. They could be filled up with hot water. Her body hair was real, and so were the brown locks falling over her shoulders. All things considered, there was nothing new about her— merely a vulgar doll. The scornful and happy Inventor left at once but Dreyer, always afraid of missing something entertaining, strolled through all the rooms. He examined the faces of criminals, enlarged photographs of ears, messy fingerprints, kitchen knives, ropes, faded shreds of clothing, dusty jars, dirty test tubes—a thousand trivial articles that had been wronged—and again rows of photographs, the pasty faces of unwashed, badly dressed murderers, and the puffy faces of their victims who in death came to resemble them; and it was all so shabby, so stupid, that Dreyer could not help smiling. He was thinking what a talentless person one must be, what a poor thinker or hysterical fool, to murder one's neighbor. The deathly gray of the exhibits, the banality of crime, pieces of bourgeois furniture, a frightened little console on which a bloody imprint had been found, hazel nuts injected with strychnine, buttons, a tin basin, again photographs—all this trash expressed the very essence of crime. How much those simpletons were missing! Missing not only the wonders of everyday life, the simple pleasure of existence, but even such instants as this, the ability to look with curiosity upon what was essentially boring. And then the final Bore: at dawn, breakfastless, pale, top-hatted city fathers driving to the execution. The weather is cold and foggy. What an ass one must feel in a top hat at five in the morning! The condemned man is led into the prison yard. The executioner's assistants plead with him to behave decently, and not to struggle. Ah, here's the axe. Presto—the audience is shown the severed head. What should a frock-coated burgher do when looking at it—give it a nod of commiseration, a frown of reproach, a smile of encouragement as if to say: "See, how simple and quick it all was"? Dreyer caught himself thinking that it might be interesting to wake up at the crack of dawn and, after a thorough shave and a hearty meal, go out in striped prison pajamas into the yard, touch the plump executioner's muscles with some appropriate joke, give the whole assembly a friendly wave of the hand, take a good last stare at the white official faces. . . . Yes, all those faces are uncommonly pale. Here, for example, is a young chap who chopped his parents to death: how big-eared and pimply he is. Here is a sullen gentleman who left a trunk at the station with his fiancée's corpse. And here's Dr. Guillotin's invention—oh, no, that's a medieval Swiss contraption of exactly the same type—board, wooden collar, two uprights, the blade between them. Monsieur Guillotin, you are an impostor! Ah, the American dentist's chair. The dentist is masked. The patient also has a mask with holes for the eyes. They slit his trouserleg at the calf to attach the electrode. Aha. The current is turned on. Hop-hop, as over a bumpy road. What dreary fools! A collection of idiotic faces and tormented objects.

It was lovely outside, a lush wind was blowing. The soles of passers-by left silver traces on the sun-glorified asphalt. How lovely, blue and fragrant, our Berlin is in the summer. It wouldn't be bad by the sea either. Those clouds are radiant —vacation clouds. Workmen lazily repairing the pavement. How good it all is. How amusing it would be, he thought, to search the faces of those workmen, of those passers-by, for the facial expressions he had just seen in countless photographs. And to his surprise, in everyone he met Dreyer recognized a criminal, past, present, or future; soon he was so carried away with this game that he began inventing a special crime for each. He watched a round-shouldered man with a suspicious suitcase; he went up to him and asked for a light. The man shook the ashes off his cigarette and made the commonplace little connection but Dreyer noticed how that hand trembled, and felt sorry that he could not reveal a detective's badge. Face after face slipped by, eyes avoided his, and even in plump, motherly housewives he distinguished the skeletons of murder. Thus he walked, spinning his cane like a propeller, having an exceptionally good time, grinning involuntarily at strangers, and noting with pleasure their momentary embarrassment. Then he grew tired of the game, felt hungry and thirsty, and quickened his step. As he drew near the gate, he noticed his wife and nephew in the garden. They were standing motionless side by side, watching him approach. And he felt a pleasant relief at seeing at last two familiar, two perfectly human faces.

11

"Please, my dear," said Willy Wald, "don't. You have already taken two stealthy looks at your wrist and then at your husband. Really, it's not late."

"And have some more strawberries," said Willy's wife.

Dreyer said: "We'll have to stay a while, my love. Because I can't remember my story."

"Please try to recall it," said Willy from the depths of his armchair.

". . . or some liqueur, perhaps," said Mrs. Wald in her tired, melodious, affected voice.

Dreyer pounded his forehead with his fist. "I've got the beginning and the middle. My emporium for the end!"

"Don't worry, it will come," said Willy. "If you go on worrying your wife will get even more bored. She's a strict lady. I'm afraid of her."

". . . at this time tomorrow we shall be on our way to Paris," said Mrs. Wald, gathering momentum, but her husband interrupted.

"She's taking me to Paris! I know it's a fizzy city, but it always gives me heartburn. Still I'm going, I'm going. By the way, you haven't told me of your own summer plans. I've heard of a fellow who could not remember a funny story and burst a blood vessel."

"It's not the fact that I can't remember it that hurts," Dreyer said plaintively. "What hurts is that I'll remember it the minute we part. No, we haven't decided yet. Isn't that so, my love? We haven't decided yet? In fact" (turning to Willy), "we haven't discussed it at all. I know she hates the Alps. Venice means nothing to her. It's all very difficult. There was a twist at the end, such an amusing one. . . ."

"Drop it, drop it," puffed Willy. "How come you haven't decided yet? It's the end of June. High time."

"Perhaps," said Dreyer with a quizzical glance at his wife, "perhaps we might go to the seaside."

"Water," nodded Willy. "Lots of blue water. That's good. So would I, with delight. But I'm being dragged off to Paris. I am a remarkably good diver, though you wouldn't believe it."

"I can't even swim," glumly answered Dreyer. "I'm no good at some sports. Same thing with skiing. I seem always to stay at the same point: the swing, the knack, the equipoise, just aren't there. I'm not sure those new skis were the right ones for me. My love, I know you hate the seaside but let's go there once more. We'll take Franz and Tom with us. We'll splash and puddle. And you'll go boating with Franz, and get as brown as milk chocolate."

And Martha smiled. Not that she realized whence came that breath of moist freshness. The magic lantern of fancy slipped a colored slide in—a long sandy beach on the Baltic where they had once been in 1924, a white pier, bright flags, striped booths, a thousand striped booths—and now they were thinning, they broke off, and beyond for many miles westward stretched the empty whiteness of the sands between heather and water. Water. What do you do to extinguish a fire? An infant could tell you that.

"We'll go to Gravitz," she said, turning to Willy.

She grew unusually animated. Her glossy lips parted. Her elongated eyes flashed like jewels. Two sickle-shaped dimples appeared on her flaming cheeks. Excitedly she began telling Elsa Wald about a little dressmaker (they are always "little") whom she had discovered. And ecstatically she praised Elsa's perfume. Dreyer, eating strawberries, watched her and rejoiced. She had simply never beamed and babbled so prettily when visiting the Walds ("they are your friends, not mine").

"We'll have to have a serious talk," she said on the way home. "Sometimes you do get good ideas. Look, tomorrow morning you write and reserve two adjacent rooms and a single one at the Seaview Hotel. But the dog we'll leave—it would only be a bother. You'd better make haste or there'll be no rooms left."

Being a little drunk, he glued himself to her warm nape. She pushed him away quite good-naturedly and said:

"I see you're not only a lecher but also a liar."

He suddenly looked worried. "What do you mean?"

"I thought," she said, "you told me—when was that? A year ago?—that you were taking lessons at the Freibad, and that you now swam like a fish."

"An inexcusable exaggeration," he answered, much relieved. "A very poor fish, really. I keep afloat for three meters, and then I sink like a log."

"Except that logs don't sink," said Martha merrily.

Make haste! But now haste was lighthearted. With waves and sunlight all around, how easy to breathe, to kill, to love. The single word "water" had resolved everything. Although

Martha knew nothing about mathematical problems and the pleasure of elegant proof, she recognized the solution of her problem at once by its simplicity and limpidity. This harmonious obviousness, this elementary grace made her ashamed—as well she might be—of her gropings and clumsy fancies. She felt an inordinate desire to see Franz that very minute, or at least to do something—to cable him the code word at once, but for the time being the message ran MIDNIGHT TAXI STOP RAIN GATE FRONT HALL STAIRS BEDROOM PLEASE STOP ALL RIGHT HURRY UP GOOD NIGHT. And tomorrow was Sunday—how do you like that! She had warned Franz that if the weather did not improve she would not go to see him because Dreyer would not be playing tennis. But even this delay, which once would have driven her into a rage, now seemed trifling in the light of her newfound confidence.

She woke up a little later than usual, and her first sensation was that the night before something exquisite had happened. On the terrace Dreyer had finished his coffee and was reading the newspaper. When she came down, radiant, wearing pale-green crepe, he rose and kissed her cool hand as he always did at their Sunday morning meetings, but this time he added to it a good-natured twinkle of gratitude. The silver sugar bowl blazed blindingly in the sun, dimmed slowly, and flamed forth again.

"Can the courts still be wet?" said Martha.

"I've telephoned," he answered, and went back to his paper. "They are soaked. An archeologist has found a tomb in Egypt with toys and blue thistles three thousand years old."

"Thistles are not blue," said Martha, reaching for the coffee pot. "Have you written about the rooms?"

He nodded without raising his eyes and went on nodding

[213]

even more gently as he read his paper, cheerfully reminding himself between the nods and the lines to dictate it tomorrow at the office.

Oh, keep nodding . . . keep playing the fool . . . it does not matter now. He's a first-rate swimmer—that's not tennis for you! She, too, was born on the banks of a big river, and could stay afloat for hours, for days, forever.

She used to lie on her back, and the water would lap and rock her, so delicious, so cool. And the bracing breeze penetrating you as you sat naked with a naked boy of your age among the forget-me-nots. These thoughts came without effort. She need not invent, she had only to develop what was already there in outline. How happy her darling would be! Should she ring him up and say only one word: *Wasser?*

Dreyer noisily folded his paper as if wrapping a bird in it and said: "Let's go and have a walk, eh? What do you say?"

"You go," she replied. "I have to write some letters. We must head off Hilda, you know."

He thought: what if I ask her, tenderly, tenderly. It's a free morning. We are lovers again.

But emotional energy had never been his forte, and he said nothing.

A minute later, Martha, from the terrace, saw him walk to the gate with his raincoat over his arm, open the wicket, let Tom pass first like a lady, and saunter off, lighting up a cigar as he went.

She sat motionless. The sugar bowl alternately blazed and dimmed. All at once a gray little spot appeared on the tablecloth; then another beside it. A drop fell on her hand. She rose, looking up. Frieda began hurriedly clearing away the dishes and the tablecloth, also glancing now and then at the sky. Thunder rumbled, and an astonished sparrow landed on the balustrade—and darted away. Martha went into the house. The door of the hallway toilet was banging. Frieda, already half-drenched, with the tablecloth in her embrace, laughing and muttering to herself, rushed from the terrace kitchenward. Martha stood at the center of the oddly dark parlor. Now everything outside was gurgling, murmuring, breathing. She wondered if she should first ring him up, but her impatience was too strong—the fuss with the telephone would be a waste of time. She put on her mackintosh with a rustling sound and snatched up an umbrella. Frieda brought her hat and handbag from the bedroom. "You ought to wait it out," said Frieda. "It's a regular deluge." Martha laughed and said she had quite forgotten an appointment at a café with Mrs. Bayader and another lady, an expert in rhythmic respiration ("Mixed respiration," Frieda, who knew more than she ought to have known, kept snorting every now and then the whole morning.) The rain began drumming on the taut silk of her umbrella. The wicket swung shut, splashing her hand. She walked quickly along the mirrory sidewalk, hurrying toward the taxi stand. The sun struck the long streams of rain causing them to slant, as it were, and presently they turned golden and mute. Again and again the sun struck, and the shattered rain now flew in single fiery drops, and the asphalt cast reflections of iridescent violet, and everything grew so bright and hot that wet-haired Dreyer shed his raincoat as he walked, and Tom, who was somewhat darker after the rain, perked up and marched on a brown dachshund. Tom and the dachshund circled in one spot, or rather Tom circled while the dackel turned abruptly in one piece every now and then, until Dreyer whistled. He walked slowly, looking right and left, trying to find the newly built cinema that Willy had mentioned the night before. He found himself in a district he had seldom visited although it was not far from his house. He turned into a park to give the dog more exercise and then cut across a piece of wasteland adjoining an unfamiliar boulevard. A little farther he crossed a square and saw at the corner of the next street a tall house bared of most of its scaffolding: its first story was ornamented with a huge picture, advertising the film to be shown on the opening night, July 15, based on Goldemar's play *King, Queen, Knave* which had been such a hit several years ago. The display consisted of three gigantic transparent-looking playing cards resembling stained-glass windows which would probably be very effective when lit up at night: the King wore a maroon dressing gown, the Knave a red turtleneck sweater, and the Queen a black bathing suit. "Must not forget to order those rooms tomorrow," reflected Dreyer, and another important note that the faithful Miss Reich would write over her signature: Dr. Eier must leave the city and to his great regret cannot continue to pay for the flat where you persist in receiving other idiots, or something along those lines.

He was about to turn back when Tom gave a short muffled bark and Franz came out of a little café wiping his mouth with his knuckles.

"Well, well, well, fancy running into you," exclaimed Dreyer. "Starting the day with a schnapps, eh?"

"My landlord has stopped serving me breakfast," said Franz. What a horrible encounter. Side by side they walked, eyed by luminous puddles.

They almost never had occasion to be alone together, and Dreyer now realized that they had absolutely nothing to talk about. It was an odd feeling. He tried to clarify it for himself. He saw Franz practically every other evening at his house but always in Martha's presence; Franz fitted naturally into those usual surroundings, occupying a place long since set aside for him, and Dreyer never spoke to him in any but a joking casual way seeking no information, and expressing no feeling, accepting Franz on trust amid the rest of the familiar objects and people, and interrupting with irrelevant remarks the silly and dull narratives that Franz vaguely directed at Martha. Dreyer was well aware of his own secret shyness, of his inability to have a frank, serious, heart-to-heart talk with a person whom ruthless chance confronted him with. Now he felt both apprehension and an urge to laugh at the silence that was being wedged between him and Franz. He had not the least idea what to do about it. Ask him where he was going? He cleared his throat and gave Franz a sidelong glance. Franz looked at the ground as he walked.

"Where are you going?" asked Dreyer.

"I live near here," said Franz with an indefinite gesture. Dreyer was looking at him not unkindly. Let him look, thought Franz. Everything in life is senseless, and this walk is senseless too.

"Fine, fine," said Dreyer. "I think I've never been here. I cut through a wilderness of kitchen gardens, and then suddenly there were half-built houses all around me. By the way, you know what—why don't you show me your apartment?"

Franz nodded. Silence. Presently he pointed to the right and both involuntarily quickened their step in order to accomplish at least one not wholly aimless act—a right turn. Tom, too, looked ennuied. He was not overfond of Franz.

"How stupid," thought Dreyer. "I must find something to tell him. We are not following a hearse." He wondered if he should not tell him about the electric mannequins. It might interest a young man. The subject in fact was so entertaining that he had to make quite an effort not to gush about it at home. Lately the Inventor had asked him not to visit the workshop, saying he wanted to prepare a surprise, and then the other day, looking very smug, he invited Dreyer to come. The sculptor who looked like a scientist and the professor who looked like an artist also seemed extremely pleased with themselves. Two young men from the store, Moritz and Max, could hardly hide their giggles. Pulling at a cord, the Inventor drew open a black curtain, also an innovation, and a pale dignified gentleman in dinner jacket, with a carnation in his buttonhole, walked out of the side door at the left, crossed the room at a lifelike though somewhat somnambulic gait, and left by the side door at the right. Behind the scenes he was seized by Moritz and Max, who changed his clothes while a youth in white, with a racket under his arm, wandered across the room in his turn and was immediately followed by somnambule number one, now wearing a gray suit with an elegant tie and carrying a briefcase. He dropped it absentmindedly before leaving the stage but Moritz retrieved it and followed him to the exit. Meanwhile the youth reappeared, now sporting a cherry-red blazer, and after him the older man, soberly clad in a raincoat, ambled along in his melancholy and mysterious dream.

Dreyer found the show absolutely entrancing: not only did those grandly trousered legs and properly shod feet move with a stylized grace that no mechanical toy had ever achieved before, but the two faces were fashioned with exquisite care in the same wax-like substance as the hands. And when vulgar young Max humorously impersonated the younger automannequin by stalking and prancing in his wake on the delightful youth's final appearance, none could doubt which of the two personages had more human charm, though one Inventor was so much more experienced than the other. Presently the mature gentleman came by for the last time, and at this point his creator had devised matters in such a way as to have the re-tuxedoed one (minus the carnation mislaid in some avatar) stop in mid-stage, jiggle his feet a little as if demonstrating a dance step, and then continue toward the exit with his arm crooked as if escorting an invisible lady. "Next time," said the Inventor, "a woman will be added. Beauty is easy to render because beauty is based on the rendering of beauty, but we are still working on her hips, we want her to roll them, and that is difficult."

But could one describe all this to Franz? Told in a jocular tone it would be of no interest, and if made serious, Franz might not believe it since Dreyer had pulled his leg too frequently in the past. All at once a saving thought flashed through his mind. Franz did not know yet that he was being invited to the seaside and of course should be told the good news; and simultaneously Dreyer recalled the end of the anecdote that had eluded him on the eve. First, though, he told him about the trip, saving the anecdote for the last. Franz mumbled that he was very grateful. Dreyer explained to him what to buy for the trip, charging everything to Uncle, *selbstverständlich!* Franz, reviving a little, thanked him again more eloquently.

"Are you thinking of marriage?" asked Dreyer (Franz made the gesture of a clown's stooge when presented with a conundrum). "Because I might find you a very amorous bride."

Franz grinned. "I'm too poor," he replied. "Perhaps if I got a raise."

"That's an idea," said Dreyer.

"We are almost there," said Franz, and almost fell over Tom, who had stopped.

Dreyer decided he would wait to tell his story—which was really an extremely funny one—until they were in Franz's room: certain vehement gestures and extravagant attitudes had to accompany the story. This was a fatal post-ponement. He never told it. They were now in front of the house where another good anecdote was in the process of what botanically minded folklorists call "exfoliating." Tom stopped again, looking up and then back. "March-march," said Dreyer, and with his knee pushed the intelligent hound.

"I live there," said Franz pointing at the fifth floor.

"Well, let's go in by all means," said Dreyer, and held the door open for Tom, who shot upstairs with a whimper of excitement.

"Good Lord, I must get him some other quarters. No nephew of mine should live in a slum," reflected Dreyer, as he climbed the stairs whose meager carpeting disappeared at an elevation well below timberline. While they climbed Martha had time to finish darning a last hole. She was sitting on the dear decrepit couch leaning over her work, her lips puckering and moving in a happy domestic pout. The land-lord had said that Franz would be back in a moment. He had popped out to eat a bigger breakfast than a sick old woman could prepare. Martha got up to return the socks to their drawer. She was already wearing the emblematic slip-pers and had laid out the little rubber basin coquettishly covered with a clean towel. She stopped in a half-bent atti-tude holding her breath. "He's here," she thought and gave a blissful sigh. Then a strange patter of nonhuman footfalls came along the corridor; a horribly familiar bark rang out. "Quiet, Tom, behave yourself," said Dreyer's cheerful voice. "Third door on your right," said Franz's voice. Martha made for the door in order to turn the key in the lock. The key was on the other side. "Here?" asked Dreyer, and the handle moved. She braced her whole body against the door, holding the handle with her strong hand. The key was heard to turn this way and that. Tom was ardently sniffing under the door.

The handle attempted to jerk again. There were now two men against her. She slipped and lost a slipper, which had happened already in another life. "What's the matter?" said Dreyer's voice. "Your door doesn't open." Her efficient lover was helping to press on the door. "Two idiots," thought Martha coldly, and started to slide again. She heaved with her shoulder and forced it shut. Franz was muttering: "I don't understand it at all. Maybe it's some joke of my landlord's." Tom was barking his head off. He shall be destroyed tomorrow. Dreyer was chuckling and advising Franz to call the police. "Let's kick it in," he said. Martha felt she could not hold the door any longer. Suddenly there was silence, and in the silence a squeaky querulous voice uttered the magic anti-sesame: "Your girl is in there."

Dreyer turned. An old man in a dressing gown, clutching a kettle, was shaking his shaggy gray head at the young imbecile who had covered his face with his hands. Tom was sniffing at the old man. Dreyer burst out laughing and, dragging the dog by the collar, started to walk away. Franz accompanied him to the hallway, and tripped over a pail. "Aha, that's what you're up to," said Dreyer. He winked, nudged Franz in the solar plexus, and went out. Tom looked back—and then followed his master. Franz, wooden-faced and a bit unsteady on his feet, returned along the corridor and opened the now unresisting door. Rosy, dishevelled, panting, as though after a fight, Martha was looking for her slippers.

Impetuously she embraced Franz. Beaming and laughing, she kissed him on the lips, on the nose, on his spectacles, then sat him down beside her on the bed, gave him a drink of water, he rocked limply, and dropped his head in her lap; she stroked his hair and softly, soothingly, explained to him the only, the liquid, the resplendent solution.

She was home before her husband, and when he arrived, and Tom trotted up to her, she gave the dog a withering derisive look.

"Listen," said Dreyer, "our little Franz—no, just imagine—" he spluttered and shook his head for a long time until he finally told her. The image of his somber and awkward nephew fondling a big, hefty sweetheart was unspeakably comic. He recalled Franz hopping on one foot in soiled underpants and his mirth increased. "I think you're simply envious," said Martha, and he tried to hug her.

The very next time Franz came to supper his clever uncle began poking fun at him. Martha kicked her husband under the table. "My dear Franz," said Dreyer, moving out of her shoe's range, "perhaps you don't feel like going away to a distant shore, perhaps you are perfectly happy in town. You can speak frankly. After all I was young myself."

Or else he would turn to Martha and casually observe: "You know, I've hired a private detective. His job is to see that my clerks lead an ascetic life, do not drink, do not gamble, and especially do not—" Here he pressed his fingers to his lips as if he had said too much, and glanced at his victim. "Of course I'm joking," he continued in mock confusion, and added in a thin artificial voice, as if changing the subject: "What lovely weather we're having."

Only a few days remained before the scheduled departure. Martha was so happy, so calm, that nothing could now affect her very deeply: her husband's witticisms would soon end as would everything else—his cigar, his eau de cologne, his shadow with the shadow of a book on the white terrace. One thing only—the fact that the director of the Seaview Hotel had had the impudence to take advantage of the vacational influx and demand a colossal price for the rooms—only this could still perturb her. It was certainly a pity that

Dreyer's removal would be so expensive—especially now, when they had to save every penny because before you knew it he could in those last few days lose, she said, his entire fortune. Some grounds for such apprehension did exist. But at the same time she experienced a certain odd satisfaction at the thought that now, at the very moment when he was to die under her supervision, Dreyer seemed to have exhausted the brilliant business imagination, the gift of daring enterprise, thanks to which he had prepared a fortune to leave to his not ungrateful widow.

She did not know·that paradoxically, at that period of decline and indolence, Dreyer had quietly started on the very expensive affair of the automannequins. Question: Were they not too glamorous, too extravagant, too original and luxurious, for the needs of a stodgy bourgeois store in Berlin? On the other hand, he did not doubt one minute that the invention would fetch a spectacular price if one could dazzle and enchant the prospective buyer. Mr. Ritter, an American businessman who had the knack of making fancy stuff work for him, was soon to arrive. I'll sell it, reflected Dreyer. Wouldn't mind selling the whole store as well.

Secretly he realized that he was a businessman by accident and that *his* fantasies were not salable. His father had wanted to be an actor, had been a make-up man in a travelling circus, had tried to design theatrical scenery, wonderful velvet costumes, and had ended as a moderately successful tailor. In his boyhood Kurt had wanted to be an artist—any kind of artist—but instead had spent many dull years working in his father's shop. The greatest artistic satisfaction he ever derived was from his commercial ventures during the inflation. But he knew quite well that he would appreciate even more other arts, other inventions. What prevented him from seeing the world? He had the means—but there was some fatal veil between him and every dream that beckoned to him. He was a bachelor with a beautiful marble wife, a passionate hobbyist without anything to collect, an explorer not knowing on what mountain to die, a voracious reader of unmemorable books, a happy and healthy failure. Instead of arts and adventures, he meanly contented himself with a suburban villa, with a humdrum vacation at a Baltic resort —and even that thrilled him as the smell of a cheap circus used to intoxicate his gentle bumbling father.

That little trip to Pomerania Bay was in fact proving to be quite a boon for everybody concerned, including the god of chance (Cazelty or Sluch, or whatever his real name was), once you imagined that god in the role of a novelist or a playwright, as Goldemar had in his most famous work. Martha was getting ready for the seaside with systematic and blissful zest. Lying on Franz's breast, sprawling all over him, strong and heavy, and a little sticky from the heat, she whispered into his mouth and ear that his torments would be soon allayed. She purchased—not at her husband's store— oh, no—various festive fripperies, a black bathing suit, a beachrobe zigzagged with blue and green, flannel slacks, a new camera, and a lot of bright clothes, which, she chided herself with a smile, was reckless since she would be so soon in mourning. Dreyer depended on the emporium for a tremendous beach ball and a new type of water wings.

She wrote to her sister Hilda, who had tentatively suggested they all spend summer together, that this year plans were uncertain, they might go for a few days to the seaside, or again they might not, she would write if they did and found they wanted to stay longer. She permitted Frieda to remain in the attic but forbade her to receive visitors there. She told the gardener that hysterical Tom had bitten her, that she did not wish to upset her husband, but that she wanted the beast to be put quickly to sleep as soon as they left for Gravitz. The gardener seemed about to demur, but she pushed a fifty-mark note into his honest, caterpillar-stained claw, and the old soldier shrugged his consent.

On the eve of their departure she inspected all the rooms of the villa, furniture, dishes, pictures, whispering to herself and to them that in a very short time she would return, she would return free and happy. That day Franz showed her a letter from his mother. The woman wrote that Emmy would be getting married in a year. "In a year," smiled Martha, "in a year, my darling, another wedding will be taking place too. Come on, cheer up, stop picking your navel. Everything is fine."

They were meeting for the last time in the shabby room which already had an apprehensive unnatural look as happens when a furnished room parts with its tenant forever. Martha had already taken the red slippers home with her and hidden them in a trunk but she did not quite know what to do with the doilies, the two pretty cushions, and the dainty implementa so full of memories. With a heavy heart she advised Franz to wrap it all up and mail it to his sister as a thoughtful wedding present. The little room was aware it was being talked about and was assuming a more and more strained expression. The lewd bidders were appraising the big-nippled bronze-bangled slave girl for the last time. The pattern on the wallpaper—bouquets of blood-brown flowers in a regular succession of repeated variations—arrived at the door from three directions but then there was no further place to go, and they could not leave the room, just as human thoughts, admirably coordinated though they may be, cannot escape the confines of their private circle of hell. Two suitcases stood in a corner, one brand-new in brown leatherette, with its pretty little key still attached to the grip, a sweetheart's gift; the other, a black fibrous affair, bought a year ago at a market stall, and still quite usable except that one lock would sometimes fly open without provocation. All that had been brought into this room, or had accumulated there in the course of ten months, disappeared in those two suitcases which were to depart on the morrow—forever.

That last night Franz did not go out for supper. He closed the empty chest-of-drawers, looked around, opened the window, and seated himself with his feet on the ledge. He must somehow get through this night. The best thing was not to move, not to think, to sit and listen to the far-off automobile horns, to gaze at the blue ink of the sky, at a distant balcony where a lamp glowed under its orange shade, and two happy, innocent, carefree people were playing chess, bent over the bright oasis of the happy table. That third of a man's consciousness, the imaginable future, had ceased to exist for Franz except as a dark cage full of monstrous tomorrows huddled up in an amorphous heap. What had struck Martha as the first realistic, logical solution of all their problems had all but dealt the last blow to his sanity. It would be as she had said—or would it? A flutter of panic brushed his heart. Maybe it was not yet too late. . . . Maybe he should write to his mother, or to his sister and her fiancé to come and take him away. Last Sunday fate had almost saved him, it might save him again, yes—send a telegram home, come down with typhus, or perhaps lean forward a little and slip into the ever-ready embrace of greedy gravity. But the flutter passed. It would be as she had said.

Barefoot, coatless, he sat there a long time hugging his knees without moving, without changing the position of his thighs, even though a knob on the ledge hurt him and a humming mosquito was preparing to strike at his temple. It was by now quite dark in the doomed room, but there was nobody to turn on the light and there would never be anybody if he fell off the sill. On the distant balcony the chess game had long since ended. One by one, or by twos and even threes, all the windows had grown dark. Presently he felt stiff and cold, and slowly clambered back into the room and went to bed. Sometime after midnight the landlord passed noiselessly along the corridor. He checked if there was a slit of light under Franz's door, listened with bent head, and went back to his room. He knew perfectly well that there was no Franz behind the door, that he had created Franz with a few deft dabs of his facile fancy. Yet the jest had to be brought to some natural conclusion. It would be silly to have a figment of one's imagination using up expensive electricity or trying to open a jugular vein with a razor. Besides, old Enricht was getting bored with this particular creature of his. It was time to dispose of him, and replace him with a new one. One sweep of his thought arranged the matter: let this be the fictitious lodger's last night; let him go tomorrow morning—leaving the usual insolent mess as they all do. He postulated, therefore, that tomorrow was the first of the month, that the lodger himself wished to leave—that, in fact, he had paid what he owed. Everything now was in order. Thus, having invented the necessary conclusion, old Enricht, alias Pharsin, dragged up in retrospect and added to it in a lump that which in the past must have led up to this conclusion. For he knew perfectly well—had known for the last eight years at least—that the whole world was but a trick of his, and that all those people—eight former lodgers, doctors, policemen, garbage collectors, Franz, Franz's lady friend, the noisy gentleman with the noisy dog, and even his own, Pharsin's, wife, a quiet little old lady in a lace cap, and he himself, or rather his inner roommate, an elder companion, so to speak, who had been a teacher of mathematics eight years ago, owed their existence to the power of his imagination and suggestion and the dexterity of his hands. In fact, he himself could at any moment turn into a mousetrap, a mouse, an old couch, a slave girl led away by the highest bidder. Such magicians should be made emperors.

The waking hour struck. With a scream, shielding his head with his arms, Franz leapt off the bed and rushed to the door; there he stopped, trembling, looking around myopically, already aware that nothing special had happened, that it was seven a.m. on a hazy, tender, melting morning with its hullabaloo of sparrows and an express train that was to leave in an hour and a half.

He had slept in his day shirt and had sweated profusely. His clean linen was already packed and anyway it was not worth the trouble of changing. The washstand was bare except for the thin relic of what had been a beige cake of violet-scented soap. He spent a long time scraping up with his fingernail a hair that was stuck to the soap; the hair would assume a different curve but refuse to come off. Dry soap collected under his fingernails. He started to wash his face. That single hair now stuck to his cheek, then to his neck, then tickled his lip. The day before he had packed the landlord's towel. He paused pondering—and dried himself with a corner of the bed sheet. There was no point in shaving. His hairbrush was packed but he had a pocket comb. His scalp felt scaly and itched. He buttoned up his wrinkled shirt. Never mind. Nothing mattered. Trying to ignore loathsome contacts, he attached his soft collar, which immediately grasped him around the neck like a cold compress. A broken fingernail caught in the silk of his tie. His second-best trousers, which had lain where they had been shed, at the foot of the bed, had gathered some nameless fluff. The clothes brush was packed. The ultimate disaster occurred while he was putting on his shoes: a shoelace broke. He had to suck the tip and ease it into its hole with the result that two short ends were diabolically difficult to make into a knot. Not only animals, but so-called inanimate objects, feared and hated Franz.

At last he was ready. He put on his wristwatch and pocketed the alarm clock. Yes, it was time to leave for the station. He donned his raincoat and hat, responded with a shudder to his reflection in the mirror, picked up the suitcases, and, bumping against the doorjamb as if he were a clumsy passenger in a speeding train, went out into the corridor. The remnants of his physical self that he left behind were a little dirty water at the bottom of the wash basin and a full chamber pot in the middle of the room.

He stopped in the passage, stunned by an unpleasant thought: good manners bade him take leave of old Enricht. He put down the suitcases and knocked hurriedly at the landlord's bedroom door. No answer. He pushed the door and stepped in. The old woman whose face he had never seen sat with her back to him in her usual place. "I'm leaving; I want to say good-by," he said, advancing toward the armchair. There was no old woman at all—only a gray wig stuck on a stick and a knitted shawl. He knocked the whole dusty contraption to the floor. Old Enricht came out from behind a screen. He was stark naked and had a paper fan in his hand. "You no longer exist, Franz Bubendorf," he said dryly, indicating the door with his fan.

Franz bowed and went out without a word. On the stairs he felt dizzy. Setting down his load on a step, he stood clutching the banister. Then he bent over it as over a ship's side and was noisily and hideously sick. Weeping, he collected his valises, re-clicked the reluctant lock. As he proceeded downstairs, he kept meeting various traces of his misadventure. At last the house opened, let him out, and closed again.

12

The main thing of course was the sea: grayish blue, with a blurred horizon, immediately above which a series of cloudlets glided single-file as if along a straight groove, all alike, all in profile. Next came the curve of the bathing beach with its army of striped booth-like shelters, clustering especially densely at the root of the pier which stretched far out amid a flock of rowboats for hire. If one looked from the Seaview Hotel, the best at Gravitz, one could catch now and then one of the booths suddenly leaning forward and crawling over to a new location, like a red-and-white scarab. On the land side of the beach ran a stone promenade, bordered by locust trees on whose black trunks, after the rain, snails would come to life and stick out of their round shells a pair of sensitive yellow little horns that made no less sensitive Franz's flesh creep. Still farther inland came in a row the facades of lesser hotels, pensions, souvenir shops. The balcony of the Dreyers acted the hotel's name. Franz's room sulkily faced a town street parallel to the promenade. Beyond that stretched the second-class hotels, then another parallel lane with the third-class accommodations. The further from the sea the cheaper they grew as if the sea were a stage and they, rows of seats. Their names attempted in one way or another to suggest the sea's presence. Some of them did it with matter-of-fact pride, others preferred metaphors and symbols. Here and there occurred feminine names such as "Aphrodite" to which no boarding house could really live up. There was one villa that either in irony or owing to a topographical error called itself Helvetia. As the distance from the beach increased, the names grew more and more poetical. Then abruptly they gave up and became Central Hotel, Post Hotel, and the inevitable Continental. Hardly anybody hired any of the poor boats near the pier, and no wonder. Dreyer, a wretched sailor, could not imagine how he or any other tourist would care to go out rowing on that desolate expanse of water, when there were so many other things to do at the seaside. For instance? Well, sunbathing; but the sun was a little cruel to the russet of his skin. Sitting around in cafés was not unpleasant although it could be overdone too. There was the Blue Terrace café where the pastry, he thought, was so good. The other day as they were having ice chocolate there, Martha counted at least three foreigners among the crowd. One, judging by his newspaper, was a Dane. The other two were a less easily determinable pair: the girl was trying in vain to attract the attention of the café cat, a small black animal sitting on a chair and licking one hind paw rigidly raised like a shouldered club. Her companion, a suntanned fellow, smoked and smiled. What language were they speaking? Polish? Esthonian? Leaning near them against the wall was some kind of net: a bag of pale-bluish gauze on a ring fixed to a rod of light metal.

"Shrimp catchers," said Martha. "I want shrimps for dinner tonight." (She clicked her front teeth.)

"No," said Franz. "That's not a fisherman's net. That's for catching mosquitoes."

"Butterflies," said Dreyer, lifting an index finger.

"Who wants to catch butterflies?" remarked Martha.

"Oh, it must be good sport," said Dreyer. "In fact, I think to have a passion for something is the greatest happiness on earth."

"Finish your chocolate," said Martha.

"Yes," said Dreyer. "I think it's fascinating, the secrets you find in most ordinary people. That reminds me: Piffke—yes, yes, fat pink Piffke—collects beetles and is a famous expert on them."

"Let's go," said Martha. "Those arrogant foreigners are staring at you."

"Let's go for a good ramble," suggested Dreyer.

"Why don't we hire a boat?" said Martha for a change.

"Count me out," said Dreyer.

"Anyway, let's go somewhere else," said Martha.

As she passed the cat's chair, she tilted it and said "Shoo," and the cat, magically four-legged again, slipped off the seat and vanished.

Dreyer strolled off alone, leaving his wife and nephew on another terrace. This was the second or third tour he was making of the local display windows. Immemorial souvenirs. Picture postcards. The most frequent object of their derision was human obesity and its necessary opposite, Herr and Frau Matchshin of Hungerburg. A monstrous bottom in bathing tights was being pinched by a red crab (resurrected from the boiled), but the nipped lady beamed, thinking it was the hand of an admirer. A red dome above the water was the belly of a fat man floating on his back. There was a "Kiss at Sunset," emblemized by a pair of huge pygal-shaped impressions left on the sand. Skinny, spindle-legged husbands in shorts accompanied pumpkin-bosomed wives. Dreyer was touched by the many photographs going back to the preceding century: the same beach, the same sea, but women in broad-shouldered blouses and men in straw hats. And to think that those over-dressed kiddies were now businessmen, officials, dead soldiers, engravers, engravers' widows.

A sea breeze made the awnings clack. Little bags of pink muslin were crammed with seashells—or was it hard candy? A barometer in the image of a gents' and ladies' lavatory with different sexes emerging according to differences in the weather engaged for a while his awed attention. A second-rate store of men's clothes advertised a liquidation sale. Local seascapists depicted storm-tossed ships, foam-spattered rocks, and the reflection of a yellow moon in an indigo sea. And for no particular reason Dreyer suddenly felt very sad.

Weaving his way among the ramparts of sand that surrounded each bather's ephemeral domain, hurrying to nowhere in order to prove by a great show of haste how much his merchandise was in demand, an itinerant photographer, ignored by the lazy crowd, walked with his camera, yelling into the wind: "The artist is coming! The divinely favored, *der gottbegnadete* artist is coming!"

On the threshold of a shop that sold only Oriental wares—silks, vases, idols (who needed all that at the seaside?)—stood an ordinary untanned little man who followed with his dark eyes the promenaders as he waited in vain for a customer. Whom did he resemble? Yes, poor old Sarah's sick husband.

In the café where he presently joined our two farcical schemers, Martha was brought the wrong pastry and flew into a rage; for a long time she called to the overworked waiter, a mere boy, while the pastry (a splendid cream-oozing éclair) lay on its plate, lonely, despised, unwanted.

Less than a week had passed, and several times already that tender melancholy had come over Dreyer. True, he had experienced it before ("the melting heart of an egotist," Erica had once called it, adding: "You can hurt people or humiliate them, you are touched not by the blind man but by his dog"); but of late the melancholy had become less tender, or the tenderness more demanding. Perhaps it was the sun that had softened him up or maybe he was growing old, losing maybe something, and coming to resemble in some obscure way the pictureman whose services no one wanted and whose cry the children mocked.

When he went to bed that night he could not go to sleep —an unusual occurrence. On the previous day the sun, under the pretense of a caress, had so mutilated his back that he yearned for a spell of dull weather. They had been playing plop-catch, standing in the water up to their hips, Martha, Franz, two other young men, one of them a dancing instructor, the other a college student, the son of a Leipzig furrier. The dancing instructor had knocked Franz's blue glasses off with the ball, and the glasses had nearly drowned. Afterwards Franz and Martha had swum far out. He had stood and watched from the beach, cursing his lack of buoyancy. He borrowed a telescope from a kind ten-year-old stranger and for quite a while had kept an envious round eye on the two dark heads bobbing side by side in their blue safe round world. As soon as his back healed, he thought, he would start to take lessons in the hotel pool. Ouch, really burns! Impossible to find a painless position. Wooing sleep, he lay with closed eyes and saw the circular moat they had been digging to make their beach booth stand more cozily; he saw the tensed hairy leg of Franz digging nearby; then, the impossibly bright page of the verse anthology he had tried to read as he lay in the sun. Oh, how it burns! Martha had promised it would get well tomorrow, definitely, would never hurt again. Yes, of course, the skin would grow stronger. Skin or no skin, I must win that bet tomorrow. Silly bet. Women can measure distances in centimeters, up skirts and down sleeves, but not leagues of water or miles of sand, or the upright glare of a door ajar. He turned over to the wall and in order to put himself asleep (not realizing how drowsy he was already despite the upright glare now between his shoulders) he began to repeat in his mind their sunset walk to Rockpoint. She liked bets and boats. She had maintained that a rowing-boat would make it faster there than a man on foot—even a man whose back burned in each of the four positions. He re-assumed the initial one, facing her door, and started to walk westward again but this time alone—she was in the other bedroom, and had not yet put out her light. If one walked westward with the slit of the sun in one's eyes along the bay after leaving the populated part of the beach, one found that the sandy strip between the heath on your left and the sea on your right gradually narrowed until your progress was stopped by an agony of jumbled rocks. I think I shall turn . . . good God. . . .

If instead of following the concave brink of the bay one takes a concentric path slightly inland as I am doing now, Rockpoint is reachable, I think, in twenty minutes or less, let us rearrange our left arm . . . how much more comfortable a limbless sleeper would be . . . and here is that path leading west from the poor back of the hotel. I traverse a hamlet and continue through a beech grove for a couple of kilometers. How quiet, how soft. . . . He stopped to rest on a bed in the grove but then gave a start and again saw the vertical line of burning pain.

He continued his wager walk. Oh, he must hurry. Or was

his pedometer slow? Or was that aspirin working at last? He emerged from the woods into heather, and presently the path, turning right, with a change of pillow, joined the coastline again at the spur called Rockpoint. Here one could stop and wait for the absurd little boat with Martha rowing like mad and enjoy the view. He enjoyed the view. He heard himself emitting a hippopotamian snore and regained consciousness. Rockpoint was a lonely little promontory, but she would come to one's bed if one won the bet. On one's right. . . . He rolled onto his right side and stopped hearing his heart. That's better. Aspirin comes from *sperare, speculum, spiegel*. Now he could see the sweep of the beach parallel to the trail one had followed, and followed, and followed. That shimmer over there, beyond a tiny rocky island, three kilometers east as the acrobat flies, was our stretch of the Gravitz beach with the sugar lumps of hotels. The little black boat with Martha in black evening dress, her eardrops blazing, had to skirt of course that little black island on the outside but otherwise geometrically speaking the seaway was shorter, the string of the bow, the sting of the bay, though even so, even a weary walker. . . .

When finally her husband's snore found a permanent rhythm, Martha got up, closed the door, and went back to her uncomfortable bed—it was much too soft and too far from the window which was open: beyond, there rose a steady soft incessant noise as if the black garden were a bath being run. Alas, it was not the sounding sea but the rain. Never mind, rain or no rain. Let him take an umbrella.

She put out the light, but it was no use trying to sleep. She stepped with Franz into the fatal bark, and he rowed her to the promontory. The process that had put her husband to sleep kept her awake. The rustle of the rain mingled with the buzz in her ears. Two hours passed—it was a much longer journey than anybody could have expected. She picked up her watch from the bed table and pondered its phosphorescent information. The sun was still in Siberia.

At half past seven Franz stirred. He had been told to get up at exactly half past seven. It was exactly half past seven. A baker in the encyclopedia who had poisoned an entire parish told the prison barber who was shaving his neck that never in his life had he slept so well. Franz had slept nine hours. His own contribution to the murder was up to now an accurate calculation of the distance to Rockpoint by land and by sea. The victim had to be there a few minutes before the boat arrived. He would be dead tired and grateful to be ferried back.

Franz opened his window, which faced south with no sea to view, but at least it revealed a small balcony one story lower on which on three consecutive afternoons at the siesta hour he had watched the spread-eagled barmaid sunning herself on a towel. The floor of the balcony was darkly damp. It might dry in time for her siesta if the sun came out before noon. "By this evening it will all be over," he reflected mechanically and was unable to imagine either that evening or the following day, as one is unable to imagine eternity.

Gritting his teeth he pulled on his clammy bathing trunks. The pockets of his robe were full of sand. He softly closed the door behind him and set out along the long white corridors. There was sand also in the toes of his canvas shoes, producing there a blunt blind sensation. His uncle and aunt were already sitting on their balcony having coffee. It was a sunless day, with a white sky, a gray sea, and a cheerless breeze. Aunt Martha poured Franz some coffee. She was also wearing her robe over a bathing suit. Green designs ran across the fluffy dark blue. She held back the broad sleeve with her free hand as she passed the cup to Franz.

Dreyer in blazer and flannel pants was reading the resort's guest list, occasionally pronouncing aloud a funny name. He had intended to wear a delicate pale-lemon Chinese tie that had cost fifty marks but Martha said it looked like rain and the tie would be ruined. So he had put on another, an old lavender one. In such trifles Martha usually was right. Dreyer drank two cups of coffee and enjoyed a roll with delicious transparent honey trickling over the edges. Martha drank three cups and did not eat anything. Franz had half a cup and ate nothing either. The wind swept across the balcony.

"Professor Klister of Swister," read Dreyer. "Sorry. Lister of Swistok."

"If you're finished, let's go," said Martha.

"Blavdak Vinomori," read Dreyer triumphantly.

"Let's go," said Martha, wrapping her robe around her and trying to keep her teeth from chattering. "Before it starts raining again."

"It's so early, my love," he drawled, casting a furtive glance at the plate of rolls. "Why does nobody at home ever give butter that curly shape?"

"Let's go," repeated Martha, rising. Franz got up also. Dreyer looked at his golden watch.

"I'll beat you anyway," he said gleefully. "You two go on ahead. I'll give you fifteen minutes. I could spare even more."

"Fine," said Martha.

"We'll see who wins," said Dreyer.

"We'll see," said Martha.

"Your oars or my calves," said Dreyer.

"Let me through, I can't get out," she exclaimed sharply, pushing with her knee and still fumbling at her robe.

Dreyer moved his chair, she passed.

"My back is much better," he said, "but Franz is seasick or something."

Franz, without looking at him, shook his head. With sunglasses over his usual spectacles and his bright red robe he looked like Blavdak Vinomori should look.

"Don't get drowned, Blavdak," said Dreyer and began his second roll.

The glass door closed. Chewing, and sucking his honey-smeared fingers, Dreyer considered with disapproval the big pale sea. A bit of beach was visible from the balcony, with its striped shelter boxes untidily scattered and slightly askew. He did not envy the hardy bathers. The spot where one rented boats was a little farther to the west, near the pier, and could not be seen from the balcony. An old man dressed like an opera captain let them. How chilly, soggy, and uninteresting everything was without the sun. Never mind. It would be a brisk bracing walk. As in the old days, the very old days, Martha had agreed to play with him a little and had not refused at the last minute because of the bad weather as he had secretly feared.

He looked again at his watch. Yesterday and the day before his office had called precisely at this time. Today, more than likely, Sarah would telephone again. He would call her back later. It was not worth waiting.

He wiped his lips firmly, brushed the crumbs off his lap, and went to the bathroom. That cold shower had been agony but now he felt fine. He paused before the mirror and ran his little silver brush right and left over his English mustache. His German nose was peeling. Not very attractive. A knock at the door.

The office had managed to catch him. Dreyer, beating his pocket, hurried to the telephone. The talk was brief. He wavered—should he take an umbrella—decided he would not and went out by the back entrance.

The two young fellows whom they had met yesterday were sitting sideways on a bench playing chess. Both held their legs crossed. White had his hand ensconced between the knee of the left leg and the calf of the other leg and dangled his right foot slightly. Black's arms were folded on his breast. Their gaze left the board as they greeted Dreyer. He stopped for a moment and gaily warned White that Black's knight was planning to attack White's king and queen with a forked check. Martha, who loved bets but thought them undignified, had asked him not to tell anybody about their little rendezvous at Rockpoint, so he said nothing about it and went on his way. "Old idiot," muttered Black, whose position was desperate.

Dreyer followed a boulevard of sorts, then a path, then walked through the hamlet where he observed that the bus to Swistok was leaving the post office and looked at his watch. It would catch the express to Berlin. As he turned right to rejoin the coastline, he glimpsed the sea and saw the speck of a boat in the blurry distance. He thought he distinguished two bright bathrobes but was not sure, and, quickening his step almost to a trot, entered the beechwood.

Franz rowed in silence, now grimly lowering his face, then in a sweep of despair turning it skyward. Martha sat at the helm. Before renting the boat, she had gone in the water for a minute, thinking it would warm her up. That had been a mistake. The sun that had made a half-promise had not kept it. The cold wet suit now stuck to her chest, hips, and sides. She was too excited and happy to pay much attention to such trifles. A delightfully compliant mist veiled the receding beach. The boat started to round the little rocky island where seagulls were the only witnesses. The oarlocks creaked ponderously.

"You don't want to ask anything, you remember everything, darling?"

Leaning forward on the back stroke, Franz nodded. And again stared at the empty sky as he pushed the resilient water.

". . . when I say, only when I say—remember?"

Another grim nod.

"Let us go over it quickly—all right? You remain in the bow—"

The oarlocks creaked, an inquisitive gull circled over them, a wave lifted the boat to inspect it. Franz bowed in answer. He tried not to look at his insane aunt but whether he stared at the damp bottom of the boat along which lay a second pair of oars or followed the happy seagull with his eyes, he nevertheless perceived Martha with his entire being and saw, even without looking, her rubber cap, her broad-jawed dreadful face, her shaven shins, her heavy coronation robes. And he knew exactly how it would all be, how Martha would cry out the password, how both rowers would stand up to change places . . . the boat would rock . . . not easy to get past each other . . . careful . . . one more step . . . nearer . . . now!

". . . remember—just one big push, with your whole body," said Martha, and he slowly bent forward again.

"You must send him flying out, toppling in, face forward, and then you row like hell."

Now a chill breeze was penetrating her body with dampness and yet the elation persisted. She gazed intently at the in-curved shore, at its fringe of forest, at the mauve stretch of heather, searching for the place, near a pointed rock, where they were to land. She saw it. She pulled taut the left rope of the rudder.

Franz, as he swung backwards with a soundless moan, heard Martha laugh hoarsely, cough, clear her throat, cough, and laugh again. A sizable wave took possession of the boat. He stopped rowing for a moment. The sweat trickled down his temples in spite of the cold. Martha rose and fell with the wave's motion, shivering, aged beyond belief, her gray face shining like rubber.

She was watching a tiny dark figure that had suddenly appeared on the deserted strip of jutting land.

"Quicker," she said, trembling and plucking at the icy-cold clinging bathing suit as if it were a sheet, and she dying. "Oh, please! He's waiting."

Franz laid down the oars, slowly took off both pairs of glasses, slowly wiped the lenses of both on the flap of his robe.

"I told you to hurry!" she shouted. "You don't need those silly sunglasses. Franz, do you hear?"

He put the sunglasses into the pocket of his robe. He raised the other pair skyward. He looked through the lenses at the clouds; then he slowly put them on and took up the oars again.

The dark little figure became more distinct and acquired a face like a grain of maize. Martha was moving her torso back and forth, perhaps repeating Franz's movements, perhaps trying to speed up the boat.

Now the blue jacket and gray pants were distinguishable. He stood with his feet planted apart and his arms akimbo.

"This is the critical moment," said Martha, already speaking in a whisper. "He will never get into a boat if he does not now. Try to look more cheerful."

She was twisting the end of the rudder ropes in her hands. The shore was drawing near.

Dreyer stood looking at them and smiling. In his palm he held a flat gold watch. He had arrived eight minutes ahead of them, eight whole minutes. The boat was called "Lindy." Cute.

"Welcome," he said, putting the watch back in his pocket.

"You must have run all the way," said Martha, breathing heavily and glancing around.

"Nothing of the sort. Took it easy. Even stopped to rest along the way."

She continued her survey. Sand, rocks, and further on, heathery slopes and woods. Not a soul, not a dog ever came here.

"Get into the boat," she said.

Lapping little waves jolted the boat ever so slightly. Franz was listlessly fussing with the second pair of oars.

Dreyer said: "Oh, I'll return the same way. It's wonderful in the woods. I made friends with a squirrel. We'll meet at the Siren Café."

"Get in," she repeated sharply. "You can row a little. You're getting fat. Look how tired Franz is. I can't row alone."

"Really, my love, I don't feel like it at all. I hate rowing, and my back smarts again."

"All right," she said, "it was part of the bet and if you don't get in at once, I'm not playing, the bet is cancelled."

Martha was slapping her palm with the rudder rope. He rolled up his eyes, sighed and, trying not to wet his feet, started awkwardly, cautiously, to get into the boat. "Illogical and unfair," he said, and fell down heavily in the middle seat.

The second pair of oars were in the locks. Dreyer took off his blazer. The boat moved off.

A sense of blissful peace now descended on Martha. The plan had worked, the dream had come true. A deserted beach, a deserted sea, and fog. Just to be safe they should go out some distance north of the shore. An odd, cool, not unpleasant emptiness was in her chest and head as if the breeze had blown right through her, cleaning her inwardly, removing all the trash. And through that cool vibration she heard his carefree voice.

"You keep getting tangled up in my oars, Franz—that's no way to row. You have never rowed in your life, I suspect. Of course, I can understand that your thoughts are far away. . . . There again. You must pay a little more attention to what I'm trying to do. Together, together! She hasn't forgotten you. I hope you left her your address. One, two. I'm positive there'll be a letter for you today saying she's with child. Rhythm! Rhythm!"

Franz watched his firm stout neck, the yellow strands of hair thinning on pink suede, the white shirt now growing taut on his back, then ballooning. But he saw it all as if through a dream.

"Ah, children, it was glorious in the woods," the voice was saying. "The beeches, the gloom, the bindweed. Keep in rhythm!"

Martha, through half-closed eyes, was looking with interest at this face which she was seeing for the last time. Beside her lay his blazer; it contained the golden timepiece, the silver mustache brush, and a plump wallet. She was glad these things would not be lost. A little bonus. Somehow, she did not realize at that moment that the jacket with its contents would have to be thrown in the water too. This rather complicated question arose only later when the main matter had already been settled. Now her thoughts were circling slowly, almost languidly. The anticipation of hard-won happiness was ravishing.

"I must admit I was wrong in thinking this would irritate my back. You promised, darling, it would be all right today, and sure enough it's much better. Remember, I've won the bet. And I can row a hundred times better than that rascal behind me. My shirt keeps rubbing the itchy spots, and that feels good. I think I shall take off my tie."

They were now sufficiently far from the shore. It was drizzling. A number of white spectators had found their seats on their black island. The tie joined the blazer. The wavelets broke and foamed around the boat.

"Actually, it's my last day," said Dreyer, energetically rowing.

That tragic pronouncement left Franz unmoved; there was already nothing in the world that could shock him. Martha, however, gave her husband a curious glance. Premonitions, eh?

"I have to leave for the city early tomorrow," he explained. "I just had a call."

The rain was growing stronger. Martha glanced around, then looked at Franz. They could begin.

"Listen, Kurt," she said quietly, "I feel like rowing a bit. You take Franz's place, and Franz will steer."

"No, wait, my love," said Dreyer, trying to do as Franz was doing—to flatten his oars over the water, swallow-like on the backstroke. "I'm just getting warmed up. Franz and I have got our rhythm synchronized. His form is improving. Sorry, my love—I think I splashed you."

"I'm cold," said Martha. "Please get up and let me row."

"Five more minutes," said Dreyer, trying again to feather his oars, and again failing.

Martha shrugged. The sensation of power was ecstatic; she was willing to prolong that sensation.

"Eight more strokes," she said with a smile. "The years of our marriage. I'll count."

"Come on, don't spoil it. We'll let you row soon. After all, I'm leaving tomorrow."

He felt hurt that she was not interested to know why he had to go. She must think it was just a routine trip, some ordinary office business.

"An amusing surprise," he said casually.

She was moving her lips with singular concentration.

"Tomorrow," he said, "I'm making a hundred thousand dollars at one stroke."

Martha, who had got to the end of her count, raised her head.

"I'm selling an extraordinary patent. That's the kind of business we are doing."

Franz suddenly laid down his oars and began wiping his glasses. For some reason he thought Dreyer was talking to him and as he wiped the sweat and the rain away, he nodded and cleared his throat. Actually he had reached a stage at which human speech, unless representing a command, was meaningless.

"You didn't think I was so smart, eh?" said Dreyer, who had also stopped rowing. "At one stroke—just think!"

"I suppose this is one of your jokes," she said, frowning.

"Word of honor," he said plaintively. "I'm the sole owner of a miraculous invention, and I'm going to sell it to Mr. Ritter, whom you know."

"What is it—some kind of trouser press?"

He shook his head.

"Something to do with sports, with tennis?"

"It's a big glorious secret," he said, "and you're a goose not to believe me."

She turned away, biting her chapped underlip, and stared for a long time at the inky horizon, where a gray fringe of rain hung against a narrow light-colored band of sky.

"You're sure it's a hundred thousand dollars? Is that definite?"

It was not, but he nodded, and pulled at the oars, hearing that the rower behind him had resumed his work.

"Can't you tell me a little more?" she asked, still looking away. "You're sure it won't drag on? You'll have that money in a few days?"

"Why yes, I hope so. And I'll come back here and we'll go rowing again. And Franz will teach me to swim."

"It can't be; you're deceiving me," she cried.

Dreyer started to laugh, not understanding why she chose not to believe him.

"I shall return with a great bag of gold," he said. "Like a medieval merchant back from Bagdad on a donkey. Oh, I'm pretty certain I'll clinch that deal tomorrow."

The rain would stop one moment and the next start pouring again, as if practicing. Dreyer, noticing how far out they had gone, began turning the boat with his right oar; Franz mechanically backed water with his left. Martha sat lost in thought, now consulting the filling of a back tooth with her tongue, now running it over her lips. Presently Dreyer offered to let her row. She gave a silent shake of her head.

The rain now came down in earnest, and Dreyer felt its soothing coolness through the raw silk of his shirt. He tingled with vigor, this was great fun, with every stroke he rowed better. The shore appeared through the mist; one could make out the flags and the striped shelters; the long pier was beginning slowly and carefully to take aim at the moving target of their boat.

"So you'll be back Saturday, not later than Saturday?" asked Martha.

Franz could see, through Dreyer's soaked shirt, flesh-colored patches which showed now here, now there, a geography of hideous pink, depending on which country adhered to the skin in the process of rowing.

"Saturday or Sunday," Dreyer said zestfully and, as the surf adopted him, caught a crab.

The rain lashed down. Martha's robe enveloped her in heavy humidity that made her ribs ache. What could she care about neuralgia, bronchitis, irregular heart beat? She was entirely immersed in the question—was she doing the right thing or not. Yes, she was. Yes, the sun would again shine. They would go boating again, now that he had dis-covered this new sport. Every now and then she would glance past her husband at Franz. He must be perplexed and disappointed, poor pet. He is tired. His poor mouth is open. My baby! Never mind, we'll soon be back, and you'll rest, and I'll bring you some brandy, and we'll lock the door.

"Lindy" was returned intact. Bending their heads under the fierce downpour, our three holidayers walked across soggy dark sand and then up slippery steps to the desolate promenade. When they finally reached their apartment, Martha was unpleasantly surprised to find her door open. The two maids she disliked most, one a thief, the other a slut, were busy, too busy, making her room, which she had told them to do always *punkt* at ten, and now it was almost noon. But a strange apathy weighed upon her. She said noth-ing, and went to wait in Dreyer's bedroom. There she pulled off her heavy robe and sank into an armchair, feeling too tired to peel off her bathing suit and get a towel from the bathroom. Anyway, her husband was in the bathroom; she saw him through the open door. Naked, full of ruddy life, various parts of his anatomy leaping, he was giving himself a robust rub-down, and helling every time he touched his red-blotched shoulders. One of the girls knocked to say Madam's room was ready, and Martha had to make a great effort in order to undertake the long journey into the next room.

She washed and dressed—with infinite intervals of languor. A turtleneck thick red sweater which Franz had lent her on the esplanade the night before—or was it two nights? —looked a little too masculine but it was the warmest thing she could find. However, it hardly muffled the fits of shivering that kept tormenting her body, while her mind was enjoying such peace, such euphoria. Of course, she had done the right thing. Moreover, the dress rehearsal had gone perfectly. Everything was under control.

"Everything is under control," said Dreyer through the door. "I hope you are as hungry as I am. We'll have lunch in the grill in ten minutes. I'll be waiting for you in the reading room."

All she could envisage was a cup of black coffee, and a little brandy. When her husband had gone, she stepped across the corridor and knocked at Franz's door. It was unlocked, the room was empty. His robe sprawled on the floor, and there were other untidy details, but she did not have the strength to do anything about it. She found him in a corner of the lounge. The barmaid, a skinny artificial blonde, was bothering him with vulgar small talk.

Meanwhile the rain did not cease. The needle that marked on a roll the violet graph of atmospheric pressure acquired a sacred significance. People on the promenade approached it as they would a crystal ball. Its competitor in the gallery, a conservative barometer, also refused to be propitiated either by prayer or knuckleknock. Someone had forgotten a little red pail on the beach and it was already filled to the brim with rain water. The photographers moped; the restaurateurs rejoiced. One could find all the same faces now in one café, now in another. Toward evening the rain thinned, and then stopped. Dreyer held his breath as he made carom shots. The word spread that the needle had risen one millimeter. "Fine weather tomorrow," said a prophet, expressively striking his palm with his fist. Red at night, sailor's delight. Despite the cool air, many dined on public verandas. The evening mail arrived: a major event. On the promenade the after-dinner shuffling of many feet began under the lights, bemisted by the damp. There was dancing at the *kursaal*.

In the afternoon, she had lain down under a quilt and two blankets; but the chill endured. For supper she could eat only a pickle and a couple of pale cooked cherries. Now, in the Tanz Salon, she felt a stranger to the icy noise around. The black petals of her vaporous dress did not seem right, as if they would come apart at any moment. The tight touch of silk on her calves and the strip of garter along her bare thigh were infernal contacts. A colored snowstorm of confetti left its flakes sticking to her bare back, and at the same time, limbs and spine did not belong to her. A pain, of another musical tone than intercostal neuralgia or that strange ache which a great cardiologist had told her came from a "shadow behind the heart," entered into excruciating concords with the orchestra. The dance rhythm did not lull or delight her as it usually did, but, instead, traced an angular line, the graph of her fever, along the surface of her skin. With every movement of her head, a compact pain rolled like a bowling ball from temple to temple. At one of the best tables around the hall, she had for a right-hand neighbor the dance instructor, a famous young man who flitted all summer from resort to resort like a velvet butterfly; on her left was Schwarz, the dark-eyed student, son of a Leipzig millionaire. The slipper under the table had apparently been kicked off by her. She heard Martha Dreyer ask questions, supply answers, comment on the horror of the thundering hall. The fizzy little stars of champagne pricked an unfamiliar tongue, without warming her blood or quenching her thirst. With an invisible hand she took Martha by the left wrist and felt her pulse. It was not there, however, but somewhere behind her ear or in the neck, or in the grinning instruments of the band, or in Franz and Dreyer, sitting opposite her. All around, growing from the hands of the dancers, glossy blue, red, green balloons bobbed on long strings and each contained the entire ballroom, and the chandeliers, and the tables, and herself. The tight embrace of the foxtrot engendered no heat in her body. She noticed that Martha was dancing also, holding high a green world. Her partner in full erection against her leg was declaring his love in panting sentences from some lewd book. Again the stars of champagne crept upwards, and the balloons resumed their bobbing, and again most of Martha's leg was in Weiss's crotch, and he moaned as his cheek touched hers, and his fingers explored her naked back.

She was sitting again at the table. Red, blue, green spots were swimming in Franz's glasses. Dreyer was guffawing vulgarly slapping the table with his palm and leaning back. She extended her foot beneath the table and pressed. Franz gave a start, stood up, and bowed. She placed her hand on his dear bony shoulder. How happy they had been in the rhythm of that earlier novel in those first chapters, under the picture of the dancing slave girl between the whirling dervishes. For one delicious moment the music pierced her private fog, reached her, enveloped her. Everything was fine again, for this was he, Franz, his shy hands, his breath, the soft fuzz on the back of his neck, under her fingernails, and those precious, adorable motions that *she* had taught him.

"Closer, closer," she murmured. "Make me feel warm."

"I'm tired," he murmured back. "I'm tired to death. Please don't do what you are doing, please."

The music reared its trumpets and then collapsed. Franz followed her back to the table. People around her were clapping. The dancing instructor slipped past her with a bright-yellow girl. Walnut-brown Mr. Vinomori, the iris brimming meaningfully in the white of his eyes, was bowing to her, enticing. She saw Martha Dreyer nestle up to him and begin a tango.

Uncle and nephew remained sitting alone. Dreyer was beating time with his finger, watching the dancers, waiting for the recurrent return of his wife's green earrings, and, with a kind of awe, listening to the strong voice of a girl singer. Stocky and joyless, she bawled out, straining her throat and prancing in time to the music: "Montevideo, Montevideo is not the right place for *meinen Leo*." She was jostled by the dancers; endlessly she repeated the ear-splitting refrain; a fat man in tuxedo, her owner, hissed at her, telling her to choose some other song because nobody was enjoying it; Dreyer had heard this *Montevideo* both yesterday and the day before, and he was again filled with a bizarre melancholy, and felt embarrassed for the poor dumpy girl when her voice cracked on a note and she recovered the tune with a brave smile. Franz sat beside him, shoulder to shoulder, and seemed also to be watching the dancers. He was a little drunk and his muscles ached from that morning rowing. He felt like letting his forehead fall onto the table to remain thus forever, between a full ashtray and an empty bottle. A reptile, a supple dragon was tormenting him elaborately and hideously, turning him inside out—and there was no end to that torment. A human being, and after all he was a human being, was not supposed to go on enduring such oppression.

It was at that moment that Franz regained consciousness like an insufficiently drugged patient on the operating table. As he came to, he knew he was being cut open, and he would have howled horribly if he were not in an invented ballroom. He looked around, toying with the string of a balloon tied to a bottle. He saw, reflected in a rococo mirror, the meek back of Dreyer's head nodding in time to the music.

Franz looked away; his gaze became entangled amid the legs of the dancers and attached itself desperately to a gleaming blue dress. The foreign girl in the blue dress danced with a remarkably handsome man in an old-fashioned dinner jacket. Franz had long since noticed this couple; they had appeared to him in fleeting glimpses, like a recurrent dream image or a subtle leitmotiv—now at the beach, now in a café, now on the promenade. Sometimes the man carried a butterfly net. The girl had a delicately painted mouth and tender gray-blue eyes, and her fiancé or husband, slender, elegantly balding, contemptuous of everything on earth but her, was looking at her with pride; and Franz felt envious of that unusual pair, so envious that his oppression, one is sorry to say, grew even more bitter, and the music stopped. They walked past him. They were speaking loudly. They were speaking a totally incomprehensible language.

"Your aunt dances like a goddess," said the student, sitting down beside him.

"I'm very tired," remarked Franz irrelevantly. "I rowed a lot today. Rowing is a very healthy sport."

Meanwhile Dreyer was saying with an ingratiating wink: "Am I also permitted to invite you for a dance? If I promise not to tread on your feet?"

"Get me out of here," said Martha. "I'm not feeling well."

13

Barely awake and still blinking, his yellow pajamas unbuttoned on his pink stomach, Dreyer went out on the balcony. The wet foliage scintillated blindingly. The sea was milky-bluish, sparked with silver. On the adjacent balcony his wife's bathing suit was drying. He returned to his darkish bedroom, in a hurry to dress and leave for Berlin. At eight o'clock there was a bus that took forty minutes to reach Swistok and its railway; a taxi would bring him there in less than half an hour to catch an earlier train. He tried not to sing under the shower so as not to disturb neighbors. He had an enjoyable shave on the balcony in front of an absolutely stable and unbreakable new type of mirror screwed onto the balustrade. Diving back into the penumbra, he briskly dressed.

Very softly he opened the door into the adjacent bedroom. From the bed came Martha's rapid voice: "We're going to a tombola in a gondola. Please hurry."

She often talked in her sleep babbling about Franz, Frieda, Oriental gymnastics.

As he slapped his sides to check if he had distributed

everything among the proper pockets, Dreyer laughed and said: "Good-by, my love. I'm leaving for the city."

She muttered something in a waking voice, then said distinctly: "Give me some water."

"I'm in a hurry," he said. "You get it yourself. Okay? Time for you to go swimming with Franz. Heavenly morning."

He bent over the dark bed, kissed her hair and walked through his own bedroom into the long corridor leading to the lift.

He had his coffee on the Kurhaus terrace. He had two rolls with butter and honey. He consulted his watch and ate a third. On the beach one could see the bright robes of early swimmers and the sea was growing more and more luminous. He lit a cigarette and popped into the taxi that the concierge had called.

The sea was left behind. By that time a few more bathers were dotting the flashing green-blue. From every balcony came the delicate tinkle of breakfast. Automatically tucking a hateful ball under his arm, Franz marched down the corridor and knocked at Martha's door. Silence. The door was locked. He knocked at Dreyer's door, entered and found his uncle's room in disorder. He concluded, correctly, that Dreyer had already left for Berlin. A terrible day was in store. The door into Martha's room was ajar. It was dark there. Let her sleep. This was good. He started to tiptoe away but from the darkness came Martha's voice. "Why don't you give me that water?" she said with listless insistence.

Franz located a decanter and a glass and moved toward the bed. Martha slowly raised herself, freed a bare arm, and drank avidly. He put the decanter back on the dresser and was about to resume his stealthy retreat.

"Franz, come here," she called in that same toneless voice.

He sat down on the edge of her bed, grimly expecting she would command him to fulfill a duty that he had managed to evade since they came here.

"I think I am very ill," she said pensively, not raising her head from the pillow.

"Let me ring for your coffee," said Franz. "It's sunny today and here it's so dark."

She began to speak again. "He's used up all the aspirin. Go to the pharmacy and get me some. And tell them to take that oar away—it keeps hurting me."

"Oar? That's your hot-water bottle. What's the matter with you?"

"Please, Franz. I can't speak. And I'm cold. I need lots of blankets."

He brought one from Dreyer's room, and clumsily, carelessly, fuming at a woman's whim, covered her with it.

"I don't know where the pharmacy is," he said.

Martha asked: "You brought it? What have you brought?"

He shrugged and went out.

He found the pharmacy without difficulty. Besides the aspirin tablets he bought a tube of shaving cream and a postcard with a view of the bay. The package had safely arrived but Emmy wondered in her last letter if he was quite right in the head and he thought he'd send her a few words of protest and reassurance. As he walked back to the hotel along the sunny promenade, he stopped to look down at the beach. He had separated the aspirin container from the shaving cream which he now put into his pocket. A sudden breeze took possession of the paper baglet which had contained both. At that moment the puzzling foreign couple overtook him. They were both in beach robes and walked rapidly, rapidly conversing in their mysterious tongue. He thought that they glanced at him and fell silent for an instant. After passing him they began talking again; he had the impression they were discussing him, and even pronouncing his name. It embarrassed, it incensed him, that this damned happy foreigner hastening to the beach with his tanned, pale-haired, lovely companion, knew absolutely everything about his predicament and perhaps pitied, not without some derision, an honest young man who had been seduced and appropriated by an older woman who, despite her fine dresses and face lotions, resembled a large white toad. And generally speaking, tourists at these swanky resorts are always inquisitive, mocking, cruel people. He felt the shame of his hairy nudity barely concealed by the charlatan robe. He cursed the breeze and the sea and, clutching the container with the tablets, entered the lobby of his hotel. The flimsy paper he had lost fluttered along the promenade, settled, fluttered again, and slithered past the happy couple; then it was wafted toward a bench in an embrasure of the balustrade, where an old man sitting in the sun meditatively pierced it with the point of his cane. What happened to it next is not known. Those hurrying to the beach did not follow its fate. Wooden steps led down to the sand. One was anxious to reach the sea's slow shining folds. The white sand sung underfoot. Among a hundred similarly striped shelters it was easy to recognize one's own—and not only by the number it bore: those rentable objects grow accustomed to their chance owner remarkably fast, becoming part of his life simply and trustfully. Three or four shelters away was the Dreyers' niche; now it stood empty—neither Dreyer, nor his wife, nor his nephew was there. A huge rampart of sand surrounded it. A little boy in red trunks was climbing all over that rampart, and the sand trickled down, sparkling, and presently a whole chunk of it crumbled. Mrs. Dreyer would not have liked to see strange children ruining her fortress. Within its confines and around them the impatient elements had already had time to scramble the prints of bare feet. None could distinguish now Dreyer's robust imprint from Franz's narrow sole. A while later Schwarz and Weiss came over, saw with surprise that nobody was there yet. "Fascinating, adorable woman," one of them said, and the other looked across the beach at the promenade, at the hotels beyond it, and replied: "Oh, I'm sure they'll be down in a few minutes. Let's go for a swim and come back later." The shelter and its moat remained deserted. The little boy had run back to his sister who had brought a blue pailful of toy water and after magic manipulations and pattings was carefully shaking out of the pail an impeccably formed cone of chocolate sand. A white butterfly went by, battling the breeze. Flags flapped. The photographer's shout approached. Bathers entering the shallow water moved their legs like skiers without their poles.

And in the meantime a cluster of these seaside images—gleams on the green folding wave—were travelling south at fifty miles an hour comfortably collected in Dreyer's mind, and the further he travelled from the sea in the Berlin express, the more insistently they demanded attention. The foretaste of the affairs awaiting him in the city grew a little insipid at the thought that at the very moment he was being transformed again into a businessman with a businessman's schemes and fancies, and that there, by the sea, on the white sand of true reality, he was leaving freedom behind. And the closer he came to the metropolis, the more attractive seemed to him that shimmering *plage* that one could see like a mirage from Rockpoint.

At home, the gardener informed him of Tom's death: the dog, he thought, had been hit by a truck, it was found unconscious and had died, he said, in his arms. Dreyer gave

him fifty marks for his sympathy, reflecting sadly that nobody besides that rather coarse old soldier had really loved
the poor beast. At the office he learned that Mr. Ritter would
meet him not in the lobby of the Adlerhof but at the bar of
the Royal. Before going there, he rang up Isolda at her
mother's at Spandau and pleaded abjectly for a brief date
later in the evening, but Isolda said she was busy, and suggested he call her again tomorrow or the day after tomorrow
and take her to the premiere of the film, *King, Queen,
Knave*, and then one would see.

His American guest, a pleasant, cultured person with steel-
gray hair and a triple chin, asked about Martha, whom he
had met a couple of years before, and Dreyer was disappointed to discover that all the English learned since the day
of that pleasant party was not sufficient to cope with the
nasal pronunciation of Mr. Ritter—whereupon the latter
courteously switched to an old-fashioned brand of German.
Another disappointment awaited Dreyer at the "laboratory."
Instead of the three automannequins promised him, only
two were available for the show—the initial elderly gentleman, wearing a replica of Dreyer's blue blazer, and a stiff-
looking, bronze-wigged lady in a green dress with high
cheekbones and a masculine chin.

"You might have thrown in a little more bosom," observed
Dreyer reproachfully.

"Scandinavian type," said the Inventor.

"Scandinavian type," said Dreyer. "Female impersonator,
rather."

"An amalgam, if you like. We ran into some trouble, a rib
failed to function properly. After all, I need more time than
God did, Mr. Director. But I'm sure you'll love the way her
hips work."

"Another thing," said Dreyer. "I don't much care for the

old chap's necktie. You must have got it in Croatia or Liechtenstein. Anyway it is not one of those my store provided. In fact, I remember the one he had on last time; it was a beautiful light blue like yours."

Moritz and Max tittered.

"I confess," said the Inventor calmly, "to have borrowed it for this important occasion." He started to worry the front stud of the tall collar under his rustling beard, but before it could spring, Dreyer had already swished off his own pearl-gray tie and remained with an open shirt collar for the rest of his known existence.

Mr. Ritter was dozing in an armchair in the "theater." Dreyer coughed loudly. His guest woke up rubbing his eyes like a child. The show started.

Gyrating her angular hips, the woman passed across the stage more like a streetwalker than a sleepwalker. She was followed by the drunken viveur. Presently she jerked by again in a mink coat, reeled, recovered, completed her agonizing stretch, and the sound of a massive thud came from the wings. Her would-be client did not appear. There was a long pause.

"That meal you bought me was certainly something," said Mr. Ritter. "I'll have my revanche when madame and you visit me in Miami next spring. I have a Spanish chef who worked for years in a French restaurant in London so you do really get quite a cosmopolitan menu."

This time the woman drifted past on slow roller skates, in a black evening dress, her legs rigid, her profile like that of a skull, her décolleté revealing a tricot smudged by the hasty hands of her maker. His two accomplices failed to catch her behind the scenes where her brief career ended in an ominous clatter. There was another pause. Dreyer wondered what aberration of the mind had ever made him accept, let alone admire, those tipsy dummies. He hoped the end of the show had come but Mr. Ritter and he had not yet seen the best number.

White-gloved, in evening dress, one hand raised to his top hat, the old chap entered, looking refreshed and gay. He stopped in front of the spectators and started to remove his hat in a complicated, much too complicated, salute. Something crunched.

"*Halt*," howled the Inventor with great presence of mind and darted toward the mechanical maniac. "Too late!" The hat was doffed with a flourish but the arm came off too.

A photographer's black curtain was mercifully drawn.

"*How have you liked?*" asked Dreyer in English.

"Fascinating," said Mr. Ritter and started to leave. "You'll hear from me in a couple of days. I have to decide, you see, which of two projects to finance.

"Is the other similar?"

"Oh, no. Oh, goodness, no. The other has to do with running water in luxury hotels. Water made to produce recognizable tunes. The music of water in a literal sense. An orchestra of faucets. Wash your hands in a barcarolla, bathe in *Lohengrin*, rinse your silver in Debussy."

"Or drown in a Bach," punned Dreyer.

He spent the rest of the evening at home, trying to read an English play called *Candida*, and every now and then lapsing into lazy thought. The automannequins had given all they could give. Alas, they had been pushed too far. Bluebeard had squandered his hypnotic force, and now they had lost all significance, all life and charm. He was grateful to them, in a vague sort of way, for the magical task they had performed, the excitement, the expectations. But they only disgusted him now.

He worked through another scene, dutifully leafing

through his dictionary at every stumble. He would ring up Isolda tomorrow. He would hire a pretty English girl to teach him the language of Shaw and Galsworthy. He would simply resell the invention to Bluebeard. Ah, brilliant idea! For a token sum of ten dollars.

How quiet the house was. No Tom, no Martha. She was not a good loser, poor girl. All at once he understood what subtle extra was added to the lifeless silence: all the clocks had stopped in the house.

A little after eleven he rose from his comfortable seat and was about to go up to the bedroom when the telephone placed a cold hand on his shoulder.

He was now speeding in a hired limousine driven by a broad-shouldered chauffeur through an infinite nocturnal expanse of woods and field, and northern towns, their names garbled by the impatient darkness—Nauesack, Wusterbeck, Pritzburg, Nebukow. Their weak lights fumbled at him in passing, the car shook and swayed, he had been promised they would make it in five hours, but they did not, and a gray morning was already abustle with bicycles weaving among crawling trucks when he reached Swistok, from which it was twenty miles to Gravitz.

The desk clerk, a dark-haired young man with hollow cheeks and big glasses, informed him that one of their guests happened to be Professor Lister of international fame; he had visited Madame last night, and was with her now.

As Dreyer strode toward his apartment, the doctor, a tall bald old man in a monastic-looking dressing gown with a brown satchel under his arm, came out of Martha's room. "It is unheard-of," he growled at Dreyer without bothering to shake hands with him. "A woman has pneumonia with a temperature of 106 and nobody bothers. Her husband leaves her in that state and goes for a trip. Her nephew is a nincompoop. If a maid had not alerted me last night you would be still carousing in Berlin."

"So the situation is serious," said Dreyer.

"Serious? The respiratory count is fifty. The heart behaves fantastically. It is not a normal organ for a woman of twenty-nine."

"Thirty-four," said Dreyer. "There is a mistake in her passport."

"Or thirty-four. Anyway, she should be transported at once to the Swistok clinic where I can have her treated adequately."

"Yes, at once," said Dreyer.

The old man nodded crossly and swept away. One of the maids Martha disliked, the one who had stolen at least three handkerchiefs in as many days, was now dressed as a nurse (she had worked in winter at the clinic).

Plain brown or the heather tweed? Franz on the terrace of a café was in the middle of a nervous yawn when the doctor billowed past, heading for a quick swim before going to Swistok. Plain brown. Gruff Lister could not help being touched by the young fellow's dejection and shouted to him from the promenade: "Your uncle is here."

Franz went up to Dreyer's room and stood listening to the moaning and muttering in the adjacent room. Would fate allow her to divulge their secrets? He knocked very lightly on the door. Dreyer came out of the sickroom, and he likewise was touched by Franz's distraught appearance. Presently from the balcony they saw the ambulance enter the drive.

Over the waves, small angular waves, that rose and fell in time to her breathing, Martha floated in a white boat, and at the oars sat Dreyer and Franz. Franz smiled at her over Dreyer's bent head, and she saw her gay parasol reflected in the happy gleam of his glasses. Franz was wearing one of the long nightshirts that had belonged to his father, and continued to smile at her expectantly as the boat dipped and creaked as if on springs. And Martha said: "It's time. We can begin." Dreyer stood up, Franz stood up also, and both reeled, laughing heartily, locked in an involuntary embrace. Franz's long shirt rippled in the wind, and now he was standing alone, still laughing and swaying, and out of the water a hand protruded. "Take the oar, hit him," cried Martha, choking with laughter. Franz, standing firmly on the blue glass of the water, raised the oar, and the hand disappeared. They were now alone in the boat, which was no longer a boat but a café with one large marble table, and Franz was sitting opposite her, and his odd attire had ceased to matter. They were drinking beer (how thirsty she was). Franz shared her unsteady glass while Dreyer kept slapping the table with his wallet to summon the waiter. "Now," she said, and Franz said something in Dreyer's ear, and Dreyer got up, laughing, and they both went away. While Martha waited her chair rose and fell, it was a floating café. Franz came back alone carrying her late husband's blue jacket over his arm; he nodded to her significantly and tossed it on the empty chair. Martha wanted to kiss Franz but the table separated them and the marble edge bit into her chest. Coffee was brought—three pots, three cups—and it took her some time to realize there was one portion too many. The coffee was too hot, so she decided that since a drizzle had set in, it was best to wait for the rain to dilute the coffee, but the rain was hot too and Franz kept urging her to go home, pointing at their villa across the road. "Let's begin," she said. All three got up, and Dreyer, pale and sweaty, started to pull on his blue jacket. That perturbed her. It was dishonest, it was illegal. She gestured in mute indignation. Franz understood and, talking to him firmly, began leading away Dreyer, who staggered as he fumbled for the armhole of his blazer. Franz returned alone but no sooner had he sat down than Dreyer appeared from another direction, furtively making his way back, and his face was now utterly ghastly and inadmissible. With a sidelong glance at her he shook his head and seated himself without a word at the oars of the bed. Martha was overcome by such impatience that as soon as the bed began to move she screamed. The new boat rode through long corridors. She wanted to stand up but an oar blocked her way. Franz rowed steadily. Something kept telling her that not all had been properly done. She remembered—the jacket! The blue jacket lay at the bottom of the boat, its arms looked empty but the back was not flat enough, in fact it bulged, it humped suspiciously, and now the two sleeves were swelling. She saw the thing trying to rise on all fours, and grabbed it, and Franz and she swung it back and forth and hurled it out of the boat. But it would not sink. It slithered from wave to wave as if alive. She nudged it with an oar; it clutched at the oar, trying to clamber aboard. Franz reminded her that it still contained the watch, and the coat, now a blue mackintosh because of the water, slowly sank, limply moving its exhausted sleeves. They watched it disappear. Now the job was done, and an enormous, turbulent joy engulfed her. Now it was easy to breathe, that drink they had given her was a wonderful poison, Benedictine and bile, and her husband was already dressed, saying: "Hurry up, I'm taking you to a ball," but Franz had mislaid her jewels.

Before leaving with her for the hospital, Dreyer told Franz to hold the fort, they would be back in a few days. There was probably not much difference basically between Martha's delirium and her wretched lover's state of mind. Once, on the eve of a school examination, when he desperately needed a passing mark in order not to repeat a whole class year, a clever sly boy said to him there was a trick that always worked if you knew how to apply it. With the utmost clarity, with all the forces of your mind bunched up in an iron fist, you had to visualize not what you wanted, not the passing mark, not her death, not freedom, but the other possibility, failure, the absence of your name from the list of those who had passed, and a healthy, ravenous, implacable Martha returning to her merry seaside inferno to make him carry out the scheme they had postponed. But according to the boy's advice, that did not suffice: the really hard part of the trick was ignoring success utterly and naturally as if the very thought of it did not exist in one's mind. Franz could not recall if he had achieved that feat in the case of the examination (which eventually he did pass) but he knew that he was incapable of managing it now. No matter how distinctly he imagined the three of them sitting again on the terrace of the Marmora tavern, and renewing the wager, and again getting Dreyer into the boat, he would notice out of the corner of his eye that the boat had floated away without them and that Dreyer was telephoning from the hospital to say she was dead.

Going to the other extreme, he allowed himself the dangerous luxury of imagining the freedom, the ecstasy of freedom awaiting him. Then, after that awful volupty of thought, he tried other ways of tricking fate. He counted the boats for hire and added their sum to that of the number of people in the open-air café on the beach, telling himself that odd would mean death. The number was odd but now he wondered if somebody had not left or come while he counted.

The day before he had resolved to take advantage of solitude and make a purchase that Dreyer might have ridiculed with his usual wit, and Martha thought frivolous at such a critical time in their lives. It was his old dream of fashionable plus-fours. He had spent a couple of hours in several shops. He had practically bought a pair but then had said he'd think it over, and decide which he wanted, the brown or the purplish tweed. He now returned to that shop and tried on the plain brown pair and it turned out to be a little too wide in the waist. He said he would take it if they could make the adjustment before closing time. This they promised. He also bought two pairs of brown woollen stockings. Then he went for a swim, and after that had three or four brandies at the bar, vainly waiting for the attractive blonde to get rid of two elderly men flirting with her, ponderously and obscenely. Suddenly it occurred to him that his choosing the more conservative tint meant his having envisaged death rather than life which those confetti-like specks in the tweed might suggest. But when he returned to the tailor's the plus-fours were ready, and he did not have the courage to change his order.

Next morning Franz, wearing the new plus-fours and a turtleneck sweater, was looking at the rain over his second cup of after-lunch coffee when the desk clerk—who resembled him according to Uncle Clown—brought him two messages. Dreyer had telephoned that madame wanted her emerald earrings—and Franz immediately realized that if madame contemplated going to a dance, no death was expected. The clerk explained that Mr. Director Dreyer wanted his nephew to get those jewels from his aunt's dresser and drive in a taxi to Swistok without delay. She had evidently recovered from her slight cold so swiftly that the doctor allowed her to go out that very night. Franz reflected bitterly that, of all the contingencies he had attempted to forestall, this was the only one he had not imagined specifically. The other message was a telegram that had been read over the telephone and transcribed thus by the multilingual desk: WISCH TU CLYNCH DEEL MUSS HAVE THAT DRUNK STOP HUNDRED OAKEY RITTER. It made no sense, but who cared. Cursing Lister, the miracle worker, he rode up in the lift with the pseudo-Franz, and a stout locksmith, hoarse-voiced and reeking of beer. The key was in Martha's handbag which had gone with her to Swistok. The locksmith started working on the lock of the dresser. He wiped his nose and went down on one knee, then on both. The false Franz and the more or less real one stood side by side, staring at his dirty soles.

The drawer was finally extricated. Franz opened a black jewel box and showed the emeralds to the gloomy clerk.

Half an hour later he arrived at the hospital—a new white building in a pine grove on the outskirts of the town. The taximan demanded a tip and slammed the door angrily when Franz shook his head. A remarkably cheerful nurse had another message for him. His uncle, she said with a happy smile, was expecting him at the inn—about a mile down the highway. Franz walked the distance with his left hand pressed to his left side where the jewel box bulged. They chafed slightly between the thighs. As he approached the inn, he saw Martha come out of it briskly and consult the sky, one finger on the trigger of her umbrella. She gave Franz a quick look and went the way he had come. She was younger than Martha, and the mouth was different, but the eyes and the walk were Martha's. That meant a gay reunion in a Swistok inn. Uncle, nephew, and two aunts.

He found Dreyer in the hall of the inn. He was inspecting an ornamental pewter and kept looking at it even when Franz was already thrusting the black box and the telegram into the vicinity of his person. Dreyer thrust both in his pocket without opening either, and replaced the pewter on its hook.

He turned toward Franz, who saw only then that it was not Dreyer but a demented stranger in a rumpled open shirt, with swollen eyes and a tawny-stubbled trembling jaw.

"It's too late," he said, "too late to put on for the dance, but still not too late to wear—"

He pulled Franz by the sleeve with such force that Franz almost lost his balance, but Dreyer only wanted to lead him to the desk.

"Take him up," he said to the innkeeper's widow. And then, turning to Franz: "We'll have to stay here till tomorrow. The worst formalities begin afterwards. Go to your room now. Hilda has just come from Hamburg. She will fetch you in a couple of hours."

"Is it—" began an amazed Franz, "is it—?"

"Is it all over?" asked the new sobbing Dreyer. "Oh, it is over! Now go."

Franz attempted to catch his benefactor's hand and shake it in token of ardent condolence but Dreyer dreadfully mistook the adumbrated gesture for the rudiment of an embrace, and wet bristles came into brief contact with Franz's glowing cheek.

Her last words had been (in a sweet remote voice he had never heard before): "Darling, where did you put my emerald slippers—no, I mean earrings? I want them. We shall all dance, we shall all die." And then—with her good old familiar sharpness: "Frieda, why is the dog here again? He was killed. He can't be here any more."

And the fools say second sight does not exist.

Franz followed the old woman upstairs. She led him into a

darkened room. Quickly she threw back the shutters, quickly she opened the lower stage of the bed table to see if the nightpot was there. Quickly she left.

Franz marched to the open window. Dreyer crossed the road and sat down on a bench under a tree. Franz closed the window. He was now alone. A woman in the next room, a miserable tramp whom a commercial traveller had jilted, heard through the thin wall what sounded like several revellers all talking together, and roaring with laughter, and interrupting one another, and roaring again in a frenzy of young mirth.

Catalog

If you are interested in a list of fine Paperback
books, covering a wide range of subjects
and interests, send your name and address,
requesting your free catalog, to:

McGraw-Hill Paperbacks
1221 Avenue of Americas
New York, N.Y. 10020